The Girl
I Thought
I Knew

BOOKS BY KELLY HEARD

Before You Go

KELLY HEARD

The Girl I Thought I Knew

Bookouture

Published by Bookouture in 2020

An imprint of Storyfire Ltd.
Carmelite House
50 Victoria Embankment
London EC4Y 0DZ

www.bookouture.com

ISBN: 978-1-83888-008-8
eBook ISBN: 978-1-83888-007-1

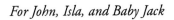

For John, Isla, and Baby Jack

CHAPTER ONE
Before

After the fire, Daisy was frightened of the dark. It was easy enough to handle on its own, but add another wild card, and all of Daisy's senses fired. Any attempt to flee, to escape the memories, felt like running through a thicket. Cheery music rolled over the film previews, but the dimly lit movie theater turned suddenly into the forest: the girl's dying body at her feet, the chestnut-bronze eyes looking up at her all too alive. Stella's friends laughed at her confusion in the cruel, chattery way that only high schoolers can, one of them still half reclining on the floor, playing dead.

Daisy's mind clawed for a foothold in the dark and found it. *You're indoors, not out. This isn't real. If you were outside, if it were happening again, you'd see the fireflies.*

Daisy blinked and the memories disappeared. Surrounded by the sharp laughter of the teenaged girls, she could have been in the midst of a flock of crows. She held her hands to her face, making to block the noise, and fumbled along the row of seats and through the dark theater for the exit. She hurried to the bathrooms and found a long line. At least having to cry in public guaranteed her admission to the front.

She ducked into a stall and pressed the heels of her hands against her eyes until the tears stopped, as if applying pressure to a wound. When Daisy exited the stall, she stepped over to the mirror and looked up, finding, instead of her own reflection, the girl she considered her best friend.

"What do you want, Stella?" Though her voice was cool, it released a rush of relief: Stella was sorry. She had followed her out. "You could have stuck up for me back there. God, that was horrible."

Stella inched away, reached up and tucked her shiny brown hair behind one ear. "Nothing." She spoke in a low voice, looked back over her shoulder. "I—I just had to go to the bathroom."

Daisy felt the heat in her clenched palms cool, a blue, removed anger streaming down to her toes, her mud-tinged sneakers almost touching Stella's patent leather flats.

"Got it. You know what, Stella? I saw her. I don't need you to believe me." Daisy's voice wavered. She had always been a bad liar.

"I'll see you at school tomorrow. Daisy—"

Daisy exited the bathroom and let the door swing closed with a clap behind her, a single note of applause to top off the evening. The corridor to the back exit was dark, but this time, Daisy felt her eyes adjust. It was one thing to write off her mother, but Daisy had the sense that she was losing her best friend, and it had been a truth too awful to see by daylight.

CHAPTER TWO

Now

The thing about New Mexico was the sunlight. It was bright blue days and cloudless nights, tied together with sunsets and sunrises that seemed to clean the sky of all the previous hours. Daisy had always been an early riser, disliking the idea that somebody might learn something before she did. Today, she spent the sleepless hour before dawn waiting for her newest article to go live. By 6 a.m., the rising sun backlit the blinds with its yellow warmth. She turned to the sleeping figure in the bed with a smile, then approached.

It was the way Anderson slept that had stolen her heart, all those years ago. Daisy had liked him from the first minute—though, back then, an honest offer of help would have been enough to make her like anyone. The first night they were together, when he had stretched across a lumpy hotel bed and slept in absolute comfort, one arm tossed back above his head, his chin tilted up just so—exactly as he was doing now—she had begun to fall in love. How young she'd been, and how lost.

Daisy traced his hair, deep brown, then let her fingertip whisper across his brow. She still felt the loss a little bit, every day when she woke. That was okay: it got her up early. Kept her working. The doctor had said there was no reason for it, though it was uncommon for it to happen so far along.

"How old are you, Daisy?" the doctor had asked. She had looked up from her phone, still waiting for Anderson's response to her frantic messages.

"Thirty-five," she'd replied. The doctor had said nothing, but a certain look had crossed his face. "I feel young," she'd said. "I feel really healthy."

The doctor had assured her that she was healthy, that many women had healthy pregnancies and babies at thirty-five, or older. A shelf on the wall held a row of medical brochures. Daisy had reached over and selected one on egg freezing. She'd taken it home, tucked it into the top drawer of her bedside table, the information at the ready but not out in the open, an unwelcome reminder. It wasn't that Daisy was old, that wasn't it. But she wasn't as young as she had thought she was.

Daisy felt a sigh lingering in her throat, so she leaned near, laid her cheek against his warm shoulder. "Anderson," she whispered. "Are you ready?"

He stretched, broad arms almost spanning the bedframe, smiled up at her as she adjusted his pillow. "This is your big day, right? Let's see it."

Daisy opened her tablet and typed the web address. "Hold on." She rose from the bed, crossed the room to the wide picture windows that filled the east-facing wall. Pulling the cord with both hands, she filled the room with marigold-hued light one window at a time, then returned to his side. Anderson protested with a teasing groan, one forearm raised to shield his eyes.

"I'm definitely awake now."

She dropped onto the bed beside him. "I've been up," she murmured.

"Still waking early?"

Daisy's eyes met his, holding a quick, quiet moment of silence. *Not this morning*, it said. *Today, we are not sad.* She picked up the tablet again, held it out in front of her, and reloaded the website.

"There it is," she said, pointing with glee as the article appeared. "My own feature with my own byline. My own name, as soon as you visit the page."

Anderson clapped his hands together, then pulled her close and pressed his lips to hers. "You deserve it."

She let the sun warm her face, soaking in the morning. "It's not that it changes anything materially, but it feels good to see it."

"You've worked for it, Daisy," Anderson answered, scratching at his stubble as he looked at his phone.

"For this, today, or for this—" She swept her eyes across the spacious bedroom, the windows that looked out over the desert, the work that was starting to come in steadily. This life, here. Both were true.

"Hm?" He placed the phone back on his bedside table, returning his attention to her.

With a sharp clap of a noise and a puff of gray feathers, a pigeon struck the window and dropped out of sight and into the garden.

"Oh, shit." She hurried to the window, peering down to the ground below. "Not again."

"You keep those windows too clean," he answered with a smile. "I'll remember to pick that one up before the neighbor's cat comes over."

Daisy's eyebrows drew together. She gathered a floral bathrobe from the back of the chair and wrapped it over her pajamas.

"Daisy." Anderson's eyes had a way of softening and also focusing in on her. Like a shift in light, she felt his expression change. "Don't. You were so upset last time."

"Nonsense. I'm completely fine," she said. His smile was indulgent, half doubtful, as if to say *but are you really?* "I just need to see if it's alive."

CHAPTER THREE

Now

Daisy descended the staircase, nudged her toes into her sandals, and opened the front door. She took in another moment of gratitude for the incredible brightness of this place, the clean, dry air. Even the city seemed to wake up gently, the sounds of nearby vehicles and far-off voices, the neighborhood coming to life. Back home, the humid, close air seemed to get inside your clothes, inside your very skin. She drew in a deep breath and hurried around to the side of the house, scanning the ground beneath the windows. She took a careful step, placing her foot down between the red poppies and ornamental grasses, then another step, avoiding the flowering cactus, and nearly walked right over it.

Leaning close, her chin almost brushed the ground. Daisy could imagine Anderson teasing her: *What will the neighbors think?* She eyed the pigeon, which was not visibly damaged.

"Get up," she whispered, extending a curious hand. Maybe she could pick it up, call the animal control department, or a vet. "Come on."

As Daisy brushed the top of the bird's head with her fingertip, she noticed with a sigh that she had managed to chip her nail polish, and made a note to touch it up later. She brought her focus back to the bird, staring intently as it lay there, unmoving. Then, with an annoyed squeak and a flutter, the bird hopped to one foot, tottered a few steps, and flapped into the air, taking refuge on the eaves of the house next door.

Daisy laughed, following the bird with her eyes as she walked back inside. It was dark, but she opened the blinds to an angle instead of raising them. She circled through the living room, passed Anderson's office, and went into the kitchen to wash her hands. As she heated the kettle for tea, she spied a stack of mail resting on the granite bar by the stove. She thumbed through it, sorting junk—a credit card offer, a pamphlet of coupons—from more junk. At the bottom of the stack, a cream-colored envelope peered out, heavyweight paper that was pleasant and smooth to the touch. When she read the name on the return address, she almost jumped back from it, letting it fall to the floor. The kettle whistled. She poured two cups of tea, loaded them on a tray, and cautiously retrieved her mail, placing it face down beside the drinks.

"Babe, did you get the mail yesterday?" She pushed the bedroom door open with one hip and set the tray on the coffee table.

"Yes, I did." Anderson, still in bed, looked up from his computer to smile at her. "Why? Are you waiting for something?"

"No," she answered, adding honey to her tea. In the full light of morning, with Anderson right there, no imagining, she turned the envelope over and reread the name. Stella Whitten. "I'm just wondering how long this has been here."

"Worked late last night," he said, rising from the bed. "I didn't want to wake you. I knew you'd find it in the morning." With a hint of concern, he approached her, took his tea. "Why—is everything alright?"

"Fine, I think." Daisy tore open the envelope and traced the edges of the card. *You are cordially invited to the wedding of Stella Whitten and Bryson Crane, of Zion, North Carolina.* Biting her lip, she traced the letters with her fingertip: lacy calligraphy letters in navy-blue ink. Below the address block, a handwritten line, *Daisy, hope to see you. Best wishes, S.* Daisy squeezed her eyes shut. This was no mistake.

It's a mean prank, she wanted to say. *Another excuse to laugh at the crazy girl. No*, she thought, *no, that was years ago. Another life entirely.*

Memories flickered and swarmed before her closed eyes like a flock of hummingbirds. She pictured the sparkling, warlike, little ruby-throated birds from back home with wings abuzz around her. In spite of the thorny panic that still sprang up, the idea of home remained pervasive, sweet, a lullaby, the recollection of the lush, chirping landscape of her childhood still holding onto her somewhere in her body. That place was a lull, the myriad sounds of crickets, the rustling forest, birds, engines, blurring against the snapping beams and shouts of a long-ago afternoon. The word *panic*, Daisy had read, came from Pan, the deity of the forest, and other things, those little noises attributed to him.

There was another face that flickered through Daisy's memory, a girl whose name she had never learned; the singed stubs of eyelashes framing moss-brown eyes, the same color as her own. The wooden beam across her midsection, which surely would have killed her slowly if the fire and chemical smoke had not done the heavy lifting already. Her hands reaching upward, toward Daisy's own, the cheaply made ring on her finger. Daisy's memory clouded. Wasn't there an inscription printed on the ring? It was a word she knew, she was certain of it. Of how her hands held tight to the dying girl's, until she was pulled away, how the ring slipped off the thin fingers into her own fist. Her own voice whispering, *What is your name?*

"Babe, you listening?"

"No," she said. "Sorry—what? I was distracted."

"Who's Stella?"

"Someone from home. You know," she answered with a firm smile that was something less than happy.

"Rather not talk about it now?"

"It's not that." Daisy sipped her tea and looked out the windows, the sky turning from sunset yellow into clear blue. "We were best friends, once. Years ago. There's nothing to say or feel or think about it. And I wouldn't say we left things on happy terms. So…" She picked up the invitation and handed it to Anderson. "The question remains: why?"

"Who knows, Daisy?" He placed it face down on the table and took her hand. "If you don't want to think about it, let's not think about it."

"You're exactly right." She stood up and paced across the room with an excess of energy. Opened her tablet again, traced her finger over her name on the screen. *That's Daisy Ritter*, she thought. *Not that other girl, from way back. Not the girl Stella betrayed. This Daisy is the only one that matters, and Stella might have found my address, but she doesn't know I'm on a different planet altogether.* But something squeezed inside her chest, and it was gentle and soft, propelling her back to Anderson's side. She wrapped her arms around him tight, only exhaling when she felt him return the embrace.

"I love you, Daisy."

"I love you, too."

"Hey," he said, remembering. "How's your dead bird?"

She turned her chin up and beamed at him. "It wasn't dead," she said. "It was alive."

CHAPTER FOUR

Now

When Anderson left for his morning run, Daisy put the invitation on the other side of the room, under a magazine. She glared in its direction, then returned to bed. *Avoid strenuous exercise*, the doctor had said. *Don't lose any weight.* To watch Anderson leave to breathe past city blocks, feel the concrete pushing him back up, made her jealous.

Daisy had to admit she had never excelled at sitting still. But she was remembering that she'd been awake since half past four. She closed her eyes and pulled the blanket over her face to block the light. Ten minutes later, she walked back across the room, lifted the magazine and looked at the invitation again. Bryson Crane—why did that name sound familiar? When you're from a small town, every name sounds familiar. But she was certain she'd heard it somewhere before. Who cared who Stella ended up married to, anyway?

Daisy put the magazine back and sat at her desk, scanning the multitude of tabs open on her browser. She had an interview scheduled with a candidate for city council, and a column on local tourism to write. A write-up on wedding trends was due the following Friday. *Damn.* If it meant working to put Stella's wedding out of her mind, that was just as well; she was no stranger to hard work. She always had at least six projects on the go. She clicked on another tab, only to scroll past an advertisement for nursery furniture. *Damn targeted ads*, she thought. *Someone should tell them that if you do a web search for 'miscarriage' they should probably stop running the pregnancy ads.* She pushed the desk chair away from the computer and rolled to a stop in the middle of the floor.

Anderson didn't need to propose to her. Daisy felt their love was somehow bigger than a need for marriage, the way they'd always looked out for each other. She had kept house and cooked for years while he finished law school, though, to be fair, that was about all she'd considered herself qualified for at the time, writing late at night while he caught up on studying or sleep. In his early years at work, while he was still an intern at the law firm, he'd invited her to every party, introduced her to some of her first contacts for interviews and newspapers. Even when he was studying to pass the bar, he had always made time to help her, looking over her articles. Nearly seventeen years of having each other's backs. They didn't need a ceremony or a piece of paper to make that real.

When Daisy heard the back door open downstairs as Anderson returned from his run, she smiled. "How'd it go?" she called, hearing his footsteps on the stairs. "You're back sooner than I expected."

"Three miles," he replied. "Short run today. I'm going into the office early." Anderson gave Daisy's rolling chair a playful push, then spun her around to face him, kneeling down so that their eyes were level. "You're looking pensive. Work going okay?"

"Yes." Daisy glanced back toward the computer. "Still lots of advertisements for baby stuff. I'm just taking a breather."

"Ah." Anderson brushed Daisy's cheek, swept his fingers across her hair. "You're so stunning in the morning."

"Not as much as you." She leaned closer and wrapped her arms around him, then traced the faint, pale scar that dashed across his chin, a souvenir of a childhood fall.

"Nonsense." Anderson squirmed, pulling back just slightly. Daisy adored that scar, though she knew he disliked it. He rose to his feet, passed through the bedroom, and took a clean towel from the closet. "I'm going to take a shower. Be right back."

Daisy smiled and pushed the rolling chair back to her desk. She clicked through her usual roster of news and social media websites, landing finally on the *Zion Daily*. Daisy told herself that she only checked the Zion news periodically, only to remind herself that she was glad to live far away. Zion. Home. Strange word. All these years later, the distance between her and that town written in stone, and still, the word, *home*, called to mind that hillside North Carolina town. That town, and everything that had happened there.

The too-large font and shabby margins of a cheaply designed website loaded, a banner image of the skyline of her hometown sharpening across the screen. The *Zion Daily* had been around for decades, and their website still reflected the small-town paper's discomfort with newer forms of media. Still, she checked it as though picking a scab—marriage announcements, real estate sales—devouring every word. Even in the comment sections beneath articles, she saw names she recognized, people she had gone to high school or church with, now married, replicating the lives their parents had lived. But she didn't expect to see the headline that cycled across the screen next. Beside it, an image of a chain-link fence enclosing an overgrown yard, a fire-blackened structure that sagged with the weight of years but still, somehow, stood. Daisy inhaled sharply, then clicked on the words *Local Developer Finalizes Sale of Zion Chemical Site*. Daisy instinctively looked over her shoulder, huddled closer to the screen.

> Seventeen years after a fire permanently shut down the Zion Chemical Company, local real estate developer Bryson Crane will finalize purchase of the site. Rumored plans for development include retail, recreation, or industrial. Decades may pass before the groundwater

supply is cleared for residential or foodservice. The fire,
in which four workers were killed…

Not now, she thought, rising from her chair. Surely she could
allow herself a quick run. She'd keep an easy pace. Daisy pulled
off her t-shirt and stepped out of the cotton pajama shorts. She
pulled on a pair of leggings, then wrestled a black sports bra over
her shoulders and into place. Daisy drew deep breaths, stretching
each leg as she pulled on her socks and laced her sneakers, already
craving the fresh morning air.

She tapped on the bathroom door before opening it. "Anderson,
I'm going for a quick run."

"Run?" He raised an eyebrow without turning to face her,
frowning at his reflection. "Do you see gray hair?"

"I don't think so. Well, maybe just one or two." She stood next
to him, glanced at their reflections: her mess of blonde waves,
his darker brown hair. "Looking dapper as ever, Mr. Moreland."

He stood up to his full height and picked up his aftershave.
"Miss Ritter, I think you already know you're not supposed to be
running anywhere."

"Jog," Daisy countered. She took a clean tank top from the
drying rack and pulled it on over her bra.

"Walk." He patted the aftershave onto his neck, twisted the cap
back onto the bottle, and replaced it on the shelf above the sink.

"Jog," Daisy answered firmly. "I won't be gone long. I know
my limits." She drew close and leaned her chin on his shoulder,
turning away from the mirror as she spoke. "You know, the doctor
said we could start trying again anytime."

He tilted his chin and smiled back at her, and it seemed to Daisy
that the warmth of his expression reached her from a distance, or
perhaps too close to focus. She blew him a kiss and turned to leave,
heading down the stairs at a trot and breaking into a jog as soon as
she was out the door. Maybe it was harder for him than he let on.

What mattered was that, whatever that inscrutable distance was, they still reached each other. Always had. She turned the corner, jogging in place as she waited for the light to change. This was the relationship that had saved her, that had helped her build her life into something she cherished. Her life with him. The reason Zion, and whoever lived there and whatever poisoned, backhanded things they were up to, didn't have to matter to her one bit. The light turned green and she ran.

CHAPTER FIVE

Before

Zion Chemical sat on a large, fenced-in lot, just a mile, as the crow flies, up the steep hillside behind the graying-white ranch home where Daisy and her parents lived. As the hill rose, the trees thickened, and the rocks began to jut out of the ground, standing like the protruding fossilized bones of some long-extinct creature, alongside the remnants of old stone fences. Daisy supposed the fences had been built by mountain settlers from years back, their land now grown over. Because of how the land became complicated as it merged into the mountain, the roadway couldn't go straight up, instead winding around a series of switchback turns that took nearly twenty minutes by car.

Daisy's father was named William, though it had been decades since anyone, with the exception of his wife, had called him anything but Tracker. A deer hunter, the story went that he had once successfully tracked an elusive buck through the woods for weeks before finally shooting it. These days, though Tracker left the house regularly for hunting trips, Daisy had never seen him return from his excursions with anything more useful than a cooler full of empty beer cans.

Whether his trips were solitary or with friends, he always left and returned alone. There was a silent rule in their house against begrudging him this. Daisy's mother Ellen had come from a family where drink and violence were daily bread, and she seemed to have some deep resolve against ever speaking ungratefulness for her relatively quiet, boring life. Ellen never pursued an explanation for Tracker's fruitless hunting trips. They were his own time. She had a roof. Suggesting ungraciousness for his ways, however, seemed sanctioned.

"It's a miracle," Ellen used to say when Daisy was a child, "how your father always manages to find money for beer." She had repeated this so many times that Daisy didn't realize it was a joke until she was nearly ten.

But Ellen never begrudged Tracker his relaxation, after the long days at work.

It was early that summer, the summer before Daisy turned eighteen, that Tracker got it into his head that Daisy should take a job at the plant. Zion Chemical employed only a few dozen men and no women, although Tracker had often pressured Daisy to take part-time work there. It would be off the books, he promised her, and entirely safe, just sweeping the floors. Just some spending cash, for her to help out with groceries.

Exactly what the employees dealt with there, whatever might make it other than safe, was a mystery to Daisy. She could remember two occasions when the fish downstream from the plant had died in the creeks. She could remember four times her mother had miscarried pregnancies. A handful of times there had been the sound of a small explosion, metallic-smelling smoke spilling down the hillside. It was only strange if asked about, which Ellen would not permit. Not directly.

So when Tracker offered her the job, an offer that was not meant to be questioned, Daisy's first thought was a resounding, *hell, no.* Not because of the uncertain safety so much as the time commitment. The summer before her last year of high school was precious free time. Daisy had become pretty, her skin golden and freckled from the sun, her curves generous and full. Ellen, who was pale and slim, seemed to grow anxious to see her daughter taking up space, filling out her clothes. So Daisy knew Ellen would not come to her rescue if she were to vocalize her outright refusal.

"I won't have time," she had said, looking down at her dinner plate. "The summer's shorter than you think. Plus, I have algebra."

Tracker drank from his beer and set it down heavily on the table. "Algebra? It's summer."

"I failed the class this spring," Daisy said. "I'm taking it again."

That, at least, was true. Daisy couldn't have cared much less about the subject of algebra, although she had begun to take some interest in the boy from school who was helping her with the homework.

So, Daisy had refused to work at Zion Chemical, and the subject was put aside.

"Imagine that," Tracker grumbled, his big voice giving way to an awkward laugh. "Never thought I'd see the day a girl refused a paying job. Times sure have changed. Figured you'd want a chance to pitch in, at least help a little with gas and groceries."

Ellen soothed Tracker with a long, soft stare that tapered into a wise nod of her chin. As she nodded, her fine hair tangled in the top button of her dressing gown. Daisy felt herself a sort of mark or target, a hidden dollar value on her hours, a value she owed for living.

"You never bring back any food from your hunting," she said. "You don't pitch in as much as you could." It wasn't Tracker, but Ellen who turned and slapped her. Maybe so Tracker wouldn't, or because Ellen was the one who was more frightened of having their fragile peace disturbed.

"Don't you ever talk like that again."

"Sorry, Mama."

Daisy swallowed her anger. There was a mean current in Ellen's piety, a part of her that stood guard over Tracker's shortcomings and twisted the rest of the world around him until it was Daisy's fault for pointing out the obvious. That same summer, at seventeen, Daisy had begun to sneak cans of beer from the back of the fridge. She could usually get one of Stella's brothers to buy enough to replace it. There was too much risk in hiding any other sort of alcohol around the house. And besides, she didn't drink it for the taste, or the rush, although she came in time to appreciate both. She did it for the act of theft. An act of secrecy, however small, to prove her life was her own, even if it didn't always feel like it.

CHAPTER SIX

Before

In the overcrowded high school auditorium, Stella and Daisy sat shoulder to shoulder, watching the senior graduation. Both their foreheads were misted with sweat, and every few minutes, Stella took a powder compact from her purse and dabbed at her face. Though their classmates around them chattered and whispered, the pair sat in silence, the significance of the moment holding an unexpected gravity.

"Just think," Stella said, leaning close to Daisy. "Next year, that will be us."

Daisy turned, smiling back at her friend. The dim lights caught Stella's gleaming eyes, her harmonious features glowing with promise.

"I don't think so." Daisy's smile faltered. The room was dimly lit, but she nearly felt a shadow pass between them. "For some reason, I don't think it will."

"What?" Stella spoke aloud, several heads turning their way. "Why would you say something like that?"

"I'm sorry. I don't even know." Daisy shook her head to clear the sense of foreboding. "Just a feeling." Finally, after what felt like hours of acknowledgments and rounds of applause, the classes were permitted to file out, one row at a time. As the space began to clear, Daisy and Stella hung back, occupying the last two seats in the darkened row.

"I can't think of any reason we wouldn't be graduating together," Stella said.

"God willing, we will." Daisy extended her tanned legs and propped them on the back of the row ahead of theirs. Stella stretched her legs out to imitate her relaxed pose, but, a few inches shorter than Daisy, she only brushed the next row with her toes. "I'm failing algebra."

"Still?"

"Yeah." Daisy tilted her chin back, rolling her eyes. She stood up and began to approach the door, adjusting her backpack as Stella caught up. "Failed, really. Past tense. I'll be in summer school again."

"Well, all that matters is you pass it, so that you don't fall behind."

"Yeah. Otherwise, maybe it won't be both of us up there a year from now."

"Just think," Stella whispered, holding the door open for Daisy as they walked into the corridor. "When we come back to this building, we'll be *seniors*."

"You're forgetting," Daisy said once again. "Summer school. When I walk in here again, it's going to be next week."

It was a half-day, the last day of school, and they collected their backpacks from their lockers and hurried outside. Crowds of students lingered by the row of idling school buses. Daisy and Stella walked together across the hot pavement, offering their yearbooks to friends to sign, writing cryptic jokes and warm messages whenever friends' yearbooks were exchanged.

It wasn't a long walk, but the May sunshine was already warm, and they moved slowly alongside the two-lane road that led to Tucker Swamp Road.

"It's bright," Daisy murmured. "I forgot my shades."

"Do you want my sunglasses?" Stella pulled the frames halfway off her face.

"No, thanks," Daisy answered. "You remembered yours. It's only fair you wear them."

"Let's take turns." Stella handed them over. "You can have them till we pass the cow pond."

"I'll miss you after graduation," Daisy said. She took the sunglasses from Stella and put them on, the world around her taking on a protected violet tint.

"Don't be silly."

"What's it going to be like?"

"We're best friends," Stella said, huffing as they walked uphill. "That's not going to change."

As the two girls passed by the algae-speckled pond beyond the cow field, Daisy removed the sunglasses and returned them to Stella. She blinked and squinted at the bright sun. They were almost home. Stella's house was up a long drive, number 405. A quarter-mile down the road was the gravel stretch that led to Daisy's house, number 407. They walked up Stella's driveway together, shaded by willow trees, the grasping, swishing branches hanging low around their shoulders. Daisy looked toward Stella's house with some longing, but knew that she was expected at home. If the Ritter house was full of quiet chaos, Stella's family's house exploded with energy, the out-loud kind, with five siblings and twice as many pets. With all their mess and arguments out loud, Daisy would sit in Stella's room or outside by the pond and marvel at the satisfied lull that punctuated each uproar. In Stella's house, secrets were harmless; there were no secrets that lasted. Daisy grew up around secrets she knew by heart but didn't have words for, at least not in those days.

Past the red-brick house, they continued to the barbed wire fence that marked the border to Daisy's yard, installed by a prior inhabitant to keep livestock in or out.

"What are you doing this week?" Stella asked. "I'm so, so glad school's out."

"School's out for you," Daisy said. "Summer school starts Monday. Stupid algebra."

"You'll be fine," Stella insisted. "Come over after school, if you want. I'll be at home until we go on vacation in three weeks."

She held up one of the lines of wire while Daisy crouched and inched between them. This had been a simple maneuver when they were eight years old, to just bend over and inch through. Now, taller, with breasts to worry about, it was trickier, but the wire fence wouldn't bear her weight for climbing. Daisy stood up on the other side of the fence and smoothed her hair back.

"Here." Stella held out the sunglasses. "Wear them home. That way we have to hang out soon, so you can give them back."

"God, no. I'm afraid I'll break them. I could never replace these."

"Take them."

Before Daisy took the glasses, she held Stella's stare, both of them agreeing in the same moment. With girlish smiles, they each pushed a fingertip down against a barb, just enough to draw blood, then pressed their fingertips together, smirking at each other, a ritual that was as playful as it was deadly serious. They were blood sisters.

CHAPTER SEVEN

Now

Running felt good. A couple miles in, Daisy's lungs burned, sweat misting her forehead and shoulders. Instead of turning back, she headed to a park that bordered a neighborhood of shops and cafes. She paused by a fountain, stretched one calf and then the other, then reached her arms above her head, letting the tension in her muscles melt. Fresh air and sounds of the city occupied her senses, providing some much-needed distraction from her thoughts. She sat on a bench and felt the breeze cooling her face.

The morning was cloudless and blue. It wasn't a day to spend at the house, ruminating over things she couldn't change, questions she might not even want the answers to. Daisy repeated these lines to herself twice and then a third time. *Sale Finalizes On...* She took out her phone and opened the website, promising herself to read the summary and then forget about it. What did it matter if the land sold? It would change nothing. But she read the headline, the summary, and kept straight on reading.

The fire, in which four workers were killed, opened a cleanup that took nearly two years. Following finalization of the sale, Mr. Crane, a Zion native, looks forward to marrying his fiancée, Miss Stella Whitten, a journalist.

"I'll be damned," Daisy whispered to herself. "I knew I'd heard that name before." The journalist's thrill of finding a connection quickly settled into bewilderment. *Stella's marrying Bryson Crane, the man who's about to buy that confounded piece of land, and she's invited me—the one person with information that could prevent that sale—to her wedding?* Daisy almost laughed before she remembered. Nobody believed her. Nobody ever had.

The bond she and Stella had shared was so close and so sweet that it had fermented, turned sour without her even noticing. Yet, even now, on the other side of the country, Daisy could reach into her memory and listen for Stella's voice. Sometimes when Daisy couldn't think anything kind, she paused, asked herself what Stella would have said, and listened. *Girl friendships like that aren't meant to last*, she told herself. *This world takes them all apart. Starting with one simple betrayal. The last time I trusted her was when the adult world came calling for her, claimed her as its own.*

But she always wondered, each time she tuned in and listened for Stella in her memory, how different things could have been. Zion was tangled up with nostalgia in her mind, so that it was impossible to remember her hometown without imagining herself in an alternate life, one where she'd had the courage to stay. Against her better judgment, she wondered what Jesse's life was like now, if he had finished veterinary school, if his sweet mother still lived in the big house up the road from her parents.

She stood up, stretching again. With midday approaching, the sun was growing warmer, and she decided to head back. A guilty admission crossed her mind as she picked up pace, then slowed. Anderson was right: she wasn't supposed to run. No strenuous exercise—was that what they had said? No exercising to lose weight. Not if you're still trying. Never mind that she was carrying four months' worth of pregnancy weight with nothing to show for it. Daisy compromised with a brisk power walk, turning over the pieces in her mind. There was a link, a connection. Stella would never have invited Daisy for old times' sake; she had been a pragmatist all her life.

Daisy turned her key in the door and walked inside, savoring the rush of cool air. Anderson looked up from his seat on the sofa, startled.

"Back already?"

"It's been nearly two hours," she answered, untying her ponytail and shaking her hair loose. "Thought you had to go to work early today."

"The meeting was canceled," he said. Daisy nodded and turned away, a half-formed thought on the tip of her tongue. "What is it?" he asked, a hint in his tone giving Daisy an impression of anxiety.

She turned to face him with her fingers laced together. "I thought about Stella's wedding invitation, and I've decided I want to go."

"You do?"

"Yes." She moved behind the sofa and adjusted the blinds again, lowering them so that the glass would be visible to any birds that might otherwise mistake it for thin air. Anderson looked over his shoulder to face her with a puzzled stare.

"Why?"

"I guess I'm curious about her. That's not wrong, is it?" Avoiding his cautionary frown, she walked into the kitchen and filled a glass of water from the pitcher in the fridge.

"Of course it's not wrong," Anderson said, turning back to his phone. "Is it a good idea for you, though?"

Daisy finished her glass of water before she answered him. "I've spent nearly half my life far away from Zion. I'm not going back to dig up any of that old nonsense. I promise you, that's the last thing I want to do." She felt a chill prickle her arms. "I'll fly in, stay at a hotel, go to the wedding, and fly back."

"Let me go with you," Anderson suggested. Daisy opened the refrigerator and scanned its contents, feigning distraction. "You have a lot of memories there—not all of them good ones."

"True." She picked up a packet of cookies and pretended to scrutinize the label. Of course she wanted him to go; that wasn't the question. But she didn't want Anderson to accompany her out of obligation. Daisy felt her worry ease as he walked into the kitchen, regarded her warmly from the other side of the open refrigerator door.

"If it matters to you, then you should go," he said. "Maybe just not by yourself."

"I'm capable of going by myself," Daisy insisted.

"You know, it might be fun for us." He took the cookies from her hands, offered her one, and then closed the refrigerator door. "We haven't had a weekend away since winter."

"If there's one good thing about Zion," Daisy mused, "it's that it's beautiful in the summer." She took a bite of the cookie.

Anderson smiled. "Then it's a date."

She hugged him, savoring the warmth of his arms around her. *I'm capable of going by myself,* she thought. *But isn't it beautiful not to have to do things alone?*

CHAPTER EIGHT

Now

That Zion was accessible by airplane, or any modern form of travel, seemed somehow to besmirch it. Flying in didn't give Daisy any time to acclimate to the strange pressure in the air there, the humid climate that draped over every bit of her skin, familiar and immodest. It was the type of place, Daisy thought, that people ought to be able to get to only by car, or truck, or hitchhiking. She thought of the trail hikers who used to wander into town each summer, dirty and skinny like animals after winter, with a religious glow in their eyes. A place like this demanded some sacrifice for you to come to its door. Daisy felt a superstitious, gut-deep fear that making the journey by air would force the old place to take its ransom in some other, unexpected manner.

As Daisy felt the airplane descend to its landing, she could almost pinpoint the tiny town, which flew past in seconds. Where the brackish-green river slid through the lazy piedmont, where the hills began to rise like whipped egg whites or waves in a storm; just there. A town at the point where you knew you ought to turn back.

Yet Daisy's sense of foreboding was outmatched by her curiosity. To see Stella, now an adult, to grasp for a glimpse of what her life had grown into. This was not, Daisy told herself, absolutely not a fact-finding mission. She had no intention of finding out why Stella wanted her there, or whether it had anything to do with her fiancé's big purchase. It was a springtime weekend in the mountains with the man she loved, that only happened to be taking place in the same small town she had escaped as a wounded teenager.

"You can see it, if you look." Sitting in the middle seat, she leaned across Anderson's shoulder, letting her chin rest on his upper arm, and pointed out the window.

"What am I looking for?"

What, indeed? she wondered. A scattering of buildings that spanned four zip codes, more churches than any town its size should have needed, surrounded by the blanched arms of blighted chestnuts and fast-growing pines.

"There's not much to see," she admitted, squeezing his arm.

"Are you still okay with this idea? If you're not, we can book a return flight as soon as we land."

"I'm kind of looking forward to it." Daisy rested her head on his shoulder, then leaned up to plant a kiss on his cheekbone. "You're looking out for me, and I love it, but it's not necessary."

"Old habits die hard."

"Anyway, maybe it will be nice, you know, to have a weekend somewhere new." She didn't want to spell it out. *Somewhere different. Away from our house. Somewhere we haven't lost a baby before.*

"New?"

"New to you, at least."

If Anderson had caught her meaning, he didn't choose to answer it. She studied him as he looked out the window and suddenly grasped his hand, squeezing it gratefully.

"I've pushed you too hard to get over this," she whispered. "I'm sorry. I'll try to relax."

Daisy buckled her seatbelt when the descent began in earnest. Each moment she counted what might go wrong to prevent her arrival in Zion. If there were turbulence, and if she had not fastened her seatbelt, she might be tossed up, bump her head against the ceiling of the cabin.

She wondered if there would be a security threat, something that would delay them at the airport. There was not. Both of their checked bags arrived in short order. The rental car Anderson had reserved was ready, an oversized sedan with a sunroof.

"I don't know why I keep feeling that something could go wrong," Daisy insisted. "Oh, damn. I forgot my nail polish." Her hands, now with two fingernails chipped, squeezed into fists in the pockets of her sundress, a vibrant sky blue she'd worn for luck, to remind her of the New Mexico sky.

"They sell nail polish everywhere," Anderson said. He took her suitcase and placed it in the trunk. "Weddings are meant to be fun. Try to think of it as just another party."

The Holiday Inn just off the interstate had lost their reservation. With all of the area's high school graduations taking place the following day, there was not a single room open. Daisy stood behind Anderson's shoulder glancing with concern at the clerk. She had worried that something would go wrong. Was this the trap, the trick? She held her composure as Anderson talked with the clerk, then gave up when he realized that the hotel was truly booked out. The clerk agreed to make some phone calls while they waited.

"There's bound to be a vacancy somewhere." Minor annoyances, for Anderson, seemed to loom larger than they did for Daisy, who had learned that life often demanded flexibility.

"We'll come up with something," Daisy said. "We could always find a campground, or sleep in the car. It might be fun."

"You forget I'm almost ten years older than you." He began to smile. "If I have to sleep on the ground, or in the back seat of a car, you'll have to bring me to the wedding in a wheelchair."

"I'll carry you there if I have to," she laughed. "I didn't bring you all this way so I could go to the wedding alone."

"Daisy, you know this place. What's nearby? Anything to keep us from sleeping in a car? What about your parents?"

"That… would be a last resort." Daisy didn't add that her parents lived in such a small house, Anderson would probably have to stay on the porch. Not to mention they'd never let her share a room under their roof with a man she wasn't married to. "There are a couple of bed-and-breakfast type places, but…"

"Sir?" The clerk waved him over as she hung up the phone. "I found a room. It's at an inn just on the other side of town. They're holding a room for you until you get there."

"Thank you," Anderson said. "Can I have the address?" As the clerk read them the address, he wrote on the back of one of his business cards, took Daisy's arm, and led her back to the car.

Daisy slipped into the passenger seat, feeling the June sun unseasonably warm on her legs. She closed the door and turned up the air conditioner.

"So, where are we going?"

"Sounds like a romantic little place called…" He typed the address into the GPS as he spoke. "The Blue Ghost." Daisy stifled a gasp.

"What? You know it?" He threw the car into reverse and backed out onto the street, then made a sharp left, eyes on the GPS navigation.

"Yeah. The owner, Teresa Lopez, her son's my ex. Sort of," Daisy added. "Barely. You know, I can find a campsite for us. Or maybe the next town over has a vacancy."

"It's getting late," Anderson said. "Don't you think we could try to make it work for the night?"

"We can try," Daisy agreed. She didn't love it—this was certainly an inconvenience to her plan to pretend they were somewhere new for a romantic weekend out of town. But Teresa wouldn't recognize her now, would she? And even if she did, Daisy realized, it was inevitable that she would have run into an old acquaintance somewhere along the way. Better Teresa than her son.

As the car descended the mountainside, the dirt road widened, lined with stately magnolias, their waxy leaves glimmering as if with perspiration. It was too early for them to bloom, but some of the trees bore a few dense buds. They drove past an abandoned barn. Daisy looked through its cracked windowpanes, straight through the windows on its other side, and shivered. A quarter-mile further, Anderson pulled into the lot by a hand-painted sign, whitewashed gray wood dotted with blue orbs. The Blue Ghost.

As Anderson took the suitcases out of the trunk, Daisy pulled her hair into a ponytail and straightened her clothes, trying to sweep the lint and wrinkles of a day of travel off with her palms. She crossed the familiar parking lot to the front steps, lingering rather than climbing the old porch. Two empty rocking chairs nodded in the breeze, the deep green of the forest beyond the yard casting a kind of glow around them. Daisy heard the trickle of the creek at the edge of the property, just beyond the shadowed Victorian gazebo. The noise of the creek, she remembered, was just sufficient to cover a whispered conversation held there.

"You must be the guests from the Holiday Inn."

Standing at the edge of the porch with her hand on her suitcase, Daisy didn't turn her head when she heard Teresa's voice, instead letting Anderson approach her. She joked about his protective habits, but she could always depend on him to take the lead when she chose to hang back. As he explained the lost reservation, letting her know that they only needed a room for the night, she glanced past the edge of the porch into the forest beyond, the winking blue fireflies dotting the trees. The railing under her hand reminded her of the long afternoons she'd spent here in high school. When Teresa had bought the place, it was in disrepair, only the bones of the house holding solid.

"Thanks," she heard Anderson say. "No, we'll only need one key. Daisy, you ready to go inside?"

"Yes," she said. "Sorry. I was daydreaming." She sidled up next to him, the wheels of her suitcase clicking over the boards of the porch as she pulled it behind her. Teresa was standing in the doorway. Daisy met her eyes and looked immediately to the lantern on the wall behind her. *Like I've never been here. Like I'm a stranger from out of town.* Back then, her hair had been longer, so long that it used to catch when she rolled up the windows of the car. She'd been thinner, probably. Dirt under her fingernails. In a word, scrappy.

"Daisy Ritter, is that you?"

"Ah. Well, yes."

Teresa crossed the porch and wrapped her in a warm, fragrant hug. "If they'd said it was you, I'd have offered you my own room."

As Teresa held her shoulders, giving her an admiring look, Daisy caught Anderson's concerned stare. "My, but you look *lovely*. And we haven't seen you in *years*. Where are you living now?"

"New Mexico," Daisy answered.

"How long have you been there?"

"Since, um." Daisy paused, wondering exactly how much Teresa knew about what had happened before she left town. "Well, we've been there for a while now. This is my boyfriend, Anderson."

"And how did you two meet?" she asked. Just as Daisy lifted her mortified gaze to Teresa's eyes, she relented, her smile fading as the look of recollection crept over her features.

"I always wondered how you were doing," Daisy offered by way of apology.

"We always wondered about you too, dear," she answered. "You two must be exhausted. Wherever you've come from. Come on inside and I'll show you to your room. I'm happy to see you, Daisy," she said, "whatever it is that brings you back."

"You don't know? Stella's getting married."

"Oh, of course," she said. "Jesse told me at some point, but I didn't know it was this weekend. I don't see that much of Jesse lately. You'd never know he only lives five minutes away."

"Oh, really?" Daisy could tell her attempt to convey disinterest was shaky. The last she'd heard, he was married.

"Yes, his veterinary office is on the old farm up the street. Just past the creek—you remember the one?"

"Yes," she said. A long-disused farm property, a house with a solid stone foundation. Daisy had always known Jesse wouldn't go far from home. "I know the one."

"Now that it's just him out there, it's all work." As Teresa smiled, Daisy thought she might have winked, but she couldn't be certain.

"Some of us work hard, play hard," Daisy remembered. "Jesse was always work hard, work hard." She caught Anderson's eye and realized he hadn't spoken a word. "You're right, we're tired." She took his hand and followed Teresa up the stairs, trying not to remark out loud that the house looked exactly the same. Daisy remembered the first time Jesse had invited her to this house, how she had immediately felt welcomed.

In the front bedroom on the third floor, Anderson pushed the door closed behind Teresa with a quiet *thank you*. He put her suitcase at the foot of the bed, then his own next to it. He studied the bedroom suite and the room around them. "Beautiful place. Sounds like you knew them pretty well."

"Yeah, I did," Daisy said. "A long time ago. Is this okay with you?"

"Of course," he said. "Not what I expected, but this beats the Holiday Inn by a mile. More importantly, are you okay with staying here?"

Daisy watched him as he waited for her to answer. It had been a long day, and they were both tired and hungry. She knew he wanted her to say yes. She could do this, right? "This is the last place I wanted to be," she insisted. "Teresa's a sweet woman. That's all. Her son, however…"

"What happened?" Anderson asked.

"Just, you know, high school romance. *Young love*," Daisy sighed, rolling her eyes. "And all that absolute bull."

"Was that the guy who—"

"Let's not talk about it," Daisy answered. She exhaled, loosened the muscles in her face with a conscious effort, and turned back to Anderson with a gentle smile. "If things had worked out with him, I would have never met you."

Daisy could remember Jesse at seventeen, helping his mother paint this room when he had finished his homework. A gentle, pale violet color, like the last hint of light on the sunset horizon as the dark sky crept over. She sat on the bed and sighed, looking up toward the ceiling.

"We don't have to stay," Anderson reminded her. Daisy saw that he was tired, remembered the constant work it must have taken worrying about her. What kind of thanks was it, she wondered, for her to make him drive them somewhere else this late at night, try to find another room?

"No, babe." She stood up and wrapped her arms around his shoulders. "I'm fine. I'm more than fine. Let's go get something to eat."

"Cheers to that," he laughed. "Speaking of cheers, is there anything open around here? Preferably somewhere with alcohol?"

Daisy laughed. "Despite all the churches, this is not, in fact, a dry town."

CHAPTER NINE

Before

In retrospect, the days preceding the fire had been extraordinary. But maybe omens are always obvious in one's memory, the missed signs and warnings simply part of a sequence of events. The truth was that Daisy's life was so filled with moments of foreboding, of pregnant silence, she had long since lost any ability to identify a clear sign for what it was. The air was as thick and heavy in their home as the poisoned well water that seeped through the earth under it, growing into the veins of the flora that surrounded their small house. At seventeen, apart from Stella and her family, Daisy was the youngest person she knew of in her neighborhood. All the women she knew had either moved away or had miscarried their pregnancies, like her mother had. Though her mother was fastidious and hated any sign of blood, Daisy had seen the trace of pink at the bottom of the toilet bowl, noticed the empty laundry baskets, after nearly four months of hopefulness. Her mother was having another miscarriage. Meanwhile, the Carolina foothills were blossoming at the ripest part of spring, the grass of their small lawn freshly cut.

"This is the last time the grass will look this good," Tracker had proclaimed before leaving for work, surveying the yard from the kitchen window over the sink. "Weather's already getting hotter. Soon it'll be brown, patches of dust."

"Maybe we'll get rain," Ellen volunteered. "Last summer we had rain."

"Yeah," Tracker snorted. "More than we could stand."

"Will, dear." Ellen's tone sweetened. "I misplaced that ring you gave me. Have you seen…"

Ellen was an expert in changing the subject, in diverting Tracker's stewing anger from one dot to the next. Daisy tuned out, sitting quietly over her cereal. She remembered last summer, how water had dripped through the roof, how the gravel had washed down the driveway in rivulets of mud, drowning Ellen's modest flower gardens. The skies that summer had been a stormy gray that took on a verdigris cast with the afternoon rains, almost the same color as Tracker's eyes. Daisy had always wished she'd taken after her mother, Ellen, who embodied love, Daisy thought, in her slight softness. Instead, she was nearly the image of Tracker, long-legged, built for strength. Daisy considered it plain luck that she hadn't inherited his mean-looking eyes, too.

"Nope. Haven't seen it," Tracker replied. "Sure it'll turn up." He kissed Ellen brusquely on the cheek and headed out the door, not before ruffling the top of Daisy's head with a heavy hand. He was always like that: kisses too rough, footsteps too heavy. When Daisy was little and her father would ask for a bite of her apple, she used to marvel at the size of his bite, nearly half the fruit gone. The rest of their house fell quiet as the screen door clapped shut behind him.

"Well." Ellen folded her hands. "You want to help me pull out that wisteria?"

Daisy did not. But this wasn't the kind of question that was a question. Two months shy of starting her last year in high school, she was learning by trial and error which questions really offered an option. She washed her cereal bowl, turning the faucet on the soggy flakes in the bottom of the sink, and stood at attention.

"Not in those shorts," her mother said. "You'll sunburn. And what if someone from church drives by?"

"*Mom.*"

"Besides, there are ticks. Mosquitoes. Brambles. Go on," Ellen clucked, shepherding Daisy toward her room. "Put on jeans and sneakers. And don't forget socks! Wear long socks, and tuck the jeans into them."

Daisy's room was an afterthought, a ten-by-twelve-foot rectangle in between the stairwell and the bathroom, with a curtain hung over an open doorway at either end. She pulled the curtains to each edge of the rods, though she could still see light through them. She stood at the inner corner away from each open doorway to change into her jeans, a years-old habit. From here, she might theoretically have been visible in her undressed state through the window from outside, but that was just the forest, and nobody was looking anyway.

Already humiliated in her gardening attire, Daisy grumbled when Ellen handed her a straw hat, mumbling something about her complexion. Nobody else's mother begrudged them a suntan. She followed Ellen across the long yard, wondering if the grass under their feet would turn brown on this very day. By the edge of the forest, Ellen had started an herb garden, at her father's prompting to grow "something more useful" than the flowers she enjoyed. Rosemary, oregano, savory, sage, all perennial plants, since he disliked buying annuals, were bordered with a long plank of wood. The wisteria vine grew wild in the trees around it, and, unless they fought it back each spring and summer, would have continued to grow inland, to swallow their very house. With gloves on, Ellen and Daisy silently tugged at it by the roots. Soon it grew hot, and Daisy's peaceful mood dissipated with the morning cool. She began to quietly grow angry, wiping sweat from her forehead and neck with her bare arm.

"Pull up all the roots," Ellen chided, taking note of her lazy work. "If you don't pull all the roots out, it'll just grow back."

"I don't see why we can't let some of it grow here." Daisy waved her arm at the expanse of wisteria that hung from the oak tree above them, its vigorous vines weighing down the tree's limbs, heavy with sweetly fragrant blossoms. "It would be easy enough, and it's pretty, and it smells nice. We should just let it be."

"You don't think that might look a little disorganized?"

"No. It would be beautiful."

Ellen pursed her lips. Daisy realized that it had been a disguised question, the kind of question that was really a statement, and that she had answered it the wrong way. Ellen would never budge when it came to her garden. "It's a nasty plant," she said. "Tropical—grows too fast. Invasive, that's it. It was brought here and the native plants can't compete against it. It pulls down entire trees and houses if you let it."

"Not if you cultivate it," Daisy said. "Stella's mother lets it grow on an arbor."

"Oh, she does, does she?" Ellen rolled her eyes in the direction of their neighbor's house, then quickly smoothed her features. "I'm not interested in the choices Mrs. Whitten makes. Wisteria isn't a native plant, and we should all do our share to keep it from tearing the natural environment apart."

"Are you a native plant, Mom?" Daisy rolled her eyes.

"I have no idea what you mean."

"We're all transplants," she murmured, as if wisely, focusing on the soil, partly embarrassed by her thoughts, partly afraid of them. "You think our entire culture is a native plant here? Besides, we have bigger problems around here than wisteria."

"I have no idea," Ellen repeated. She had an incredible blind spot, Daisy thought, for drawing out metaphor. She wanted to talk about the miscarriage, but didn't know how to ask her mother directly. Ellen's stress was invisible, or maybe it was that she wore it every day, like whatever fragrance it was she used that made her smell papery and sweet, like dried roses and talcum.

"You really don't?" Daisy pushed. "You think the wisteria is the most poisonous thing about this land?" She rested a dirty, gloved hand on her knee and turned her chin over her shoulder to look up the hillside behind them, toward the plant. Ellen wasn't the only woman in the neighborhood who had lost pregnancies, one after the next. Daisy heard whispers, at church, sometimes at school. Stella's mother paid for special water filters on their showers, bottled water to drink and cook with. Stella had four younger siblings.

"You don't know what you're talking about." Ellen's face tightened and she pulled harder on a root, drawing it out of the earth with a snap and a scatter of red clay soil. Daisy felt a squeeze on her heart, the fear of having reached down too far, having struck something real. The damp ground opened where the roots had pulled free and Ellen set to it with a spade, her gloved hands wrapped tight around the handle as if it were a dagger. The dirt flew and Daisy stepped back, anxious.

"What are you doing, Mom?"

Her mother did not seem to hear her, using the spade like a knife to cut through another root portion. It looked as though she were digging a hole.

"I want to go to Stella's house," she said. "I want to shower and go to Stella's. And I have to study later."

Ellen sat up as if she'd been shocked, as if a realization had fallen over her. "You'd better," her mother said, recovering herself and speaking with a tense throat. "You had better pass algebra this time. I can't believe my own daughter is taking a remedial summer class." Daisy stood up, brushed her hands on her knees, and turned to walk away, anxious to remove the jeans stupidly tucked into her socks. As she did so, she caught a glimpse of a cardboard tissue box behind her mother's folded knees, nearly out of her line of sight. The box was covered with one of the innumerable sheets of Bible verses that were handed out at church. Ellen caught Daisy's eye by accident and Daisy had to turn away from the intensity of her pain, fearing it was contagious. The sound that came from her throat was a hybrid of a cough and a squeak. She dropped the moment as if it were a live animal and hurried away.

CHAPTER TEN

Now

A barbeque restaurant four miles away was the closest option. They arrived one hour before closing, enough time for Anderson to pout over a sandwich, and Daisy to eat his fries and finish two drinks. As he drove back, too fast, more so because it was dark now, Daisy watched for sparks of color in the woods, whether checking for fireflies, or distant fires, she wasn't sure.

"Why is it called the Blue Ghost?"

"This is one of the only places you can come to see the blue fireflies every spring. People say they're Civil War spirits. Surprised she had a room for us at all." She relaxed, watching the countryside go past outside her window. "You know how fireflies blink on and off, kind of yellowish?"

"Yeah."

"These ones don't blink, they really glow. And they're blue, almost turquoise blue." Though her tone turned wistful, she shivered.

Anderson nodded his head. An uneasy silence rested tensely between them as he sped up the road and pulled loudly into the small lot, letting the engine idle. Daisy paused to touch his wrist. "I meant what I said on the plane, earlier today. I realized I've been pushing you to get over what happened, at my pace. That wasn't fair, and I'm sorry."

"Don't be," he said, eyes focused on the soft lights of the dashboard.

"I mean it." Daisy withdrew her hand, felt her fingers curling in, nervously scratching at the pink nail polish again. Giving him space to get over things at his own pace; that was what she intended to do. "We don't need to discuss it. When you're ready to, you know, think about trying again, just say."

In the quiet that followed, Anderson's expression was difficult to read. Maybe that was what she needed to learn: not knowing precisely what he was thinking, where he was at. Trust him to his own cartography. Counterintuitive for Daisy, who'd first started learning her own way after being deserted at a roadside in a state many miles from home. But for him, for them, she would try.

As Anderson followed her through the foyer, the quaintly appointed sitting room, and up the wide staircase, she imagined herself with magical blinders on, insulating her from the familiarity of the room around her. She halfway wanted to drop to the ground and crawl, as if all her memories were a cloud of smoke that hung about the ceiling. She unlocked the door of their room, let Anderson walk in ahead of her, then locked it behind them. He seemed distant; he was tired, Daisy knew, and besides that, it was probably unpleasant for him to be here, in the same way that it was for her, if not quite so much. But how strange, to see him undressing for bed, hanging his shirt in the closet, in this house, where she had passed so many hours with Jesse.

"I think I'll take a shower and get some work done before I go to sleep," she said. "Unless you'd like to sit outside on the porch? Maybe you can still see some fireflies."

"No, I think I'll turn in early." He drew the covers back and placed the ornamental pillow on an armchair. "Besides, I'm not too sure I want to see those fireflies up close, if what you said is true."

Daisy flashed a warm smile at him. "Baby, those fireflies are the least haunted thing about this town. Trust me."

And I would know, she thought. *The most haunted thing about this town is standing right here in this room. And it's not him.*

Daisy showered and dressed in a pair of leggings and a t-shirt, combing her hair as she stood in front of the bathroom mirror. The bathroom, at least, had seen a renovation since she'd last been here. She opened the door quietly and found the lights dimmed and Anderson sleeping. His ability to fall asleep instantly, and to stay asleep, mystified her, as if he had a magical power she couldn't soak up, no matter how close she got. She cracked a window to let the breeze in, taking in the smell of leaves and brush and nighttime air.

As the sheer curtains rippled in the breeze, Daisy opened her purse and took out Stella's wedding invitation again, tracing over each line of text with her fingers, as if doing so could reveal an explanation she had not found there before. She pulled the window frame up to open it another few inches. If only there were somewhere to go for a run around here. There were no streetlights, no sidewalks this far out of town. She'd be running blind in the dark. Better to stay in, get some work done until she was tired enough to sleep.

She had forgotten, almost, the way staying in a new room disrupted routine: her purse sat on a chair by the bathroom door, both of their suitcases were open, Anderson's phone resting atop the blankets, rather than on the charger that sat by his side of the bed in their house. Daisy stretched out in the bed, the sheets cool on her toes, and snuggled close to give Anderson a kiss. He did not stir. As she settled into the bed, propping up the pillows and opening her tablet to work on some writing, she heard Anderson's phone drop to the floor and reached down to retrieve it.

It was impossible not to see the message on the screen as the phone lit up in her hand. *New message from Charlotte. 'I wish you were here, too. Kisses. Goodnight.'* Daisy dropped the phone face down on the bed between them, then crossed her arms over her knees. She sat in the dark like that, throwing a sidelong glance at Anderson's sleeping form every so often, as if holding a silent conversation with him. Could it have been a relative she didn't know? But still, *kisses* was rather much for a relative's sign-off. Maybe a message he received in error? No, the contact was named. Charlotte. Did he even know anybody named Charlotte? She glanced at him in the dark again, wishing he were awake to answer her. Then again, someone he knew casually could have sent him a message by accident, that they intended for someone else. That happened all the time, right? Sending a text to the wrong person?

Yes, Daisy decided. That was it. She turned on her tablet and began the soothing, inane ritual of checking emails, social media, news websites. She opened a half-written piece, typed a few worthless lines, then erased them.

Anderson's phone rested on the bed between them. She couldn't quite put words to the rest of her questions. Could it be possible that it wasn't an error? By daylight, Daisy was flawlessly practical, but that was the Daisy who had grown up with Anderson, who trusted him as much as, even more than, she trusted herself. For some reason, Stella's voice came to her mind, back then ever the grounded one. Stella would have told her to believe what she saw; let the facts tell their story before you build your own around it. Only once had that approach led Daisy astray, but it had been enough to break them apart.

Daisy stood at the open window and looked out into the variegated darkness, the deep, guttural greens and reds and violets of the woods at night, coming back into its vernal fullness before the lull of summer. She could hear the birdsong that haunted her dreams, the jagged outline of the mountains against the velvet sky.

Then, finally, near the forest bed, she saw them: ethereal, faint blue lights, a bioluminescent haze just above the earth. These were the ghosts she always saw. That girl that flashed before her eyes. The officer she'd spoken with back then had said wisely, *Eyewitness reports are the least reliable we have in scenarios like this*, as if he were talking to his clipboard rather than to her. Between the trees, Daisy saw, almost sensed, a faint blue glow hovering around what would have been knee height, a cloud just inches off the ground. She saw the intermittent glow of blue fireflies in the woods, old ghosts or new. If they were spirits, Daisy would not have imagined that they were specific to a particular time period, which felt somehow unfair. It seemed more likely to her that their ethereal blue lights were uneasy ghosts: here, gone, then here again.

For Anderson to cheat on her was impossible. For that reason, she decided, it wasn't happening. That made it sound simple. But she worked late into the night, the pattering of her typing blending with the noise of the tree frogs outside. Finally, when the earliest tinge of violet dawn touched the horizon, the same shade as the walls of the bedroom, Daisy closed her eyes, too exhausted to think, and fell back against the pillows.

CHAPTER ELEVEN

Before

There were moments when living on land that was toxic, intoxicated, offered other kinds of gifts. Where Daisy crossed the yard under the clothesline, a patch of clover sprouted from the ground, emerald green and robust. Over half of them sprouted four leaves, an unexplainable crop of good luck, just wide enough to lie down in. In a hurried, nonverbal explanation, Daisy considered it some sort of mutation, but took it as a consolation prize.

Daisy walked inside and pulled the unbecoming clothes off as quickly as she could. The bathroom, carpeted, was another afterthought of a room squeezed in where there happened to be access to a pipe. She wondered, as the steam warmed and filled the room, if whatever ailed her mother was in her veins, her bones, too. Probably so: she had grown up here, while Ellen had only lived here for part of her life.

As she stood in the shower, Daisy let the hot water run over her face, wondering why she couldn't speak to her mother, or even cry, even imagine the idea of a younger sibling. The real poison wasn't whatever was in the ground, seeping out of the plant. It was this paralysis, the silence between them that she struggled against like a firefly in a spiderweb, seeing but unable to change it.

Stella met Daisy at the front door. They walked past the spacious sitting room, where Stella's brothers were playing a video game at maximum volume. The house smelled cool and fresh. In the kitchen, Stella gathered an armful of snacks: name-brand Diet Coke, sliced vegetables and hummus, an organic chocolate bar. Even the inside of their refrigerator looked spotless, healthy. Stella's bedroom was Daisy's favorite: with two big windows looking out on the forest, gauzy violet curtains, and a low, simple bedframe, it had a secondhand, bohemian vibe with none of the actual cheapness. Stella got to pick out her own furniture, although she let Daisy help, knowing that Daisy never got to choose things of her own at home. They sat in the hammock chairs they had picked out together.

"Mom had another miscarriage."

"Is she okay?" Stella asked.

"I guess so," Daisy said, then admitted, "I don't know. She was okay after all the ones before. They're so stupid," she said, suddenly angry. "I wish they'd quit trying. What would make them think this time would turn out any differently?"

Stella shrugged her pretty shoulders. "Does your dad know?"

"I don't know what she tells him. All she wants to do is work in her stupid garden. She won't tell me anything," Daisy said. "I tried."

Stella leaned her head on Daisy's shoulder and offered her the chocolate bar. She began to braid their hair together, Stella's chestnut brown against Daisy's straw-colored curls. "Maybe you should talk to someone."

Daisy scoffed. "Right. Because my dad would pay for a therapist. Bottling up obviously works so well for him, he expects everyone else to do the same."

"Maybe the guidance counselor at school." Stella finished the braid and twirled the end around her fingertip.

"Yeah," Daisy said, although she knew she wouldn't. She sat up quickly, tugging the braid Stella had made and causing them both to yelp. "Sorry," she mumbled, untangling it with her fingers. "Just—the guidance counselor? I don't think so, Stella."

They finished their lunch and wandered back outside, away from the noise of the video games and the hum of the air conditioning. Outside, under the wisteria arbor, Stella and Daisy swung on the wooden bench, their feet pushing against the ground in unison. The Carolina foothills rose in the distance, unfolding away from them in greater and greater size, green up close and rolling away into violet blue.

Stella waited a judicious few minutes before changing the subject. "How is your algebra class going?"

"It's not hard," Daisy said. "The thing is, I guess it's so boring that it's difficult to pay attention to it. But when you can bear to pay attention to it, it's easy."

"What about Jesse?" Stella asked. "Does he hold your attention?"

Daisy covered a bashful smile with her hands. "Maybe."

"Is he still meeting you to study?" Stella asked.

"Yeah. We're meeting up later today."

"*Oooh.*" Stella fluttered her eyelashes and cooed. "You know, Harlow Matthews had a crush on him for over a year and he would never go out with her. Not even when she asked him to help her study."

Daisy looked at Stella skeptically. Harlow was the most popular girl in their class, and if she had ever pursued Jesse it was probably to prove a point, or for the wrong reason. "He just agreed to help me as a favor to you."

"Who knows?" Stella said. "Anyway, what matters is that you pass the class. So you can graduate and get out of here."

"Who says I want to get out of here? I like it here." Daisy studied her best friend lovingly, looking over the repertoire of features she knew so well: Stella's tidy, lush brown hair, her straight white teeth. Her features were beautiful in their simplicity; no part of her was out of tune with any other. "Besides, how do you know I could go to college or move away even if I did pass algebra?"

"What do you mean?"

"Stella, honestly," Daisy snapped, suddenly angry. "Going to college costs money, you know."

"What about scholarships?"

Daisy went silent. Stella had a kind of innocence in her privilege that Daisy found endearing and infuriating in equal measure. They kicked at the ground, rocking the wooden swing.

"Anyway," Daisy stammered, "I do like it here. If I lived anywhere else, I'd miss the fireflies, and the way the forest sounds during the summer."

"I know you do," Stella said, trying to soothe her. "But you've also never really been anywhere else."

"What is *with* you today?"

Stella's chin dropped, sullen. "I just don't want us to move away from each other."

Across the fence, a farmer was driving a hay baler across a meadow of tall, pale green grass that grew above waist height. The sweet, younger grasses were harvested in the spring and stored for the calves that would come the following winter. They watched, quietly mesmerized as the machine rolled across the field, leaving a shorn path in its wake, every several yards depositing a round hay bale.

"And you don't think your dad knows? About the miscarriages?"

"He must know something," Daisy said. "I mean, I'm sure she told him she was pregnant."

"And nobody says anything about it? Nobody talks about anything?"

Daisy shrugged her shoulders, feeling pushed away. She imagined her mother with the tissue box, imagined what was inside it. She pictured the traces of blood, heavier than the water around it, that pooled at the bottom of the toilet bowl that morning. Had Ellen brought her out there for company? She had a nonverbal sense of having failed her mother, but she didn't know she was being tested. Ellen would have said that God never tells you when he's testing you. Daisy felt swept with shame for acting like such a child, a bratty teenager, at a moment when her mother might have desperately needed a friend. She glanced over toward Stella, saw in her peaceful stare, watching the hay baler, that she was unperturbed, that her mother would never have made her wish she could act like more of an adult, be more of a friend to her, when it was her normal impulse to be what she was: a teenager. Suddenly, Daisy felt a snap of chilly anger for Stella, for how she took her nice things for granted, even in her steady willingness to share them.

With a cool removal, Daisy watched with bare satisfaction as Stella's expression turned from peaceful to confusion to shock, her hand grasping for Daisy's wrist.

"What's happening?"

"What do you mean?"

"Look."

A terrible noise came from the baler as a pair of fawns, already badly injured, attempted to flee its path. Daisy had heard, once, of a nest of foxes concealed in the tall grass, caught under a hay baler, but something about a fawn was different.

"Tell him to stop," Stella murmured, then, more loudly: "Can't someone make him stop?"

"It's too late." Daisy couldn't prevent herself from crying. She was torn between the impulse to cover her eyes and the need to watch, to bear witness to the young animals' plight.

"They don't know to run away when they sense danger," Daisy said, trying to fill the terrible silence. "They don't understand scent the way adults do, and they just duck under pressure."

The sadness of the moment made her irritation with Stella seem small and silly. Watching the wounded animals fall, both of them wept helplessly just the same. The driver stepped down, cursing, pulled off his cap and used it to wipe his forehead. Daisy could see his sorrow from where she sat. Her grief was useless. Tracker had once said, *If you keep livestock, you'd better be prepared to deal with dead stock.* Daisy found her hand squeezing Stella's, their palms clammy.

"If only there were some way they could prevent that from happening," she sniffed.

"There has to be something they could do," Stella agreed, her voice thick. "They could send a dog out to scare them away before they…"

"It's okay," Daisy interrupted. She hugged Stella tightly, sensing that her friend was somehow more vulnerable to shock than she was. "They died almost right away." The red hay bale stared at them like an eye from its distance; the farmer got back into the baler and kept working. Daisy clung onto Stella's hands, feeling them shake in hers.

"I need to go home," she realized. "I was wrong not to stay and try to get my mother to talk."

Stella nodded, her eyes glowing with compassion. Though she couldn't form words, her encouragement was evident: *Go home. Be with your family.* That was what Stella would have done. That was what made sense.

Daisy walked through the yard, cutting through the wisteria patch she had abandoned with such haste in the morning. In the wisteria's tangled clutches of roots, there was a fresh, small mound of soil, marked with a stick protruding from the earth. She breathed in the quiet of the air, thought of a half-formed body, small enough to fit inside a Kleenex box. As Daisy began to retreat, she glanced up at the wisteria, whose twisted arms, sheltering but clutching, allowed narrow, bent fingers of sunlight down to the earth. Behind the fresh mound of soil, she spied several more upright sticks, one after the other, too organized to have been placed there by accident. She was standing in a graveyard. Daisy began to cry again and hurried toward the house.

But Ellen was not at home. Daisy remembered that it was Wednesday afternoon, that she had gone to her Bible study class. And what would Daisy have said to her? She imagined herself brave enough to push the simple issue: that she was aware. That she knew there was pain, although she didn't understand it. Maybe Ellen preferred her prayers, her reading. Daisy imagined how she sat in church, so quietly, barely even part of that community, only there at its outskirts, soaking up its solidity. She pushed the image away, glad to have the house to herself. The quiet of the house was less oppressive when it belonged to her alone. When four o'clock drew near, she gathered her backpack, putting in her algebra textbook along with a couple of cans of beer from the fridge, and walked out to meet Jesse.

CHAPTER TWELVE

Now

The summer chorus of birds began early, before dawn. Daisy opened her eyes two hours after drifting off, stretched, and rolled over. She never wasted a minute lying half awake, half asleep in bed—she considered it one of her tricks for beginning each day in a productive mood. No falling back asleep, no dozing, no snoozing. But just today, she thought. Just maybe, for an hour. The weight of exhaustion pulled her back into the covers, reaching for Anderson's hand, clasping it in hers under the blanket. As Anderson slept beside her, she admired his familiar, chiseled profile, heard the hum of his exhales. Something about this pained her, something sharp, and finally, she remembered.

Daisy's heart felt cold inside her chest. By daylight, it was even more difficult to deny the truth. Anderson was hiding something, and it involved a woman named Charlotte, and she had sent him a message with kisses. That was enough. Daisy couldn't consider dealing with it—not now, not here. She would say nothing. She would wait until they were back in New Mexico, then mention it, calmly, without going on the attack. If one thing was for sure, Daisy knew that she hadn't come all this way for Stella's wedding only to let someone named Charlotte unravel her plans. Yet the room was too quiet, with Anderson still sleeping, somehow existing in a world just slightly different to hers, where he knew something she didn't, but she also knew something he didn't. Daisy quietly got dressed and walked outside, tying her hair up in a ponytail as she went.

If Zion's lack of streetlights and sidewalks made for difficult terrain after dark, its rolling meadows and forest trails made up for it by day. It was a perfect morning for a long run. Daisy jogged the perimeter of the wide meadow behind the inn. She remembered that she wasn't supposed to overexert herself, then picked up her pace. Her side cramped in a stitch and she paused, hands on her knees, breathing in, then out. The idea of keeping it in, even for the next two days until they were back at the house, caused her an almost physical pain. Daisy had learned that secrets, lies, half-truths, and all other ways of generally screwing with facts tended to lead only to trouble. Then, she remembered, sometimes telling the truth did, too.

Regardless, it wouldn't do any good to put off the discussion. *But not here*, Daisy thought. *Not now. I just need to get through this weekend.* She knew the area well: a mile or two east, her parents' house; to the north, a thin strip of houses before the mountain rose too sharply to build. And if she had kept going west, that way was the old green farmhouse, the one where Jesse had built his vet practice. The fact was, there wasn't much of anywhere to run to, even by day. Daisy turned and jogged back to the inn.

Inside, the large house was quiet. Daisy paused in the foyer and looked at the walls, the narrow, stained-glass windows that bordered the doorframe. She could almost sense the house, the surroundings she knew so well, trying to draw her in, to reacquaint her with the pieces of herself she'd left behind. It wasn't possible that Anderson could be seeing someone else, that she should have to learn about it here and now, while she was also holding all those memories off. But as she climbed the stairs, she resolved not to let it get to her. After all, she'd gotten herself through worse, and alone.

But that was years ago. Daisy wasn't sure who she might be without Anderson. *If he's seeing someone*, she told herself, *maybe we can fix it. Maybe it isn't that serious.* Her mind set to work enumerating the reasons he might have done so. Stress, maybe? Maybe she was putting too much pressure on him. That made sense, that was something she could fix. Daisy ran her hands over her hair, smoothing the unruly curls into place. She took a deep breath, unlocked the door of their room, and walked in.

"Morning, babe." Anderson was already dressed, sitting in the armchair, phone in hand. Daisy held back a wince. "I was wondering where you went. Out for a run?" He clicked his tongue, jokingly scolding her. "Should've known. You follow your own rules. Something wrong?"

She hesitated, hands on her hips. "Um. No, babe. No. How'd you sleep?"

"Great. Very comfortable. You?"

"Not too bad," Daisy answered, not meeting his eyes. "I'm a little tired, but I'll be fine." She crossed the room to the closet, where she had hung her clothes the evening before. When Daisy was younger, she never thought that having too many dresses would become an inconvenience, but she'd stared around the walk-in closet back in Santa Fe and sighed, trying to choose the right one. She'd landed on a shell-pink wrap dress, with sleeves that fluttered and a row of beading around the collar, with a pair of beige heels.

Daisy could feel Anderson watching her. She walked into the bathroom and started the shower without speaking to him. It felt good to wash off the sweat from her run, and the hot water helped her to feel more awake. She dried her hair and tamed it with a straightener, a lengthy process that was mostly an excuse not to talk. Straightening her curls gave her a feeling of polish, of armor almost, though it was true that she preferred her hair in its natural state. As she worked at finishing her makeup, it was difficult not to wonder: *What does Charlotte look like? What sort of dress would she have chosen? Where did he even meet her?*

In an attempt to put the text momentarily out of her mind, Daisy turned her thoughts again to the oddly timed wedding invitation, the news article about the sale of the old site. *I don't know if I believe you*, Stella had said. *If that story were true, you would never have acted that way. You would never have walked away from a dying person who asked you for help.* Pursing her lips in focus, Daisy patted at her cheekbones with the brush, softening and accenting the angles of her face. Maybe enough time had passed that they could forget about all of that.

She was fastening her dress when Anderson tapped at the door. "Can I come in? I need to shave before we leave."

"Sure thing," she answered, opening the door and stepping quickly past him. "I'm all done."

"Dressed already?"

"Yes," she answered, a hint of impatience tightening her lips. "It's half past twelve. You know, I think I'd like to see the flower garden. I'll wait for you outside, okay?"

"Okay." Anderson took his razor out of the travel case, looking in the mirror. "I'll be out shortly."

CHAPTER THIRTEEN

Now

Stella's wedding was to be hosted at a vineyard on an open hillside, with rows of simple wooden benches that gave a quaint impression of homeliness, as if the cost for the facility rental was any less than that of a midline new car. Daisy removed her hat, counting several familiar faces as they walked up. Soft music sounded from the side of the seating area; Daisy saw a few musicians, heard violin and mandolin. When an usher approached them, Daisy was prepared to be asked to leave.

"Welcome," he said. "Bride or groom's side?"

Daisy exhaled and smiled at Anderson. "Bride," she answered. "Thanks." The usher gestured to the left side and led them to an empty row.

The open field where they sat, surrounded by trees and rising ground, gave Daisy an eerie impression that she was on a stage, being watched on all sides by the land, like a lightning bug at the bottom of a glass jar. She didn't have the feeling, precisely, that she wasn't wanted here: she was welcomed back, by some strange energy, something that left her feeling exposed, self-accusatory.

As two young girls, who had confided almost solely in each other, Daisy and Stella could not help but become foils for each other, their various small differences appearing stark as day and night. From that vantage point, Daisy had felt a small, guilty degree of scorn for Stella's more traditional choices: her office job, three-bedroom home, the perfectly dull husband—a life gone to plan.

But maybe there was something here that she had overlooked, for Bryson seemed very much, and very genuinely, in love with Stella. She saw him adjusting his tie, looking toward the end of the aisle, the straight line of his brow softened by the anxiety in his eyes. Daisy realized that he was nervous, happy, even proud.

"Doing okay, Daisy?" Anderson whispered to her in a low voice.

"Yes," she said. "Fine." She turned her chin and looked, briefly, into his eyes, then away. She felt his gaze lingering. He knew something was wrong. Though she was not often seized with the impulse to get up and start walking, the idea glimmered, tempting, across her mind. *Just go somewhere.* Away from Anderson and Stella both. *Wouldn't that be nice, for once?* No. She'd done it before, and look how that turned out. Fine, until it wasn't. Despite her discomfort, Daisy stayed in her seat, caught by an unshakable feeling that she needed to see Stella, to talk to her, that this could be their last chance. For what? She didn't know.

That sense was vindicated when, at the end of a procession of bridesmaids, Stella appeared, her hand on her father's arm. In a white gown accented with touches of yellow, she took three short steps up the aisle, looked over each shoulder, and crossed her arms.

"I can't do it," Daisy heard her whisper, voice low, a realization meant only for Stella herself to hear. Her father placed a hand over her arm, gave her a questioning look. Then, her voice rose, calling to the nearest bridesmaid. "Tell Bryson I'm sorry."

But in a flurry of voices and movement, Bryson walked down the aisle, heads turning to watch him. He whispered Stella's name and squeezed her hands, gave her a look that was just what Daisy knew she would see: pleading, shock, realization. Stella returned his expression with the same sadness, as though she wanted to fall into his arms, but her stature seemed held up by whatever knowledge kept her mouth a firm, resolute line. Sitting in the back row of seats, Daisy felt she had been given an up-close viewing of what ought to have been a private exchange. Stella's eyes gleamed with emotion as she waved her father away and whispered to Bryson, "I can't marry you unless you tell me the truth about what happened." Daisy sat up straight, snapped into focus.

It was as if Stella had asked for the one thing in the world Bryson couldn't give her. He turned away as though she had slapped him and stared down at his shoes. Stella gathered the ample folds of the gown in her arms and took off at what must have been the fastest pace she could manage, her bare, tanned ankles reminding Daisy of their summers together outside. Stella turned a resentful look back at Bryson and all Daisy could see was the young girl who had seen a fawn die under a baler, who was overcome with her weakness and anger at her inability to make it stop.

Stella paused in her flight, whispering to one of her bridesmaids, gesturing with one fluttering hand. Before Daisy knew it, the woman was walking back toward the benches, chin turning as she scanned the crowd.

"I'm sorry," she called, "but does anyone know if a Daisy Ritter is here?"

Daisy slouched just a little and folded her hands in her lap. Curiosity wrestled with dread, with her promise to herself that this was a romantic weekend away, nothing more.

"Don't say anything," Anderson whispered. "They'll never know you're here. Everything's fine."

Anything was preferable to sitting here next to him. "Oh, Anderson," she murmured, looking straight ahead. "I'm starting to feel like you should let me worry about myself, you know that?" Before he could respond, Daisy stood up and approached the bridesmaid, whose elegantly styled waves and flawless makeup clashed with her worried expression, giving the impression of a porcelain doll. "I'm Daisy," she said, "although I don't have any idea how this involves me."

"Me either," the woman answered, showing a faint smile of relief. "Stella's asked for you. Can you come with me?"

In response, Daisy shrugged her shoulders. *At this point*, she thought, *why not?*

CHAPTER FOURTEEN

Before

Zion's public library was a three-room brick building that had been the train station, when the train still passed through there. Years of sun and dust had baked the red brick to a shade close to the concrete of the sidewalk. Without pausing, it would have taken Daisy half an hour to get there on foot, walking right up the train tracks. Today, though, she stopped to inspect a patch of hawthorn trees, the tight clusters of white blossoms barely guarding their thorns from view. The trees provided some cover, both from the sun and from the nearest house, so Daisy opened one of Tracker's beers.

In truth, she had begun to enjoy this daily walk to meet Jesse, even to imagine what the lessons might entail. Jesse Lopez, who lived three miles up the road from the Ritters with his mother, was a studious, mild-mannered boy who, Tracker said, was guilty of watching too many movies. She crept forward, placed a penny on the tracks, and retreated to the shade.

What little thing could she ask him about today? If he had many hobbies, he did not discuss them. Daisy knew that he played piano, and the day before, she had strained to think of some piano-related topic she could bring up, which resulted only in a botched pronunciation of Chopin, leaving her, she thought, sounding even more of a hick than she had before. Watching the dappled light across her shins as she sat on the grass, Daisy could smell the hot iron of the train tracks and the fragrance of the hawthorns. Jesse liked movies—she remembered someone telling her that, though he had not said it himself. That was one thing they might have had in common, though she pictured him scoffing at the titles she loved—romantic comedies, the better if they featured odd girls who turned out to be special, or quiet boys who turned out to be sweet. This time, she decided, it would be better if she just let conversation happen naturally, or not at all. Not at all was more likely. A train whistled by, bringing a tide of coal dust and deafening noise. When it passed, Daisy had finished half the beer. She poured out the rest, and tucked the empty can into the side pocket of her backpack, which she threw over one shoulder. She stopped to pick up the flattened penny, stamped out of shape and still hot to the touch.

Finally, the library crept into view. Daisy had hoped to beat him there, to give herself a moment to wash her face, but as she approached, she saw Jesse waiting at the front step, wearing his backpack with the straps over each shoulder.

"How's it going?" He stood up and reached for the door, holding it open as she climbed the stairs.

"Good. Thanks." She did not return the question, but noticed as they walked through the otherwise silent library that his blue shirt was flecked with white paint.

"It's paint." He placed his backpack at an empty table and sat down.

"I can see that." She smiled and caught his gaze, saw that he was annoyed. "What were you painting?"

"I'm helping my mom remodel her house."

Daisy knew that Jesse's parents had split up a couple of years prior, but stopped short of asking anything else. He sat patiently as she rifled through her disorganized backpack. A crumpled old quiz covered with red marks spilled onto the table as she took out the algebra textbook. Daisy stared at it, realized suddenly that the faded red marks on white had reminded her again of blood, felt a flush rise to her cheeks.

"Do you always walk here?" he asked.

Daisy closed her hand tight around the quiz and put it back into her bag, as if putting it in the wastebasket would have left evidence behind. "If you're so much smarter than me, why do you ask obvious questions?"

"Nobody said I was smarter than you." The deep brown of his eyes darkened. "And I was only asking because the last four days, you've shown up smelling like beer, so it's probably good you're not driving."

"Save it," Daisy sighed. They didn't usually talk enough to disagree about anything, though she couldn't have said what either of them was angry about. She felt disappointed. This was the hour of the day she usually savored, looked forward to.

Daisy took on a more compliant tone as she opened her workbook, trying to show that she was sorry, that she was grateful for his help, without having to embarrass herself further by saying it. What she had told Stella was true: she was half decent at math when she could bring herself to focus on it. Most of her answers were correct, though she tripped herself up when she tried to combine steps in the equations, got ahead of herself and made mistakes. Jesse worked through each equation step by step, every addition or subtraction on its own line, as though he enjoyed the process itself. Even though, Daisy thought, he probably was smarter than her, could have skipped all the steps if he wanted to work quickly.

The next lesson proved more confusing. "Is this where you solve for X by dividing Y or—hm." Daisy's pencil hovered over the worksheet. "I hate the ones with three variables."

"Divide X by Y times two," Jesse answered. When she hesitated and began to scratch out her last response, he held out his hand for her pencil, erased her work, and slowly wrote in the correct steps. She watched him with a degree of annoyance. He was handsome, with espresso-brown doe eyes, deep lashes, his hair almost black, just long enough that it couldn't decide whether it hung or stood out. Daisy, who had taken her developing body as a personal achievement, regarded it a waste that someone so handsome should be such a strait-laced bore. But she needed to pass algebra. She followed his hands working through the equation, solving for X. "They'll take points off if you don't show each step correctly," he said.

"Even if you get the right answer?" Daisy rolled her eyes.

"Even if you get the right answer," Jesse said. She noticed that his hands, too, were dotted with paint. "Do you want to do a couple of the homework questions to make sure you've got it?"

"No," she sighed, thinking of Ellen. "I should head back."

They silently packed up their bags, Daisy holding hers close to her chest, cramming papers in wherever they would fit. She studied him as they walked to the door, put her backpack on over both shoulders.

"Do you want me to drive you home?" he asked. When Daisy didn't reply, he added, "It's along the way."

She pictured the quiet hawthorn grove, imagined another stolen beer. The lure of a solitary moment outweighed the pull of another few minutes with him. "No, thanks."

"You sure?"

"Yes."

"Sorry for snapping at you before." As Jesse spoke, he moved away from her, opening his car, but when he looked back at her she felt something immediate, something close.

"If you really want to save me a walk, let's meet outside on Monday."

"Where?"

"Between our houses." Daisy shielded her eyes from the sun as she spoke, took a small step closer so she wouldn't have to raise her voice for him to hear her. "Those trails that go through the woods, behind the chemical plant. There's an old hunting blind there that nobody uses this time of year." She put her hands in her pockets, felt the flattened penny against her fingers, her nails bitten short.

"Okay. Same time?"

"Sure. Here," she said, tossing him the penny. With a quickness that surprised her, he caught it, turned it over in his hand, and looked back at her with a grin.

"Thanks."

"It's stupid."

"No, really, thanks," he said. "I like it."

"I have to go." Daisy remembered that there was red ink all over her papers, a miscarriage at home. She couldn't let him see that. "See you later."

CHAPTER FIFTEEN

Now

Daisy and the bridesmaid walked after Stella at a hurried pace. When the bridesmaid stumbled, Daisy instinctively held out her arm, catching the woman's hand.

"Thanks. How do you know Stella, anyway?" the woman asked.

"Old friends, I guess. You?"

"We work together at the newspaper."

Daisy nodded her head as they walked. She didn't know a single one of Stella's bridesmaids, not personally, although she recognized a few of the faces. Stella had an entire life that was separate from hers. And yet when Daisy saw Stella in the midst of what must have been the deepest confusion of her life, she had felt an unpleasant conviction: they were connected, still. She knew it.

Daisy followed Stella to the restored Victorian home that housed the caterer's kitchen and the dressing rooms. For a slight woman wearing a heavy dress, Stella moved quickly; not until Daisy closed the door behind them did Stella seem to realize she was there.

"Daisy," she said. "You're here."

For a moment, in a flash of empathy too brief to stifle, Daisy forgot the reasons she had come. Her former best friend seemed to have lost her bearings. Whatever she chose to do next might have a huge effect on the rest of her life—not that Daisy knew what the right choice was. The rest of the house, their surroundings, the bridesmaid waiting by her side, might as well have been imaginary.

"Yes," Daisy agreed, betraying the fact that she had attended at all shocked her as much as it did Stella. "Would you like to tell me what I'm doing here?"

Stella, magnificently dressed in a pearl-white gown that somehow both floated and swept the floor, swung to face her. "Are we still blood sisters, Daisy?"

"Come on, Stella, you know the answer to that," Daisy answered in a plain, gentle voice, reminding her. "You ruined my life."

"I was trying to help you fix your life," Stella cried. "I didn't know what was going to happen. Anyway," she sniffled, "that's not what I wanted to talk about with you."

Daisy did her best to steady her breath, trying not to think of what Stella's betrayal had cost her. "I'm listening," she said.

With the resplendent gown crumpling around her ankles, Stella crouched at Daisy's feet. "I'm sorry, Deborah, but could you give us a minute?" she asked, waving to the bridesmaid, who left the room, timidly closing the door behind her. "I can't marry him," she said. "I want to, but I can't. I thought I could."

"Yeah, I can see that." Daisy pulled out a chair and Stella sat down with a deflated flounce. "I'm still not clear on why I'm here."

"It might take a while to explain."

"Well, try to make it fast," Daisy said. "The last time I saw you, I told you something you promised never to tell anyone. And the next thing I knew…"

"I know. I—I'm sorry for…"

"Please don't." Daisy shook her head. A cursory apology only belittled what she could barely stand to remember. "Not now. So, what should I do? Do you want me to hold your hand? Tell you to go back outside and marry what's-his-name?"

"No. Not until I know I can trust him."

"If it's something between you two, maybe I should go get him so you can talk. Then will you let me leave?"

"He doesn't want to talk about it," Stella said. "Don't you think I tried? I thought I could marry him anyway, but it turns out…"

"You can't?"

She nodded her head and finished the glass of water. "Besides, it isn't just about me and him. It's about us."

"Us, as in—"

"You and me, Daisy."

"Stella, not that I'm interested in talking about it, but I have enough on my own plate to worry about right now." Daisy stood up and approached the door. "I respectfully decline any involvement in ruining your wedding."

"You're involved already," Stella answered, sniffling. She wiped at her eyes, smearing the professionally done makeup with a careless, tanned fist. "He just took over as chair of his father's company. The board wants him to buy the land."

"I know," Daisy said. "It was in the paper."

"He says he's going to do it. The chemical plant's selling it. They gave him the real estate papers, even some information on the accident and the cleanup. It's as good as done. The thing is, I…"

Stella crossed her arms and met Daisy's eyes, speaking the words Daisy had long since given up on hearing. "I want to know what really happened."

Daisy imagined throwing a glass of water through the window, imagined raising her voice. Something the old Daisy might have done, but not any longer. She smoothed her dress with her palms. "So, just to clarify, you invited me to your wedding, to what you must know is my least favorite place on earth—just so that you could make me relive the worst time of my life? For your *own* peace of mind, Stella? Or have I got it wrong?"

"Daisy, I know it sounds awful, but a part of me just wanted to see you again."

"How do you know I care about that?"

"Well, you did come all the way here," Stella murmured.

"If you want me to give you permission to be okay with what happened back then, I can't do that. And what happened there was exactly what I told you all those years ago. You want to marry someone who's buying a crime scene to turn it into a vineyard, be my guest."

"I don't..."

"It's been years since I cared what you did. Why do you think I left?" Daisy said. "Because I don't care about anything in this place."

"I'm not going to marry him," Stella said. "I can't do it."

Daisy remembered Stella's low whisper to Bryson: *I can't marry you unless you tell me the truth about what happened.*

"Maybe it's better left alone," Daisy said. "Maybe you should go back out there. I'm sure Bryson would understand."

"But then why'd you come?" Stella said. "You're a part of this. You know it, even if you don't want to admit it."

This place seemed to want her, despite her years-long attempts to get away. She couldn't even remember why she'd come, only that she couldn't see any other option. That it had felt like a question she couldn't refuse to answer. Yet, to revisit all of that, that entire summer, pulled a number of things into question that Daisy wasn't sure she wanted to exhume.

"I'm leaving," Stella said. "This is the last place I want to be right now."

"That's one thing I can sympathize with," Daisy muttered. Stella coughed out a near laugh in response, shaking her head unhappily.

Stella removed her shoes and stepped out of the voluminous underskirt with surprising grace, leaving the skirt of the gown deflated around her like the petals of a wilting flower.

"Where are you going to go?" Daisy asked.

"Home," Stella said with a shrug of her shoulders.

"Where are you living now?" Daisy couldn't help wondering.

"Just outside of town, near Mulberry Street," Stella answered. She walked up a set of stairs to a dressing room, appointed with white and floral decor, and began to change into a casual sundress, as easily as if they were still teenagers in the locker room. "Bryson's going on the honeymoon either way. It's kind of a combination honeymoon and business trip."

Daisy rolled her eyes. "Sounds fun."

Stella zipped the wedding gown lovingly into a protective garment bag, then laid it in its box. "I might still need this. God, I hope we can sort this out."

"You gonna have another wedding like this if you do?"

Stella looked at the box in her arms. "I still want to marry him, Daisy."

"Then I hope you do," Daisy said. She suddenly felt forlorn, sorry to be leaving home again in only a day, back to the desert which, when not concretely in front of her, seemed imaginary. Back to a conversation with Anderson she desperately needed, and just as desperately wanted to avoid. Here, now, all the years of unspoken thoughts seemed more real than her house with Anderson. "I hope everything works out for you."

"Yeah, you too," Stella said. "You want to come over and catch up later?"

"No," Daisy said. "This isn't like that, Stella. What you did had an effect on my life. Not just that you broke your promise, but, you know, before you stopped talking to me, it really did feel like we were sisters. I don't think we can be friends again."

"Oh." Stella's shoulders sagged just barely. "Well, maybe some other—I don't know. My door's always open, okay? And my phone number hasn't changed."

"Sure."

Stella offered a hug, but Daisy stepped back. She took Stella's hand in her own: it felt clammy, just like hers. Finally, the long moment growing too awkward, Daisy glanced at Stella with a serious nod of her head. "Good luck, I guess."

Stella returned her nod, walked down the stairs, and out a back door into the parking lot. She opened her car door, carefully placed the dress box in the back seat, and then got in and started the engine. Daisy saw a glimpse of Stella's questioning eyes again in the rearview mirror. Then, at last, she drove away without looking back.

CHAPTER SIXTEEN

Now

Daisy watched Stella leave. She waited a moment, then walked into the kitchen. A large refrigerator held the cake, and the counters were lined with champagne flutes and hors d'oeuvres for the reception. Another bridesmaid, identifiable by her peach-toned gown, approached her.

"Have you seen the bride?"

"She just left. She said she's not getting married today."

The girl's face fell in horror and she walked out without another word. Daisy returned at a leisurely pace to her seat next to Anderson, trying to shake off a vague sense of dread. This didn't change her plans. This didn't have to change anything. Just a brief, unexpected, meaningless conversation with someone she used to know.

"What's going on?" he whispered. She shushed him and pointed as the bridesmaid rushed up the aisle to where the expectant groom waited with the pastor. As they exchanged whispers, his expression went blank, and Daisy saw his chin shaking as if there had been a mistake. Finally, he stood upright, spoke for a few moments to the pastor, then shook his hand and left, exiting across the back of the field.

The pastor approached the crowd. His deep voice rose above the whispers, a practiced skill that made a microphone unnecessary.

"Friends, although we thank you for having gathered here today, there has been a sudden change in plans," he said. "The bride's family invites you to enjoy the grounds and the meal and to please remember the couple in your prayers."

"Poor Stella," Daisy whispered as a ripple of shock moved through the crowd of guests. She didn't know if Stella realised how unkind people could be when you became a topic of conversation. Not from the outside, she didn't.

"They're not getting married? Why? What did you two talk about in there?"

Daisy managed to look him in the eyes. "It's hard to explain." She saw his phone in his pocket. "Some things just don't work out, I guess. Who can say why?"

"You're acting strange. Are you alright?"

"Maybe I am."

"Maybe you are alright," Anderson laughed, "or maybe you are acting strange?"

Daisy leaned her chin back, stared up into the cloudless blue sky. "I'm not sure, Anderson," she said. "Maybe both."

"Well, so long as they're having a party anyway, why don't we go have a drink before we leave?"

Daisy followed a few steps behind him. She discovered with some annoyance that she kept returning to Stella's expression, wondering what she was feeling. Though she was undeniably a stranger, she had been pulled back by something into that time when they were closer than sisters, and, as it always had, Stella's need seemed to conjure Daisy's grudging concern. Stella had looked at her so certainly when she'd said it: *You're involved.* Was she?

Several of the guests left immediately. Daisy did not recognize them but surmised from their expressions that they were family of the groom. She caught up to Anderson, who was approaching the open bar with purpose. "Doesn't it seem wrong to stay?"

"It won't do any harm," he said. "She invited you, after all."

"I'm not sure I want to be here."

Anderson handed her a gin and tonic; she took a long sip. "We could leave now. Maybe get an early flight back." She felt herself swaying precariously between the life she knew and the precipice of an unknown future.

"Nonsense," he said. "You came all the way here, right? You got to see Stella. You got what you wanted, didn't you?"

Daisy took another drink. He was convincing, she had to allow him that. Convincing, and charming, and all those other gifts. The way he ran his life so neatly, and somehow kept hers in balance as well. The rest of the world went into soft focus when she looked at Anderson. She didn't always like him, but some part of her needed him. Daisy walked at his side across the resort grounds, to a shallow lake lined with paddle boats.

"Come on," he said. "Care for a spin on the lake?"

"No, thanks," she said. "I'm not much of a swimmer. I'll wait at the bar."

Anderson shrugged and walked away from her, fearless, into a crowd of anxiously conversing wedding guests. Immersed in thought, Daisy continued her slow pace around the perimeter of the lake. By the time she had circled back to the reception area, Daisy felt her nerves buzzing with anxiety again. She pulled out a chair at the open-air bar and ordered another drink.

Why now? she wondered again. For a moment she wished she were back in New Mexico, then glanced up at the skyline around her, inhaled a breath of the lush, late-spring air. Something about this place knew her too intimately for comfort. It was easier to be a stranger.

When she saw Jesse Lopez stealing a glance at her from the end of the bar, she hoped it was a mistake. He ordered two drinks, leaned on one elbow in an attempt to be casual, then cleared his throat and looked her way.

Maybe it isn't him, she thought. *Seventeen years is long enough that you might not recognize someone, isn't it? It might be somebody else.* And he was different: the jawline more settled, more breadth in his shoulders, something about his eyes as sad as before but less sharp. Regardless, she would have known him anywhere. When their eyes caught the second time, she relented and broke the silence.

"Hi, Jesse."

His eyebrows rose in faux surprise. "Daisy, is that you?"

"It's me." She picked up the paper parasol from her drink and twirled it between her fingers. "You look like you've seen a ghost."

"How are you? What—what are you doing these days?" he asked. She pressed her lips around her straw and shook her head, smiling as if to say she did not know. "I didn't expect to see you here."

"I didn't expect to be here, if I'm honest," she answered as if she didn't care. Daisy watched Jesse stumbling to find something to fill the silence and found nothing to talk to him about. She could remember Jesse—the Jesse she had known, always a tad too formal, too earnest, too kind, but that was years ago. She couldn't find a reason for the numbness that descended between them, but began to feel she was watching him through a layer of soundproof glass. But she maintained a perfect politeness.

"I can't help but ask," he said. "What is your life like now? How is everything?"

"Everything is fine," she said. "I'm so sorry, but I—it's a weird day for me, okay?" Her eyes flickered up toward his and she sensed a crack in the barrier between them, felt that she needed immediately to get away from him. "Forgive me if I don't feel like catching up. This is just one surprise too many."

"I don't blame you." Their eyes met, and he waited for just a breath, an invitation to say more that she did not accept. Jesse answered her with such ready earnestness that she could feel he'd thought those words dozens of times, maybe more. *Why?* she wanted to ask. Daisy sipped her drink again until the ice rattled against the straw.

The bartender returned, placing two drinks in front of Jesse. Daisy nodded at the drinks then looked back to Jesse. "Looks like someone's waiting for you. Maybe you should get going."

"Okay, Daisy." He left a tip on the bar, picked up one drink in each hand. "Take care of yourself."

As he left, she wondered, too, what his life was like now.

From several yards away, she saw him resume his place, standing in a group of people. He handed one of the drinks to a woman with short, dark brown hair Daisy assumed to be his wife—Harlow. Her heart jumped into her throat when Jesse waved and nodded to her, only the slightest acknowledgment. She fluttered her fingers and turned away. She recalled, tipsy, something Teresa had said about him being single. So much for that. Drink in hand, she turned casually and scanned the field for Anderson.

"Excuse me," she said, turning to the bartender. "Have you seen—"

"The man you came in with?" the bartender asked. Daisy nodded. "He's over there." He pointed at the pond, where Anderson was paddling back to the shore, seated in a boat across from one of Stella's bridesmaids. The bartender offered a refill and she nodded, thanking him, then turned back to watch Anderson. Certainly, from here, their conversation appeared very polite, but on the heels of the text message she had accidentally seen the evening prior, Daisy felt a rush of anger. *He's probably wishing I weren't even here. Probably trying to imagine a way he can see her in between now and when we leave.* She cringed at the absolute discomfort of having to think such a thought, of being the woman who did the work of making excuses for her boyfriend, of wondering what he wanted instead of her. Old Daisy or new Daisy, she had always valued solitude above people who didn't treat her right.

Leaving her drink on the bar, Daisy walked toward the edge of the pond, lifted an arm up and waved to him until she saw his eyes find her. She seated herself on a bench facing the water and waited. Finally, after a few minutes had passed, the rowboat drew near the shore. She hurried to the shore to meet them as he steadied the boat with the paddle.

"Here, step up," she said, extending her hand to the girl. "I'm Daisy. Old friend of Stella's."

"Oh, I—It's nice to…"

Daisy cut her off with a nod and helped her onto dry land, then looked down at Anderson, who was still seated in the paddle boat. "I don't want to go back with you," she said.

"What are you talking about?"

"I need to stay for a few days," she said. "Anderson, I saw a text message from Charlotte on your phone last night. I didn't mean to look, but I can't pretend I didn't see it, and I need you to tell me the truth."

The bridesmaid's eyes widened. "Excuse me," she said, and walked back toward the crowd. Anderson rested his chin on his palm, fingertips tapping his brow.

"Are you telling me you looked at my phone?"

"By accident!"

"You don't trust me, Daisy?" Anderson's eyebrows rose in surprise, almost as if Daisy had struck him. "After all this time?"

"I saw it," she said. "I wish I could go back in time and just not look! But you have to tell me the truth." *Keep control of yourself*, she thought. *It isn't worth making a scene. This, of all things, is not worth my energy. I already need all of that to get through this day in one piece.* But she felt an irrational, twisting sensation between her ribs.

"If you don't trust me after everything I've done for you, then I think that says a lot more about who you are than it does about me."

"That isn't fair," Daisy said, her voice rising. Anderson's composure was untouchable, maddening, as if he existed on a different plane, where Daisy and her confusion and hurt did not matter. "It never crossed my mind that you might have been acting distant because you were seeing someone else."

"Daisy, please. Why don't you sit down for a few minutes until you can calm down?"

"All of this time," she said, "all of this time, I thought you were withdrawn because you were grieving. Because you were mourning the baby we lost. Not because you were cheating on me, Anderson."

"Christ, would you lower your voice?" he hissed. Anderson looked over Daisy's shoulder as if he were afraid they were being watched. He'd always been so thoughtful about his appearance.

"I know something's wrong," she continued. "Seeing that text was just another sign. And now you won't even tell me the truth."

Anderson gave an exasperated sigh. Extending the paddle, he pulled the little boat to a wobbly landing, then stepped to land, hissing a curse at the mud that sucked at his shoes. "If you can't control yourself, Daisy, I'm leaving. I can't always be your damage control."

"Fine, then," she shouted. "Leave." Daisy crossed her arms tight and turned her back on him, only to find that they had attracted the attention of a group standing nearby. Among them, she recognized Harlow and Jesse, and she dropped her eyes in shame.

Daisy watched Anderson leave, then called a taxi and sat at the bar to wait. An hour later, none had arrived. She remembered that it was graduation weekend and called a different company, getting no answer. Daisy felt anxiety creep up in between her ribs, vinelike. She turned her eyes to the vivid sunset, the daylight fading along with her faith in Anderson, the surest thing she had known. For the first time in years, she was alone.

CHAPTER SEVENTEEN

Now

Within an hour, the crowd had thinned to a dozen people. The sunlight was sparse and gold-tinged. The serving staff were beginning the process of polite but insistent cleaning up that meant it was time to leave. Only Daisy still sat at the bar, a line of brightly colored paper parasols at her side.

"There's an art to knowing when the bartender doesn't want to serve you anymore," Daisy chirped, smiling sadly up at the bartender as he sat a glass of water in front of her. "If you're tipping well, one of those ways is usually that they start serving water without asking if you want something else." She picked up one of the parasols and stuck it in her hair like a pin, then another.

"Not to worry," the bartender answered. "You're polite, and you're not driving. Good to stay hydrated, that's all."

"Thanks," Daisy answered, wondering if he, too, had overheard her mortifying conversation earlier. "I'm sure a cab will be available shortly. I keep calling, but they must be extra busy today." She laughed, the few drinks she'd had hitting her stomach more quickly than usual. Although Anderson had left, she half expected he would go back to the inn, pack their bags, and return to pick her up. But the sun was nearly set, and she still sat there alone, not quite ready to begin planning her next move, and yet running out of time all the same. She sipped her water.

Daisy heard someone move into the seat next to hers, and, assuming it was Anderson, turned with a wary expression to see Jesse. He looked different, the glow of youth a few years faded, a dark beard accenting his jawline. The endearing slenderness, his awkward, youthful angles, looked worn away.

"Oh." She quickly turned to face him, smoothed the skirt of her dress over her knees, folded her hands in her lap. "Sorry. I thought you were someone else."

Jesse nodded his head to acknowledge her and turned aside, holding his phone to his ear. Daisy pretended to ignore him as she eavesdropped.

"*Sí, ella está aquí. ¿Por qué?*" His eyes darted to look at her, then quickly away. "*¿Él se fue? Gracias, Mamá. Lo tengo.*"

"I'm sorry to bother you again." With his elbows leaning against the bar, facing out toward the emptying reception ground, Jesse looked as uncomfortable as he sounded.

"That's okay. You couldn't make my day any worse if you tried."

"So, I just got a very interesting phone call from my mother."

"Not that I meant to listen in, but it sounded like it," Daisy agreed. Somewhere in between high school in her nearly all-white hometown and living in New Mexico, she had picked up enough Spanish to eavesdrop effectively. "Anderson checked out of the inn? He's sure to be coming to pick me up."

Jesse coughed loudly and turned his face away. "When did you learn Spanish?"

"He's not going to leave me here," Daisy repeated. "I'm sure he'll show up any minute."

"That's probably why he left your suitcase on the front porch when he drove away, right?" Jesse asked.

"He did?" She felt a flush rise to her cheeks.

"Sorry."

"Well—" Daisy reached for her water and wished it were something stronger. "I'll—I'll call for a ride again, and go pick up my suitcase, and find a hotel." *I hope*, she added silently, remembering how every room in town had been booked the evening before. She considered her options, realized how close she was to not having a decent one. "Wait," she said. "I guess I could stay with my parents."

A scowl crossed Jesse's face. "You think that's a good idea? After everything that happened before?"

"What are they going to do—kick me out?" She laughed, glancing up at him as her smile faded. Daisy picked up another parasol and unfolded it, perched it behind her ear.

"I could ask my mother if she has another room at the house, but I remember her saying it was fully booked this weekend."

"No need." Daisy gave him a polite smile, though she continued fidgeting with the drink parasols. *I'll take my chances with them*, she thought, *over someone who left me deserted in the middle of nowhere. At least they're a known quantity.*

"I'll drive you to pick up the suitcase, then I'll drop you off," he offered.

"Fine," she answered. Though she meant to be polite, she could hear the forgotten anger welling up, chilling her voice. "If you absolutely insist."

"Alright," he answered, then added quickly: "My mother would kill me if I didn't. She's always liked you, Daisy."

Daisy left an additional tip at the bar for taking up so much time. She followed Jesse to his car, then waited while he started the engine and rolled the windows down. She was in no hurry to sit in an enclosed space with him. For one thing, she was conscious that her breath still smelled of alcohol, and another, she was afraid to sit so near him, to feel whatever lingering reverberations had scared her away just hours earlier. When he leaned over and unlocked the passenger door, she sat down.

"Seatbelt, please."

"Not now," she replied, feeling tired. "It's too warm. And it's a short drive. Plus, you're still a good driver, right?"

Daisy studied his face, the same eyes, but somehow deeper, the same hair, just trimmed shorter. Jesse had always had an impulse for kindness that she could never stop scrutinizing. Daisy was too tired to worry about what was going to happen next. She pulled her hat down over her eyes and leaned back, then woke what felt like seconds later to his hand on her elbow.

"You alright, Daisy?" he asked. Daisy awoke to the car slowing to a stop as Jesse parked outside his mother's inn.

"How long was I asleep?" She sat up with a start and looked out the window, saw that the sky was inching closer to dark.

"Not long. Fifteen minutes. You went out quick."

"Being drunk at a wedding's not a crime," she said, removing her hat and checking her makeup in the mirror. Her hair had gone frizzy with the humidity and the warmth.

"No," he agreed, his voice barely audible over the engine.

Daisy could only bear to let a few moments pass by before she spoke; the silence was too heavy. "Did you have a nice time at the... well, did you have a nice time?"

"All things considered, yes."

Even the idle chatter, though, did little to dispel all that was unspoken between them. "It doesn't really matter, Jesse," Daisy said, "and I'm probably a little prone to rambling at the moment, but—I'm not like this. Breaking up at a wedding, being—" She gestured loosely toward her chest. "Being drunk, needing a ride? This really isn't me." Needing people—being disorganized—those were things the old Daisy would have done. Somehow, she found herself anxious to convince him that things had changed, that she wasn't that girl anymore.

Jesse only smiled, barely looking away from the road. "I understand."

"This isn't my parents' house."

"Just the first stop. Picking up your bag."

"Oh, right." She pushed the door open, swung one unsteady foot out, and tried to stand up, pulled back by the seatbelt fastened in place. "What? I didn't—" She smoothed the wrinkles in her skirt, embarrassed.

"I'll get it," Jesse said. "Wait here."

She sighed and waited as he walked across the near-dark gravel lot to the steps of the front porch, retrieved her heavy bag, and carried it to the car, placed it just behind the passenger seat.

Jesse sat down in the driver's seat and closed the door. "Your parents still live in the same place?"

"As far as I know."

He started the engine again and pulled back onto the road. "Does that mean you haven't seen them since—"

"Yes," she said. "That's what it means. I haven't been back since. Now, after today, it almost feels like I don't have a home anywhere. Whatever plans I thought I had were a waste of time."

"Yeah?" His hand dropped to the gearshift, crept toward hers. "I know the feeling." Daisy crossed her arms.

"It doesn't look that way," she said. "You've got your veterinary practice. The big house down the road. Your wife. It looks like everything went to plan for you."

"No, Daisy," he said. "You know this wasn't the plan."

She crossed her arms and put her hat on again, pulled the brim low to cover her eyes, despite the dark. She stretched her legs out as far as she could, trying to relax.

"Oh, Jesse," she said. "I shouldn't have said anything. I'm sorry. I just don't feel like talking. Nothing good can come from this."

"I understand," he said. "I don't blame you."

It was a short drive to Daisy's parents' house. The minutes passed in silence as she felt the road climbing the familiar curves, the late-spring smells of honeysuckle and new leaves drifting in at the window. She waited for the click in the road as the car passed over the bridge, just before taking a right turn onto the gravelly street that would lead up the hill to the house. Jesse parked the car at the bottom of the driveway. "If you have any problems, or if you need another place to stay, just call."

"Oh, I—" Her eyes flashed. *Is he hitting on me?* Maybe she didn't know whether Anderson had cheated on her with somebody named Charlotte, but if Jesse was anything like that, he had done her a favor by deserting her. *Jump from one dishonest man to the next? Hardly.* She'd seen him with Harlow just that afternoon. Besides, even if he were single, she wasn't about to forget the history between them.

"That didn't sound right."

In the dark, she could only see his profile against the lights of the dashboard. His shy laugh, an attempt to fill the silence, made him sound like a teenager again. "I have friends—there's an attic at Mom's inn—I have a guest room. You know, if your mom and dad won't let you stay here."

Daisy looked up the drive and found her strength gathering, her posture straightening. "I'll be fine, Jesse." She exhaled with a sense of disdain. "I don't know why you'd offer me any help, anyway."

"Regardless," he said, "give me a call if you need anything."

"Goodnight," she said. "Thanks for the ride."

Some places have a pull that defies the passage of time. Sitting in Jesse's car at the bottom of her parents' driveway somehow pulled Daisy out of time, made her forget whatever years had passed, washed away all but the clearest, heart-deep wish for time to stop right here, where it was only them, for her to never have to go back to somewhere or someone else.

Ignoring his offers to assist her, Daisy unbuckled the seatbelt and climbed out of the car. She lifted her suitcase out without his help and began the walk up toward the house, trying not to think about the last time she had seen her parents, and how thin and small the shattered remains of their relationship now were.

CHAPTER EIGHTEEN

Before

As the weekend passed and Monday drew nearer, Daisy half regretted telling Jesse about Tracker's hunting blind. It was one of her favorite hideouts, a three-sided structure just on the crest of a hill. By car, the trip to the chemical plant took nearly twenty minutes, the roads circuitous around the mountain's curves. But this way, on foot, she could get directly to it in just a couple of minutes.

Mindful of their near argument before, Daisy tried to make sure that her homework was tidy, every step worked out. She wore a dress Ellen had made for her, cotton printed with tiny birds and stars, that was only a little too small around her shoulders and underarms.

Jesse, as usual, was slightly overdressed, out of place in his collared shirt there in the woods, the warmth of the sun still and close under the trees. Daisy, though, felt more in her element: she had gotten here first, for once, and she had her books spread out and ready to work.

"How are you today?" she asked.

"Good." He set down his backpack, offered her a bottle of water. "Are you doing any better?"

"Yeah, you know." Daisy's mouth pressed into a smile that meant *not really*, and then she remembered that odd closeness in his stare. "The same." While he opened his workbook, she fussed with the water bottle, peeling the label back.

"So, last week's homework?"

"Right." She pointed with her pencil to the first question, meaning to show him how she had solved the equation carefully, one operation at a time. "It says: if two times X equals…"

Though Jesse was staring into the trees above, Daisy sensed that his gaze was directed somewhere much further off. She wished she could follow it.

"I didn't ask how you're doing today," she said. "What's new?"

Jesse didn't answer, leaving Daisy wondering whether he hadn't heard her, or whether he might have been ignoring her. She decided on one more attempt at conversation. "What are you doing this weekend?"

"Nothing." When a stray leaf fluttered to the bench beside Jesse, he swatted it to the ground. His pragmatic frown softened as he looked over her answers. "You're good at this when you focus on it. These are all correct."

"I guess that's my problem," Daisy said. "Paying attention, I mean. Sometimes I wish I were more like you are."

"More like me?" He laughed, but his eyes skipped away when she looked at him, halfway between flattered and unconvinced.

"Your backpack's always organized and clean," Daisy said. "There are never scribbles in the margins of your papers."

He laughed quietly, not smiling. "Yeah—my stepbrother says I'm a nerd."

"That's not a bad thing," Daisy answered. "At least you're not stuck in summer school."

"My dad went to college on a sports scholarship," Jesse answered. "I was supposed to have dinner with him tonight, but instead he's going to my stepbrother's football game."

"Sorry." Daisy had never considered that maybe, like her, Jesse had also wished that he could be someone different, that his studious perfectionism wasn't an act. For a moment, some impulsive part of her wanted to tell him that she liked him the way he was, that she wouldn't have preferred that he was somebody else. But before she could say anything, a sharp explosion sounded from down the hill, followed by a deep, sustained blast.

There was a volley of shouts and the sound of something metal dropping, making a dappled echo through the thickening trees, though it was not more than a couple hundred yards away. Daisy looked through the sight in the blind.

"What's down there?" Jesse asked.

"That's where my dad works," she answered without looking at him. "I'm sure it's nothing. They have something blow up there every few months." There were explosions almost yearly, foul-smelling smoke and fire. Still, this was a rare enough occurrence. She kept looking.

That was when they heard the noise. At first, Daisy thought it was another minor, contained fire. But the crackling and breathless whistle of fire continued. Daisy leaned close to the hole in the blind and squinted through the darkening forest toward the plant. Jesse rose to his feet and looked over the top of the blind.

The roof and east wall of the warehouse were engulfed in flames, bright hot and reddish in the deepening evening. They moved as angrily as they glowed, and the smell that hit her nostrils burned even from back here. As the explosion sounds tapered, Daisy heard voices, shouts and screams, reminding her of a painting of damned souls in hell that she had seen in one of her history textbooks.

"Wait here," she said, giving Jesse a look that said she meant it. She was smaller than him, and couldn't meaningfully have enforced the order, but she expected he would be too timid to disobey her.

She raced through the trees, aiming for footholds on logs, rocks, soil, trying to avoid the leaves where the blue ghosts nested, issuing a breathless apology whenever her foot hit the underbrush. Finally, she drew close to the fire, the smell and the smoke nearly unbearable. She walked into the yard through the open chain-link fence. Squinting through watering eyes, she discerned that there were two groups of men: injured, and uninjured. The injured men were huddled on the ground near her; the others were running back into the building. She scanned the group of injured for her father, finally saw him leaned over with an open cut on his head. Daisy had no thought of her disdain for him, only that he was her father and she needed him. *Please let it be a scratch*, she thought, *and not a real wound, please, God*. As she began to approach him, she heard a volley of shouts, voices warning her to stay back, or, she realized, warning of something else.

With a crack and a rush of heat, the opening of a giant oven, a beam gave way and the side of the building began to heave downward. Though Daisy was fifty feet away, kneeling in the brush, she could feel the warmth of the flames on her cheeks. It was then that Daisy saw her, squinting through the smoke, her lungs burning and her head beginning to swim. Amid the confusion of the noise and smells, she thought she saw herself dart out of the collapsing building and run to the side, chin dashing back and forth in a flurry of glances left and right, trying to decide where to run.

Am I dead? Is that me? Daisy leaned forward, frightened of what she might see, and pieced the vision together: it was not herself, but another girl. *Why would a girl be in there? Why isn't she moving away? The building is about to collapse.* The girl was too slow. The burning beam fell and landed at an angle across her body, shoulder to hip, pinning her against the ground.

Isn't anyone going to help her? Daisy wondered, before realizing that there was nobody to help: everyone else there was injured, if not worse, or trying to get themselves to safety. Daisy crept closer. Her footsteps were inaudible over the noises of the fire. From the corner of her vision, she saw Tracker, gathered near the border of the fence with two other men, heard him shouting her name. His head was lifted, broad shoulders straight; he waved her in his direction as if sweeping her in, almost frantic. She realized that he was okay and kept moving.

Something compelled her footsteps to the girl's side, where the beam had dropped a few yards from the building. But the flames reflected a lifelike blush on her cheeks: singed curls, muddy green eyes. It was like looking into a mirror, if that reflection were seared to within an inch of her life. Foam flecked the stranger's lips, with speckles of blood. Daisy glanced briefly down at her midsection, then felt her stomach curdle and looked away. The girl's hand clung tight to Daisy's wrist, stinging with heat. Hovering over her, her heart racing above the volume of any of the noises around her, Daisy was confounded by an inability to speak. But what could she have said? *Can you move? What can I do? It's going to be alright.* None of those words could have served any purpose. For a moment, Daisy wrapped her hand around the girl's, feeling the desperate clutch in her fingers: fear, pain.

"Help me," the girl said, her body curling upward, an attempt to sit up on one elbow.

"Who are you?" Daisy whispered.

When Tracker's big hand closed on Daisy's arm, and she could hear the fear-turned-anger in his voice. "Didn't you hear me?" he shouted, over and over. "Didn't you hear me? I told you to get back from there. What are you doing here?"

With her father's hand on her arm and her opposite hand clasped to the girl's, Daisy felt she might break in half. Her father, she knew, would pull her away from this noise, back to the cool quiet of home, away from here. The girl on the ground next to her, that desperate grip on her fingers, the face she already knew would haunt her if she walked away.

Daisy tugged at her father's arm, raised her voice to an incoherent yell as she gestured at the girl, at the large wooden beam. Tracker looked over his shoulder then put two fingers in his mouth and whistled, waving to two men to come nearer.

"Do something," Daisy said, still held by her father and clinging to the girl's hand.

Tracker's gaze lingered over the girl on the ground, then back to Daisy. "You need to get away from here. Come on."

"But Dad," Daisy coughed. The fire was spreading. Daisy dragged her heels, still holding the girl's hand. Her tightly grasped hand collapsed as Tracker picked her up by the waist and carried her back. It wasn't until he sat her down on her feet that she noticed the tarnished, silver ring in her hand. It must have slipped off the girl's finger. She held it close, her vision blurred with smoke. An inscription on the inside of the band had the look of a familiar word, but one her mind was too scattered to register.

"Daisy, are you okay?" Tracker took both her hands. The ring fell or disappeared from sight. Without answering, Daisy took small, darting steps, trying to get around him and back to the girl.

"Stop." He scanned her face and arms for injuries. "You hurt?"

"No."

"Let's keep it that way." He turned back, approaching the girl. "Stay put, Daisy."

As soon as he turned his back, she followed him, anxious for another glance of the stranger, another chance to help. But, drawing near to her father and the building engulfed in flame, Daisy saw nobody there. The wooden beam, still smoldering, lay across the ground, but the girl was gone. Daisy looked down at her palms. They were empty. Hadn't she just been holding something? Despite the fire and the evil smells, Daisy felt a chill settle over her chest.

"Where'd she go?" Daisy looked to Tracker for reassurance.

"You have to get out of here." Tracker pushed her toward the open gate. "Go home. Tell your mother there was an accident."

"Daddy, who was that?"

"There's nobody there," he said emphatically, his big hands squeezing a threat on her shoulders. "Do you hear me? Now hurry home."

Daisy took several steps away into the trees, looking hesitantly over her shoulder. Tracker walked away from her, leaving her in the smoke-obscured yard. She swiveled on her feet, turning from the building to the girl's body. *Do people die immediately, when their bodies do?* she wondered. *Is she still in there?* The only thing that seemed impossible was to do nothing, although that was the only thing she could do, limbs heavy, mind fogged, her throat burning.

CHAPTER NINETEEN

Before

When Daisy felt arms wrapping around her shoulders, pulling her backwards, she resisted. It could have either been her body freezing or that she didn't want to leave the stranger. Her feet kicked, weakly. Daisy blinked at the smoke, finally feeling the burning pain in her eyes and nose.

But she was moved further than the yard, beyond where the men were gathering. When she finally snapped conscious and wriggled loose, she turned around, staggering, to see Jesse, his large eyes full of significance. Struggling without knowing why, Daisy shoved his hands away, her fists hitting his chest, until, unsure what else to do, he enclosed her in a hug.

"How'd you get so strong?" she mumbled, realizing that she was shaking all over.

"I don't know," he replied. His grip loosened and she clung tighter. "Tae kwon do lessons."

"Nerd," Daisy bleated. She caught a breath and began to sob, big gulps of air.

"Come on. We're still too close to the smoke." Jesse led her back through the woods. Past the light and heat of the fire, they returned to the hunting blind, walking from the orange glow into the blue glimmer of the fireflies. Their soft-lit dance lasted only through the twilight; the woods would soon be dark.

"They're supposed to be ghosts. I've heard people say the fireflies are Confederate soldiers' ghosts, or Union soldiers. I don't know why they'd be one or the other. They're all dead just the same."

"I don't know, Daisy."

Daisy realized that she was rambling and drifted into a lull of silence, watching the faint blue lights moving around them. Finally, she set about putting her things into her backpack, then stacked and closed Jesse's workbooks and handed them over to him.

"I need to go," she said. "You probably have, like, a six o'clock curfew, right?"

He shook his head.

"Well, I do. I have to…" She stood up and walked a few steps, then turned back. "Did you see it? Did you see her?"

"See what?" Jesse was neatly putting his books away, preparing to leave.

"That—that girl, Jesse. Didn't you see?"

"I wasn't as close as you were, Daisy. What happened?"

Daisy shook her head. She couldn't answer him. "I need to go home. I need my mom."

"I'll walk with you."

"Fine," Daisy sniffed, though she secretly felt relieved. He offered his hand, but she ignored it, hurrying ahead and leaving him to catch up. Shortly, Daisy stumbled over a root, landing on her hands and pulling them back stinging and scraped. She brushed her palms on her dress, then, listening for Jesse's footsteps, reached back, found his wrist, and held on.

He left her at the edge of the clearing. Daisy felt the flush of fire on her skin, touched her eyebrows and hair to make sure nothing was burned off. She looked over her shoulder, the question still unanswered, and back again to her own hands in front of her. Who was she? That girl could have been her own sister, her own self.

Daisy heard, again, her father's voice. *Who is what? There's nobody there.* Had she only imagined it? What were those fumes that kept her coughing and heaving? She made herself take deep breaths as she walked and waited for her limbs to stop trembling, for her senses to calm, knowing only that she needed to make her way home before it was too dark. In the last gray of daylight, she tripped her way through the woods, trying in the dark to avoid where the fireflies nested.

CHAPTER TWENTY

Now

Daisy set off up the driveway to her parents' place on foot, dragging the suitcase on its wheels behind her in the gravel. She looked over her shoulder once to see Jesse watching with a hint of concern. She waved her hand as if chasing him away and turned up the hill to see the familiar house.

Even the forest she had known all her life became a little bit strange close to dark. She heard a creak and whistle behind her and felt her limbs tense, her heart begin to race. Daisy dabbed at her forehead with the back of her arm and pulled the suitcase the last few steps to the door. Her heart thudded under the sweat-damp cotton of her dress. This wasn't supposed to happen. The alcohol was supposed to make her brave.

"Hello?" she called, tapping at the flimsy glass-and-screen storm door. "Mama?"

Inside, a hum of activity she hadn't even noticed dropped to silence. Daisy was sizing up her next option, which was to call a cab to pick her up and take her to a car rental place, when she saw her father's face through the rusted screen door.

"Daisy?" she heard his voice call.

"Daddy?"

Tracker sat in his chair at the kitchen table, his supper half-finished in front of him. She took in his graying hair, the net that aging had cast over his features, once so dark and certain. The skin that had been robust and suntanned was now pale. Daisy sensed her father in turn sizing her up, looking over her cocktail dress and the large suitcase she pulled behind her.

"Hi, Dad."

"Ellen," he shouted. "Your girl's here."

But her mother was already standing behind his shoulder.

"How are you?" Ellen wore a faded, striped cotton dress with a belt at her waist and a pair of worn house slippers. She almost blended into the dried flowers that stood in a vase behind her. "We had no idea you were coming." Without a backwards glance or movement, she silently alluded to Tracker.

"No. Of course you didn't. I'm sorry." Daisy looked down at the suitcase by her feet. "I didn't even remember to call. It's been a long weekend."

Tracker studied her from his seat at the table, covered in its green-and-white checkered vinyl cloth. "You look like you've had a little too much fun."

She frowned, reluctant to satisfy them with the whole truth. "I'm in town for a wedding and had a change of plans. Can I sleep in my old room tonight? It's for one night," she added. "Only one night, I promise."

Tracker glared. Ellen's feet seemed to wash forward, as if she were a wave coming onto shore. "Come in, Daisy," she said. "Of course you can stay here. You'll find your room pretty much unchanged."

"Thanks. I—"

"Oh." Ellen looked up as if just remembering. "You're alone, right?"

"Yes, Mom," Daisy answered hurriedly. The pink dress began to feel conspicuous. She looked out the window toward the road, wishing she could still count on Jesse waiting for her.

"Well, sit down and have a plate of food. Can't have a guest walk in without feeding them."

"Tracker," Ellen scolded. "She's not a guest."

"I am," Daisy interrupted. "In any case, I don't live here anymore, so."

She pushed the suitcase out of the way by the door and slid into her seat at the table, out of unspoken force of habit. Ellen brought her a plate filled with buttered green beans, fried pork chops, and boxed mashed potatoes. Daisy had always loved this food, hearty and simple but doused with salt and pepper. She set to and cleared half of the plate before she decided she should probably be conversing.

"Well, thanks for taking me in for the night." There was no way around it; this would be awkward. She decided to try to be overly polite.

"Where are you living now?" Ellen asked.

"New Mexico," Daisy said. "Santa Fe."

"Alone?"

"With my boyfriend."

"How long have you been with him?"

"Since—" Daisy paused, loaded a fork with green beans, then rested it on her plate. "A few years."

Ellen only smiled, refraining from any discussion of painful topics.

"And what is his name? Your fiancé?"

"Boyfriend," Daisy corrected her, half enjoying the wince that crossed Ellen's face.

Tracker coughed loudly. Uneasy silence settled over the table. Daisy sat up straight and picked the parasols from her hair, one at a time, lining them up next to her plate. "There's another thing. I'm—"

"You're pregnant?" her father asked.

"No," she shook her head, scowling. "I'm thirty-five, Dad. I have my own house, far away from here. I'm not here to ask you for help."

"And you're not married? No kids?"

"I can't win, can I?" Daisy directed her question to her mother, laughing. Only after a moment passed did she see the same question reflected on her mother's face. *The doctor said I'm healthy*, she wanted to say. *Maybe not young, but healthy*. Her smile faded. "Well, anyway. This isn't why I'm in town, but since I'm here anyway, can we talk about the fire?"

Ellen and Tracker looked away to somewhere alone, Ellen at her plate, Tracker into the distance. They exchanged a quick, uncoordinated glance.

"What about it?" Ellen asked. "That was a hard time for us. You know it isn't easy for your father to discuss it."

"I…" How was she supposed to ask what she wanted? What did she want? "I keep going over the memories. I believe I saw what I think I did. I—"

"Listen to that," Tracker chuckled into his beer. "You believe you saw, you think you saw… You were a little girl with your lungs full of toxic smoke. Grown men hallucinate in situations like that. You're lucky you weren't killed, sneaking around."

"You are lucky," Ellen agreed. She looked at her clasped hands. "I should tell you, I've prayed about it a lot these last few years."

"Oh, you have?" Daisy tried her best not to sound sarcastic but received a warning look from her father, regardless.

"I believe you saw another possible version of yourself, running in at the wrong moment, at just the wrong spot, and not being so lucky to survive the way you did. Imagine if your father hadn't grabbed you and pulled you away."

"It wasn't me," Daisy said. "She looked like me, but she wasn't me."

"You know I went back?" Tracker was drawing slow lines through his gravy with his fork. "After that Lopez boy pulled you away, I went back with the others to look for the girl. There was no one there." Tracker's fork clattered to the plate. "And one of them didn't make it back out."

Ellen crooned and squeezed his hand. "It's okay, dear. Sorry, Daisy, is this what you came back here for? In this house, everything is fine."

"Just as I left it," Daisy said under her breath. "No, this isn't what I came back for." She reached out briefly with each hand to squeeze her mother's and father's hands. "Thanks for dinner, Mom." She took the empty dishes to the sink. "Is it alright if I take a shower?"

"Help yourself."

Daisy walked down the step into her childhood bedroom, which, true to her mother's word, looked almost exactly the same. The wooden twin bed sat in one corner, the mismatched wooden dresser and nightstand with their feet in deep grooves on the worn carpet. Tracker was practical. He would have expected that any unneeded space should be made useful. Ellen, though, was not. Daisy realized, staring around the old room, that it meant something to find it so unchanged.

She opened her suitcase and walked into the bathroom fully dressed, changing clothes only once she was inside. Every detail of the house, even the pressure and scent of the water in the shower, seemed to embody everything that was unspoken there. The fire was difficult for her father to discuss, and so it was left alone. The entire house seemed improper and lacking in boundaries. She combed her hair back—there was no point trying to blow-dry and straighten it here—and changed into sweatpants and a light jacket.

Daisy cracked open the windows to let in the evening springtime air, despite knowing it made the curtains ripple, disturbing her privacy. She scheduled a taxi pickup for the following morning, then reclined on the old bed and stared up at the rafters in the ceiling. Her father and mother both seemed to have their lines on exactly what had happened—her father's being that she had no grip on reality, and her mother's mystical theory. The ways that people contorted themselves to avoid living with the truth.

Looking for some distraction, she picked up her phone to find a message from Anderson. *"Sorry I left, but I can't stand to watch you self-destruct. Let me know when you're calm, and we can talk."* She sighed, chewing on her thumbnail. He had to be right. She had overreacted, hadn't she? It hurt, almost physically, that Anderson had left her here, when he knew how afraid she was to come back.

She listened to the crickets and looked out the uncovered window into the dark gradations of the evening forest. She could walk from here to the old chemical plant, if she wanted to. Straight through the woods. The thought materialized in her body as if chilling it to a solid state. Half asleep, Daisy rolled over, tossing the heavier blanket away to leave only the sheet covering her body. She'd been back at home for less than twenty-four hours, and already the place seemed to be pulling her in, nearer to the center of something she could not name, that had a gravity all its own.

CHAPTER TWENTY-ONE

Now

Daisy stretched hard and knocked her toes against the end of the narrow bed, remembering where she was with a grimace. The yellow light in the windows, the angled shadows through the blinds, told her that it was mid-morning. She sat upright with a jolt. It must have been years since she had slept through sunrise, let alone past 8 a.m.

Secondary to the shock of sleeping late was the hangover, a pulsing headache and sour-sweet taste in her mouth. Daisy stood up on slightly unsteady feet.

"Daisy?" her mother's voice called. "There's coffee in the kitchen."

"Thanks, Mama," she called back, looking at her puffy, pale face in the bureau mirror.

"Can I get you anything?" Ellen asked.

Daisy leaned around the corner, poking her head out from the curtain. A radio on the counter played soft classical music and the windows were open, both of which meant Tracker was not at home. "Do you have any juice? Or iced tea? Anything cold and sweet?"

"Sure do, honey," Ellen said. "Go ahead and get dressed. I'll bring you something."

Daisy found a hairbrush in her suitcase and gave some futile effort to taming her frizzy hair, licked the tip of her thumb and tried to

smear some residual eye makeup off. It was little use. A few moments
later, Ellen appeared in the doorway, holding a glass in her hand.

"Sweet tea?"

"Thanks."

Ellen smiled wisely, as though she knew Daisy wasn't feeling
well, and why. "Where are you off to today?"

"I don't know," Daisy said.

"Not back to New Mexico?"

Daisy pressed her hands around the cool glass, imagining the
chilled blood circulating back up through her veins, calming her
throbbing head. "No," she said. "I'd rather not go back right away."

"No? Any particular reason?"

"I'm afraid he's seeing someone else," Daisy answered plainly.
"But I don't know what's going on, and I'm so scared I've messed
everything up."

"Daisy, I'm so sorry."

"I just found out. I'm not ready to decide whether—you know,
I'm not ready to deal with it right now. I need somewhere to stay
for, like, two days. Maybe three."

Ellen leaned an arm against the doorway. "I don't think that's
a good idea, baby."

"Trust me," Daisy replied curtly, hurt by Ellen's assumption,
"I am not suggesting staying here. Everything was booked for the
weekend, and I couldn't find anywhere last night." She looked up
at her mother, let their eyes join for a moment, then picked up the
tea. It was strong, as her mother had always made it, sweetened
with honey and mint leaves, and just a kick of something extra.
She coughed, then took an appreciative sip.

"Thought you could use a little hair of the dog," Ellen whispered, slim and almost girlish in her cotton dress. "You know, it's
almost noon."

Daisy gave her mother a grateful smile as she turned to her
suitcase. It was a good thing she had overpacked. She found a

pair of blue jeans and a simple gray blouse, then wondered how she would choose an outfit when she had no literal idea what she was going to do next.

"I guess I'll go to the airport," she whispered. "I'm not sure. I…" Despite her hangover and the drink in her hand, she felt the impulse to lace up her shoes and go for a run.

"Are you sure everything's okay, Daisy?" Ellen asked.

"I'm sure." Daisy felt suddenly guarded. "I really only came back to see Stella, but…" She remembered, all of a sudden, Stella's request that she should come by the house anytime. Her door was always open, right? The jeans and gray shirt would be just fine. "I'll figure everything out," Daisy said, smiling back at her mother in her innocence, taking another small sip of tea. "I think I'll go and see Stella."

"How'd you get here?"

"An old friend dropped me off."

Ellen looked over her shoulder, through the kitchen, through the windows. "You know we've got a car here we don't use regularly," she said. "You could use the old sedan, the one we taught you to drive in. Though I can't promise how far it'll get you."

"Really?"

"I drive it to church once a week, but otherwise we don't use it." She took a key from a row of hooks on the wall and stepped back a little, regretful. "I don't know what else to do for you, Daisy."

The parameters of the familiar kitchen seemed to shrink inward. "You could have found me, Mom. If you'd looked for me."

"You disappeared, Daisy."

"I didn't disappear. I never used a fake name." A flicker of anger lit Daisy's temper, weakening as soon as it hit the air. She threw back her shoulders and pursed her lips against the tightness in her throat. "I just left. You never even reported me missing."

Ellen exhaled slowly and placed her cool hands on Daisy's cheeks. Daisy wiggled her shoulders backwards and clasped her hands. "I won't be in town long. In any case, I'll see you when I return the car."

"Of course, dear."

The woman who had proved untrustworthy when she needed her most, who abandoned her to that horrible school, could call her dear and do her favors. Daisy was grateful to hear the screen door closing behind her, for every step she took away from her former home.

With the intention of waiting a little while before driving, Daisy went outside for a walk around the yard to clear her head. Toward the west, she saw the pathway that led into the forest, where she used to sneak between old hunting blinds, find paths to Teresa's house, Jesse's childhood home. She looked to the east, where the wisteria, resistant to all taming efforts and now thoroughly overgrown, cast a protective shadow over Ellen's little garden and the tiny burial mounds. Between the two, she saw the border with the Whittens' home, where she and Stella used to meet, climbing through the three wires of the barbed fence. There was nothing safe for her here. Daisy sat in Ellen's rocking chair on the front porch until her head was clear enough to drive, not because she had somewhere to go, but because she did not want to stay. Once again, the question of Stella's refusal to marry Bryson came to mind. Daisy knew she had to find out what had prompted Stella to change her mind, and what exactly she had to do with it.

CHAPTER TWENTY-TWO

Now

Daisy drove past the old landmarks of her childhood. It hadn't occurred to her to wonder how well the car had been maintained until the engine began to cough. As if in slow motion, it shuddered and rolled to a halt, giving her just enough time to pull to the curb, out of the way of traffic, the gas needle on empty. *This place has put some kind of curse on me*, she thought. *This is not me. This is not Daisy Ritter.*

Daisy threw the car into park, leaned back in the seat, and exhaled a stream of profanities. She no longer knew the town well enough to find where the nearest gas station might be, or any store that might sell a gasoline can. And besides, she appeared to be in the middle of a residential area. *Just outside of town*, Stella had said. *Near Mulberry.* Daisy glanced at the trees around her, saw them dotted with berries, birds and squirrels swarming. She couldn't remember the prior evening with enough clarity. Had she gotten Stella's phone number? She opened her phone to look through her contacts and remembered; Stella had said that her phone number hadn't changed. She scrolled through her missed calls, realizing that she had been hoping to see Anderson's name. Surely, he would have something to say, at least to apologize for the misunderstanding, if that's what it was. For leaving her here all by herself, where he knew she was frightened to be alone.

Her initial reaction to the thought of Anderson was embarrassment. What would he say if he saw her right now, here in a fifteen-year-old car, out of gas at the side of the road? Was this something Charlotte would do? *No*, she thought, *I'm not getting into a competition with an imaginary woman over a man who can't be bothered to tell me the truth. A woman who might not even exist. Not going there.* Daisy tried to remember Stella's phone number, dialed a wrong number first, then waited anxiously as the phone rang on her second try.

"Hello?"

"Stella, it's Daisy Ritter."

"Oh, hi, Daisy." Stella's smile was audible. "How are you? Are you back in New Mexico?"

"Well, no. I…" She wasn't sure where to start to catch Stella up, or if she should. "I'm still here. This is kind of a long story, but my car's out of gas, and…" *And I also don't have a place to stay.* She could add that later.

"Oh! Where are you?"

"Are you busy?"

"Not in the least," Stella answered. "I'm dying for something to do." Any upset Stella experienced had a way of transforming itself into action; she had been designed for success. "Where are you?"

"On Floyd Avenue," Daisy said, leaning forward to look at the nearest street sign. "Near Meadow."

"Oh, that's close," Stella answered. Again, Daisy sensed the nervous hum beneath the patter of activity in her voice. "Tell you what. I'll drive out, fill up a gas container at the station, and meet you there."

"Thanks," Daisy managed, ashamed again at her lack of organization.

Within twenty minutes, Stella arrived, wearing a floral sundress, leather sandals, and large sunglasses. Only her ruffled hair and hollow-looking eyes peering over the dark lenses gave away her lack of sleep. She climbed out of the car and retrieved the red gasoline container from the back seat. Daisy remembered reading that it was dangerous to drive with gasoline in the car—of course it was—but what was the better option?

"So, what have you been up to since yesterday?" Stella asked, tilting the container so the gasoline began to pour into the funnel. "And why are you still in town?"

"Do you remember yesterday, when I told you I had enough problems of my own to worry about?"

"Sure do."

"So, I—I don't want to get into it, but I had a fight with my boyfriend yesterday, after you left. He went back to New Mexico without me. I got drunk, couldn't find a single hotel room. Jesse dropped me off at my parents' house. And, as it turns out, the warm welcome there lasts about one night."

"Jesse?" Stella raised an eyebrow. "How is he doing?"

"Fine—I think." Daisy recalled waking up in the passenger seat, realizing he had fastened her seatbelt. "I don't know. We didn't talk." She remembered that Stella didn't know how things had ended with her and Jesse, and she wasn't sure she was ready for a friendly catch-up.

"Man, really?" Stella seemed disappointed, as if she had been expecting some intrigue. "You two were really in love."

"Puppy love," Daisy deadpanned. "It only feels real. Besides, you never asked what happened after I left."

Stella pushed her sunglasses up to cover her eyes entirely, dodging Daisy's glare. "I guess not. Should I?"

Daisy suddenly felt herself a heartbroken teenager again. She hugged her own shoulders. "Perhaps not."

"So where did you go?" Stella asked.

"I met Anderson not long after my parents sent me away," Daisy answered. "He was on his way to start a new job in Santa Fe. Happy ending, right?"

"Until yesterday."

Daisy started. "You heard?"

"Deborah, one of the bridesmaids, told me about the argument." The sunglasses couldn't mask the embarrassed flush in Stella's cheeks.

"Yeah, well, yesterday wasn't my finest," Daisy said.

Stella capped the gas container and put it back in her car.

"Tell me about it," Stella sighed. "Why don't you come over for lunch? How long are you in town?"

Daisy shrugged and gestured at the suitcase in the back of the car. "I haven't bought a return ticket yet. I don't know if I have anywhere to stay there. Or here, really."

"Well, that's not true. I'll drive to my house," Stella said. "Follow me there."

*

The home Stella had bought with Bryson was deceptively costly. It had no showy features, but, as Daisy climbed the steps to the well-proportioned front porch, she saw that there was nothing that was not perfectly chosen. Stella had always had good taste. The thing that Daisy had always admired about it was that it didn't change. Stella had never, since Daisy had known her, gone through a phase, a trying-something-out. She just knew what she liked. The core of her ideas, the self-knowledge from where she made every decision, from wardrobe to career choices, was grounded, flourishing. All of her choices, Daisy thought, were winning ones. Where did this most recent choice fall, leaving her dream husband at the altar because of something that should have been over years ago? Daisy parked the car, opened the trunk, and lifted her heavy suitcase to the ground. One of the wheels caught as she pulled it toward the front door, leaving her dragging it on one corner.

"Come on in," Stella yawned, stepping aside. She glanced down at Daisy's suitcase. She smiled, but her eyes held a sensitive caution that Daisy resented. "You said you had only planned to be in town for two days. What's with the giant bag?"

"I guess I may have overpacked," Daisy said. "Trust me, it's better than the alternative."

"You think?" Stella laughed.

"It's important to be prepared," Daisy said, suddenly feeling defensive.

"You're right," Stella said. "Welcome, I guess. This is our house. Bryson's not here, of course."

"Wait, really?" Daisy frowned. "He didn't, like, drop all of his plans to try to get things right with his fiancée?"

"We scheduled our honeymoon around a big meeting he had, so he couldn't really just cancel it."

"Where to?"

"The Riviera. It's not as fancy as it sounds. Bryson's family have a house there, so it's really more of a free vacation."

"Bryson's house in the Riviera," Daisy echoed, smirking. "No, you're right, that doesn't sound fancy at all."

Daisy scoffed, then bit her tongue. She had no more room to judge Stella's romantic life than Stella had to judge hers. She trailed Stella down a wide hallway that opened into the kitchen. Countertops were strewn with unopened gifts, bottles of wine from the reception, the leftovers of the canceled wedding. Stella paused at a row of custom-printed champagne flutes.

"It's a touch early for a drink, isn't it?" Daisy spoke in a low voice, only half protesting.

"You're right." Stella opened a large box instead and removed a few slices of cake, placing them haphazardly on a china dinner plate. "Let's eat first. God knows, this cake is going stale."

The living room, connected to the kitchen by a formal dining room, was broad, well-lit by two paned windows and a skylight. Stella dropped onto a deep-seated fabric sofa and crossed her legs, just as she had when she was a girl, throwing herself down with a kind of casual carelessness. Daisy sat next to her and began to feel slightly less out of place. Stella sat the plate in between them.

"If I remember correctly, this was not my favorite cake. We tried about fifteen different ones."

Daisy took a bite, the marbled raspberry buttercream melting on her tongue. "It's not bad, though."

"No," Stella agreed, shoving a forkful into her mouth. "This was the one we agreed on."

"What was your first choice?"

"A lavender cake with honey lemon frosting," Stella answered. "It was to die for. Bryson thought it was too artsy. Whatever that means."

They laughed for a few moments, then fell silent. Daisy glanced toward the front door, her suitcase a reminder of how things had changed between them. Daisy ate the rest of her cake in silence. "So," she said. "You're not sure about your fiancé."

Stella plucked a frosting rose off the cake and ate it. Her phone rang; she silenced it and stuck it between the couch cushions. "There is nobody on earth I want to talk to right now," she said. "Not besides you, anyway."

"That's not like you," Daisy said. "Is it? You usually know exactly what you want."

In response, Stella shrugged her shoulders. Daisy realized that Stella was sure about Bryson, but something was bothering her to the extent that she had pushed him away. Something that meant enough to her that she wasn't wearing her engagement ring.

"Stella, what is it? What could possibly make you change your mind about the wedding?"

Stella took a deep breath, and Daisy realized that she was trying not to cry.

"I can't marry Bryson because I found out he's keeping a secret. A terrible one."

CHAPTER TWENTY-THREE

Before

As Daisy walked through the yard to her front door, she saw the rancher coming into view, growing in size with each step she took. It looked like a moon that had come unstuck, that was falling closer and closer to the ground, yet she couldn't manage to get out of the way. She nearly walked into the side of the porch, fumbled her way up the steps.

"Mama?" She opened the back door. In her flowered robe, hair combed for bed, Ellen was seated at the kitchen table, reading her Bible by the light of a small tabletop lamp. One window was cracked, letting the breeze in, and a radio played quiet music from the kitchen counter. Both of these were signs that Daisy's father wasn't at home—the extraneous noise of the radio, as well as the wasted air conditioning from the open window, were quick to annoy him.

"Yes? You were outside this late, Daisy?" Ellen turned with a smile to face her, then, with movements as fluid and silent as a cat, rose to her feet, seemed to close the space between them in one light step. "What happened?" Her cool hands smoothed Daisy's hair, tracing the ash that smudged her face. "Are you okay?"

"Yes." Daisy felt her insides swing like a pendulum: one moment she was sure she was about to crumble with relief at her mother's presence, the next she was cool and felt far away from herself. "Mom, there was an accident at the plant. Dad said to tell you he's okay."

"What was it?"

When Daisy was a child, Ellen had seemed magical whenever an injury occurred, supplying kisses for bee stings and sneaking candies when she saw her sad. Now, to Daisy, Ellen appeared to work the same spell: a cool cloth materialized in her hand, wiped the grime from Daisy's arms and forehead.

"A fire."

"Oh, Lord Jesus. I've always feared this. Thank you for sparing him," she whispered. "Thank you. All of my days belong to you."

Somehow, this interruption, calling Jesus into the room as Ellen always had to do, snapped Daisy out of her trance. If someone else was listening, she needed to pull herself together.

"Mom, I have to tell you something."

"How many men died?"

"I don't know," Daisy admitted. "I couldn't see clearly. But there was someone else there. A girl."

"A girl?" Ellen focused in on her, momentarily pausing her flurry of movement.

"Well, someone my age, whatever that means."

"Why would a girl like you be there?"

"Mom, she was dying. The whole side of the barn fell in, and—" Daisy covered her mouth, but she couldn't stop the words coming out. "The beam fell across her, but she looked like she was hurt bad before that happened. She was trying to talk, but she could only make these horrible sounds. She was wearing a ring." Off to the right, Daisy became aware of a pinprick of tiny lights, and it occurred to her to wonder: how had the fireflies found their way inside? She swiveled her chin to see if she'd left the door open, which would surely make her father angry. The dots of light swarmed, the room turned to static around her, and the last thing Daisy heard was her mother's murmured prayer as she collapsed.

*

When Daisy opened her eyes, she was in bed in a clean nightgown. The room smelled like smoke, and Daisy couldn't tell whether it was on her skin or seeping in from outside. Light from the living room slipped in at the edges of the curtains, and she watched the variegated glow, balancing between sleep and consciousness. Daisy heard her parents' voices from the living room and found that if she held her breath, she could hear them better.

"She said she saw someone there, Will."

"What'd she say?"

"When Daisy came in—before she fainted—she was absolutely certain she'd seen a dying girl there, in the fire. She was totally spooked."

Daisy heard her father's sigh, followed by the crack of a beer can opening. "I told her to hightail it out of there and get home to you."

Ellen sighed. "Seems she's a lightning rod for bad luck."

"Could have been a lot worse," Tracker scoffed.

"Poor thing," Ellen said. "Maybe she was hallucinating. Always has her head in the clouds, that one."

"Maybe," Tracker answered.

"Thank goodness she didn't take that job there," Ellen added. "I don't know how much more heartbreak I could handle."

"Of course," Tracker replied. "Thank goodness for that. Hey, you know something else? Look what I found today."

"My ring," Ellen said. "Where was it?"

"Outside. Must have fallen off when you were gardening."

As their conversation drifted to other topics, Daisy felt herself slipping back out of consciousness, her half-formed thoughts blinking in and out, like fireflies among the trees.

CHAPTER TWENTY-FOUR

Before

Daisy held up the middle strand of barbed wire, allowing Stella to pass through between them. Stella stood up and gave Daisy an incredulous look. "So what happened?"

"Um." The secrecy Daisy felt shocked her. She rarely kept secrets from Stella. "I don't know how much you've heard."

They began to walk across the yard toward Daisy's house. On some occasions, Daisy was allowed to host Stella for dinner and a sleepover, which she looked forward to with a grain of dread: company, but embarrassment. Now, with Stella asking her point-blank about the recent event she didn't even know how to discuss herself, she found she was at a loss for words.

"Nothing," Stella said. "I haven't heard anything. Just tell me the whole story."

The sleepovers that used to be a joyful occasion had become both more necessary and more difficult; Daisy loved Stella like fresh air but began to feel ashamed of the oddities of her home. At some point, Stella had started to take notice when Daisy's father seemed drunk, when he would raise his voice at the television, when Ellen would answer quietly and passively for hours on end without ever holding real conversation. Daisy picked up her pace to try to shorten the time they had to talk before walking in for dinner.

"I was studying with Jesse. We were in the woods. I heard it—saw it." Daisy recalled the smell, as well, but stopped short of listing all five senses. She paused near the wisteria to whisper. "I ran down to see if Dad was okay. Stella…" she said, trailing off, her heart racing. "There was a girl there. Like, our age. She—she was hurt really badly."

"Who was it?"

"She grabbed onto my hand, Stella. She asked for help."

"And? What happened?" Stella looked as though she were watching a movie, Daisy thought. She still didn't get it. But why should she have? It wasn't supposed to be for young people to understand realities like this.

"My dad pulled me back. He told me I hadn't seen anything. I—I had to leave her."

Stella screwed up her face in confusion. "You left her to die?"

"I—" Daisy raised a hand to her face, bit at the nail of her index finger. "I can't believe that you would do that," Stella said. "Is this a true story? Did you really see that?"

"I touched her hand," Daisy faltered. "I looked right at her." But she, too, began to wonder.

The air between them chilled strangely and Daisy and Stella walked in silence to the front door.

Because it was Saturday, Ellen served ice cream for dinner. In place of serving a full meal followed by something sweet, she considered it healthier to skip right to dessert, one night out of the week. *Dinner and dessert is like eating two dinners*, she used to say, tightening her apron strings on her small waist, even as she heaped Daisy's plates full. But tonight, even dessert was a sober affair. Ellen dished homemade vanilla ice cream into very small bowls and handed them out at the table, first Tracker, then Stella and Daisy, then sitting one, filled with sliced strawberries, at her own place. Stella and Daisy sat quietly as Tracker heaped chocolate sauce from a squeeze bottle over his ice cream, which he passed to Stella, who passed it to Daisy.

"No chocolate sauce, Stella?" Tracker asked.

"No, thank you, sir," she answered.

"You don't like it?" Ellen asked. "I can get you something else for a topper. We have some berries—you can take some of mine. There's also…" She stopped, realizing that there was not, in fact, anything else.

"That's okay," Stella said, recovering quickly. "We don't get ice cream at home, so I like to just enjoy the vanilla." This was untrue; they had name brand ice cream at Stella's house, which she and her raucous siblings helped themselves to, whichever flavor they chose.

"Suit yourself," Tracker grunted. "It's a waste without chocolate, if you ask me."

The table fell silent. Daisy ate as quickly as she could without eliciting scolding. She nudged Stella's foot under the table in apology, forcing herself to let each bite melt in her mouth so she didn't rush.

"May we be excused?" she asked, finally. Tracker nodded, his spoon singing as he scraped the chocolate sauce from the bottom of the bowl. Daisy patted Ellen's shoulder as she pushed back her chair. "Thanks for dinner, Mama."

And with that, the girls disappeared out of the kitchen, making their way to Daisy's room.

Stella stretched across Daisy's bed. "Tough crowd in there," she said.

"I know." Daisy cracked the window to let the summer air in. Firefly season was past, but the gentle woodland noises helped to cover their conversation, giving the illusion of privacy in a room with two doorways and no doors, wedged between the living room and kitchen. She heard Ellen's footsteps as she collected dishes, then turned on the news radio. Neither of them spoke of the tense moment that had passed outside, instead diligently attending to every other topic they could think of.

"Hey, so what's going on with you and Jesse?"

Digging through a desk drawer for nail polish, Daisy smiled, her mouth sweet from the ice cream.

"I don't know," she answered. Daisy compared a shimmering blue polish with a red, offered both to Stella, who declined. "I got my nails done last week," she said. As Daisy leaned over to study Stella's subtly gleaming manicure, something she had never seen before, she heard the radio program in the kitchen tune up and sucked her breath in to listen.

"Following the fire at the Zion Chemical plant earlier this month, the investigation has been closed. A joint effort between the local police task force and company officials revealed no wrongdoing. The casualties include…"

Four men's names were listed. Daisy stood at the curtain, feeling it swing back and forth in the air conditioning as if pushed and pulled by the house's inhaling and exhaling. No more names followed. She turned to look at Stella, eyes narrowed.

"Those injured and the families of the deceased will receive monetary compensation…"

"You said there was a girl there," Stella whispered.

"She—" Daisy began to falter again. "Yes. Yes, there was. I did."

"That's not what the reporter said." With dreams of becoming a journalist, Stella gave quite some reverence to any news programming.

"I was there, Stella," Daisy said. "I know what happened."

"I don't know if I believe you," Stella whispered gravely. "Not because it's that far out of the realm of possibility. But because I know you, and I don't want to think you'd ever leave someone who was hurt and needed your help."

Daisy was filled with bitterness, after the initial hurt. How typical of Stella, who had been surrounded with things of quality all her life, to assume that Daisy was made of kinder material than she truly was.

She heard the radio turn off with a thud. Before she could move away, Tracker swept open the curtain. He had a half-poured beer mug still in his hand. He gave Daisy a long, glinting stare before speaking. "Shut those windows, girls. You trying to air-condition the whole mountain?"

Daisy hurried to push the windows closed, Stella still sitting as if invisible on the bed. The sudden reminder of the girl in the forest under the beam almost set her shaking again.

"Jesse was there with you," Stella whispered. "Did he see a girl?"

"No," Daisy answered. "He was far away."

Stella exhaled, somehow projecting a sense of judgment with her breath. "I think you should paint your nails red." She helped Daisy paint her fingernails, taking extra care on the raw, bitten cuticles, and then her toenails. Stella braided her hair, then they switched and Daisy braided Stella's. For Daisy, sleeping with a braid in would loosen her natural curls; for Stella, it would create a wave. In the morning, their hair was almost the same texture, Daisy's a wheat-like blonde, Stella's like polished chestnut. They were friendly, though neither of them spoke of the conversation the prior evening, and their manner with each other had chilled. Stella was an early riser; she left before breakfast, claiming to have some kind of lesson or meeting, but Daisy knew that even if it was the truth, she wanted to leave. The quiet chaos could be stifling. You had to know how to swim in it.

CHAPTER TWENTY-FIVE

Now

"A secret?" Daisy asked. Stella gave her a darkening look, then stood up and turned half a pace away. "What is it? Something's bothering you enough to hit pause on this."

"I'm ready for champagne," Stella announced, breezing back into the kitchen. Daisy didn't refuse. Stella returned with two flutes of champagne, filled impolitely full, printed with her and Bryson's initials and yesterday's date. She handed one to Daisy, then sat next to her. "I went to Bryson's office last week to bring him lunch. He had a report on his desk that he didn't want me to see, but it was just sitting there, and I didn't mean to read it."

"What was it?"

"It was just lying there," she repeated. "I did not mean to open this up again."

"Stella." Daisy drank some champagne and rolled her eyes. "Get on with it."

"It wasn't a police report," Stella said, looking pale. Daisy recognized the fear in her face that she would not be believed. "It was from someone at Zion Chemical. I don't know why the real estate company even had access to it. Interviews, maybe. It was an old handwritten file. All I saw, before he put it away, was a line about the bodies they found."

Daisy turned rigid. "What?" she asked. "What did it say?"

Stella gulped. "It said that there were five, not four."

Something like relief crashed over Daisy, bracing and icy-cold. "Five bodies. Right—just like I always told you." Daisy let these words sink in, watching the champagne bubbles dance. "And?"

"But Daisy, that isn't what happened!"

"Oh, it isn't?" Daisy bristled.

"It can't be." She answered with prim certainty. "Not after I ruined our friendship over it. And if that is the truth, I have to know more."

"So now you care about what I went through? But hearing it from me all these years hasn't been enough to matter?"

"And besides, Bryson wouldn't talk to me about it," Stella said. "It was the first time he's ever refused to talk to me about anything. That means he knows something's wrong. He knows it's not the same as the police report. He knows there's a secret."

"Let me be clear—this does not matter to me anymore," Daisy answered coldly. "Maybe it did once, but not anymore." She wanted those words to be the truth. Wanted the hurt of being disbelieved and cast out to only be a distant memory.

"Something tells me it still does."

"Stella, I have a life now, in Santa Fe. I have a career," Daisy insisted, though sitting there on Stella's couch, most of her necessary belongings in a suitcase, the reality behind those words didn't feel quite so solid. "You know what? I'm glad I saw you, because I needed a reminder that this is in the past. That I can fix things with Anderson and keep moving forward, not back."

"To let this get buried, forever?" Stella shook her head. "This could be our only chance to bring it to light. We're still blood sisters."

Daisy finished her champagne and felt suddenly angry. "Well, were we blood sisters when you told my parents how I was going to run away, and got me stuck in that boarding school?"

Stella dabbed at her eyes. "I didn't know that would happen. I didn't know they would do that."

"Well, if you'd asked, I would have told you!"

"What can I do, then?" Stella asked. "What should I do?"

"I don't know." Seeing her tears, Daisy awkwardly patted Stella's knee. "I'm not sure what you want me to say."

"I want to help." Stella looked at Daisy intently, a smudge of frosting on the tip of her nose. "You won't admit it, but I know you don't want them selling that land. Not before there's been a real investigation."

"What if that is what I want?" Daisy asked. "And anyway, what could the two of us do about it?"

"I'll ask around at the newspaper," Stella offered. "It's not much, but it's a platform. If we could only get people talking about it…"

"Write something, then," Daisy said. "You don't need to go and announce what you know. Trust me," she laughed. "If you go around saying there was a cover-up, nobody will believe you. I tried."

"I could write an article."

"The anniversary of the fire is coming up," Daisy said. "In a couple weeks."

"A retrospective." Stella touched her chin in thought. "I'll talk to my editor."

"Wait." Still holding her fork, Daisy looked at Stella dumbly. "Really? You will?" She sensed the inherent risk in something so public, but the idea of reopening a conversation appealed to her as much as it frightened her. "I don't know how comfortable I am with putting that topic out there, honestly."

"I'll write an article," Stella repeated. "Just so people know there are still questions. I don't know how much it'll do, but it could be a starting point. It can be as detailed or as vague as you like."

Daisy leaned over and pulled an icing rose off a slice of cake. "Actually, I like that idea."

"How'd you get into journalism?" Stella asked.

Daisy studied the icing rose, then ate it in one bite, squishing the frosting in her mouth. "I was good at it," she said. "I was putting myself through school, and writing freelance on the side, and I realized it was something I could do for a living. Besides, I like it—I like to find out what happened, and for people to care about what I have to say."

"I always wondered what you would do," Stella replied. "I knew you'd go to college, didn't I?"

They smiled at each other, and for a moment Daisy began to feel as though some thread of their friendship had survived the years of silence. But she knew she was less than sober. They had been friends as girls. Now, Stella was a woman, with a house and a man she would no doubt marry. This whim of hers had nothing to do with Daisy, nothing personal.

Stella's silence seemed to broadcast the same sense of removal. When she fished her phone out of the couch cushions and sighed, scrolling through what looked like a list of missed calls, Daisy did the same. Maybe he would have called again. Maybe, she thought, he'd be at least a little bit sorry. Then again, maybe he hadn't done anything wrong. Anything was possible, right? Daisy scratched absentmindedly at her nail polish, flakes of pink falling onto her lap. Maybe she had betrayed him, making that kind of assumption. She bit the dry skin at the edge of her nail and felt it tear. Daisy winced, half with pain and half at the thought of embarrassing him in front of all those people over a misunderstanding. But was it?

Daisy realized that Stella was watching her, toying with the last crumbs of cake. "Who's that?"

"No one. He hasn't texted since this morning."

"Are you going to answer him?"

Daisy pursed her lips. "I don't know. Seventeen years is a long time to throw away, but it feels like he already did. On the other hand, he'd never do that. Cheat, I mean. It just doesn't seem possible. I don't know if I'm ready to talk about this," she said. "No offense."

"Sure," Stella said. "Goodness knows, I've got enough on my hands to worry about. Bryson's been texting me nonstop. Talking circles around the one thing we need to discuss. How can I marry someone who thinks it's okay to hide things from me? Big things like that?"

"Don't answer him," Daisy said, a brave feeling sprouting in her heart. "Even if he's got a great salary and perfect manners, you need the important things first."

"Important things?" Stella echoed.

"Yes, the important things," Daisy said. "I don't know, honesty? Respect? On the other hand, if I knew what I was talking about, maybe I wouldn't have ended up here." *Maybe I still am the fire girl*, she thought, shivering. *Maybe I have been all this time.*

"I don't know about that," Stella answered. "You certainly sound like you do."

"Only in their absence." Daisy placed her drink on the table. "Sounding like I know what I'm talking about is part of my job. But listen."

"Yeah?"

"Don't let him off the hook," Daisy said. "Not until whatever you want fixed between the two of you is fixed. Don't let something like this slide, right at the beginning."

"I promise," Stella pressed. "Pinkie-swear? I'm going to work this out."

Daisy had always found Stella's optimism persuasive, her belief that the best would happen. She extended one pinkie and locked it with Stella's.

And just like that, Daisy thought, *I'm involved. Damn it, Stella.*

Stella sealed the promise with another sip of champagne. "Hey, how long can you stay?"

"I don't know," Daisy answered. "I don't have anywhere to go."

"Stay here for a couple days," Stella suggested. "My house is empty for the next two weeks. Unless Bryson comes back early, which he won't."

"I'm not sure," Daisy said.

"At least a day or two," Stella said.

Daisy saw that Stella did want her to stay, very badly. "I'll stay till you start on the article. See if you need my help with any of the details."

"Oh, right," Stella beamed. "That's good. It'll be fun."

"We'll see."

CHAPTER TWENTY-SIX

Before

It was late June when Daisy officially passed her algebra class. With a grade of 93 percent, she was exempt from taking the final exam. That afternoon, for the first time, she called Jesse.

"Hello?"

His voice sounded different on the phone, almost grown up.

"This is Daisy."

"Oh," he said. "Hi."

"I was just calling to tell you that I passed the class. So, thanks, I guess."

"Okay," he answered. "Well done. But wait. So, no studying today?"

"No." In the ensuing silence, she sensed disappointment, sensed that she shared it. "What is it? Are—are you doing alright?"

Standing in her bedroom with the phone cord stretched around from the kitchen, Daisy lowered her voice. "Are you home?"

"Yes. Do you want to meet at the same spot?"

"No," she said, shivering. "Not there." She couldn't stand the thought of seeing the hunting blind again. "Can—can I come over?"

Daisy had never followed the path beyond her own family's land before, at least not in the direction of Jesse's house. Before the fire, the forest had felt like home, but now, the shadows seemed to follow her. Daisy was thankful that it was a short walk. As she approached, she studied Jesse's mother's house, where he had moved in after his parents' divorce, an antebellum Queen Anne with pretty gabled windows and a carriage house. An aging gazebo in the yard bordered the creek. Daisy was surprised to find that, despite its size, and all the time they seemed to spend working on it, it looked shabby. The siding needed paint, and two of the gabled windows on the third floor were boarded over. Nevertheless, she could see that it was a beautiful house, if too large for just two people.

Jesse opened the door and Daisy saw the foyer behind him, a large mirror with elaborate carving on the wall.

"Hi." To her surprise, he seemed pleased to see her.

"This is nice."

"Thanks." Jesse turned down the path into the yard, approaching the back door. "She's fixing it up to be a bed and breakfast. Want to come in?"

"I probably shouldn't." Daisy glanced at her reflection in the mirror: blonde waves that hung loose down her back, her eyes the color of moss and soil. "I need you to drive me somewhere."

Jesse always looked a little over-concerned, perhaps because his eyes were so large. He raised an eyebrow, giving the impression of an owl. "Sure. Where?"

"I want to go to the police station," Daisy said. "Listen. Have you heard the news at all? Have you seen anything about the fire?"

"No."

"They released a list of people who died there. I heard it yesterday. There was nothing about the girl."

Jesse closed the door behind him and stepped outside, his eyes widening just slightly, giving her once again the impression that he saw more than she wanted him to. Her eyes watered and she brushed invisible soot from her arms, imagining she could still smell smoke.

"Nobody believes me," she whispered. "About…"

He met her gaze and nodded, signaling that she did not need to finish the statement. "Maybe they're still investigating."

"They said the investigation was concluded."

"They wouldn't say if it were going on in secret."

"Well, I want to ask about it," she said. "I want to tell somebody." She shook her head. "Maybe if I tell them, they'll be able to connect her to a missing person, or something. Someone must know her."

"We can go together," he said. "As long as I'm home by dinner." He opened the door and motioned for her to go inside.

"Wait." Daisy paused, hanging back. "Aren't we going to the car? Is your mom here now?"

"Yeah," he said, as if it were obvious. "I'm going to tell her we're leaving."

Daisy, who was accustomed to avoiding the step where one asked parents for permission, was stunned into silence. Jesse rapped at the back door, then opened it.

"Mom?"

A tall, beautiful woman came to the door, her dark hair pulled into a ponytail. She and Jesse exchanged a few sentences in Spanish, then he held out his arm as if pulling Daisy closer. She found herself reeled in.

"Mom, this is Daisy Ritter. I've been helping her study algebra."

"Hi, Daisy. I'm Teresa Lopez." The woman placed a warm hand on her shoulder and with the other shook her right hand. "It's great to meet you. Do you two need anything to eat?"

"No," Daisy stammered. "It's nice to meet you, too."

"Would you like a glass of water?" Teresa asked, turning to head into the kitchen. "It's so warm."

While Teresa poured two glasses of water from the refrigerator door, Jesse placed his backpack on a hook by the counter. "Daisy passed her algebra class, so we're going to drive into town to get ice cream instead of studying today," he said. "If you don't mind."

"Not at all," she said. "Unless you'll ruin your dinner. Oh, Daisy, why don't you come back for dinner?"

"My parents," she said.

"Of course, they're planning for you to eat there." Teresa's warm demeanor was not thrown off by Daisy's stammers and obvious discomfort. "Well, I hope you come for dinner one night soon."

"Thank you."

Daisy thanked Teresa at least twice more as she followed Jesse through the hallway, through a sitting room, then a family room. The home was far too large for one family, and white sheets and paint buckets marked the rooms that were not ready for use. Jesse held the front door open for her, then slowed down to walk next to her as they went to his car. She marveled again at how they had become something like friends, how they suddenly had this secret language of waiting, of pauses. Before she remembered the business at hand, it was almost nice.

"I guess we'll go to the police station in town," he said, starting the engine. His car was several years old but well kept, a small gray sedan that was almost too clean. "There's the one closer by but nobody will be there now."

"Right," Daisy agreed, as if that had been her plan all along. As they drove, he put on a playlist that seemed a little too at the ready. Soft, creaky guitar chords accented the male singer's voice, words swimming around Daisy's ears with the breeze from the open window, something about seeds buried underground and plants that could grow without sunlight. But when Jesse stopped the car, he turned to her with a removed look.

"You should go in by yourself," he said. "Make your own point."

"Right," she said. "Okay. I just wasn't expecting to go in alone. I don't know if they'll take me seriously."

"They won't take either of us seriously," Jesse said, with a certainty that surprised her. "It might be worse if I'm there with you. Are you okay to go in on your own?"

She nodded her head, although she wasn't sure.

"My parents are gonna kill me." Her eyes flickered up to meet his, to see if he understood this secret message as well, could read her nervousness between her words. "They think I made the whole thing up. I don't want to embarrass them," she insisted. "But I need to tell someone who will listen."

"You're doing the right thing." Jesse gave her a quick hug. "I'll be waiting right here."

Inside, she asked to speak to someone about the chemical plant fire. Nobody seemed to know what she was talking about, and she gave up repeating herself, finally just asking to speak to an officer. When she was paired with the female secretary, the only woman in the building, she felt there'd been a misunderstanding.

"I need to talk to someone about the fire at the plant two weeks ago," she said. "I saw someone there who wasn't on the list in the news."

"Honey, are you sure that's why you're here?" The woman leaned a little too close to her. "You can talk to me. It's safe here."

"I appreciate that," Daisy said. And she did. The woman's soft demeanor brought out a desire to please in her that genial older women always did, maybe because there was so much that seemed to fly right through Ellen's ears. "What I saw was really scary, and I don't know who to talk to about it, and I think it's maybe something the police need to know about."

"I see." The woman wasn't pleased. Even in factual conversations, Daisy had always felt a special pang when she didn't provide the right answer. "I'll get one of the officers to talk with you."

The man who came in next to talk with her was young and friendly. "So, I hear something's bothering you," he said confidentially.

"It's about the fire," she said for what felt like the hundredth time.

"Most of those files are closed," he answered. "It often goes that way, with corporate investigations."

"I don't need to see them," she said. "I was there."

"You were? How?"

"I live nearby. I was out for a walk, in the woods near the plant. I heard the explosion and went to look, since my dad works there. I—"

"Okay. Slow down."

She thought he was slowing her down so he could take notes, but then realized she was talking too fast, too emotionally. "I saw a girl, in the fire. A beam fell on her. She must have died. She died," she added. "But she wasn't on the list of people in the paper. You know, the…"

"Casualties."

"Yeah. And I don't know why."

"Is it possible you thought you saw it, but you didn't?" He crossed his arms on the table and studied her, not unkindly.

"I don't think so, no."

"Are you sure?" he repeated, in the same tone. "You would not be in trouble here. To be frank, eyewitness accounts in traumatic events are some of the least reliable evidence in any investigation."

Daisy realized that she had not had any chance of being taken seriously since she walked in the door. It would have made no difference whether Jesse was with her or not. "What would happen," she said, in a matter-of-fact way, dropping her polite and attentive tone, "if you believed me? Investigated, talked to the people who were there?"

"Nothing that hasn't already been done." The young officer shrugged his shoulders and once again tried to give her that friendly stare.

She began to ask whether there were any missing girls from nearby areas, or even this area, that she might not know about, but his stare told her to give up before his friendliness ran out. Daisy walked back outside into the summer heat as a church bus sped whistling past on the dusty highway. She let herself into Jesse's car and sat down.

"That didn't take long. Were they out for lunch?"

"No," she said. "Well, not literally. I don't know why, but I don't feel like anyone is going to take me seriously about this." She shook her head. "I should try to forget about it. Mom's acting like she'll blow her top if we don't pretend everything is fine. Let's get going."

"What about the ice cream?"

"I thought you made that up," she said. "So you could tell your mom we were leaving. She's nice."

"Yeah, she's alright," Jesse answered. "I figure if we go out for ice cream anyway, then it's not as much of a lie."

While they stopped for ice cream, Jesse explained to Daisy about his parents' divorce, his father in a bigger city somewhere near the coast, his older siblings there as well, adults with their own lives. "I think they stayed together for us," he said. "I'm not sure."

"Could you tell?"

"No," he said. "Not really. They're happier now, though."

He could do that—with algebra, with divorce—talk smoothly and easily about these complicated things that seemed to clog her mind with confusion, with fear.

"You make it sound simple," she said, looking down at her ragged fingernails.

"When someone's really listening, it's easy." Jesse hesitated, then smiled at her.

"It's almost six," Daisy said, glancing at the clock on the dashboard. "I need to be home for dinner."

Late that night, after Ellen and Tracker had retired, her to bed, him to the lounge chair with a tall beer, Daisy cracked the windows in her room and breathed in the cool evening. Midsummer was like this; nighttime was the only time worth bothering with. Days were too hot, summer had burned out all freshness. She remembered the walk to Jesse's house through the woods, wondered if he were awake, regarded this new feeling for him with caution. The pull of being a normal teenager was anchored by the heaviness of what she could not explain, leaving her no energy to marvel at what other kids found worthy of songs, of swooning. As much as people talked about it, it wasn't mysterious; it even felt familiar, though she'd never experienced it before.

It was the lingering mystery of the girl in the forest that grounded Daisy to her room, even in her mind, of that afternoon that seemed to continue happening, over and over. If the police had decided, no doubt with the help of the company owners, that there was to be no investigation, then what was there to know?

CHAPTER TWENTY-SEVEN

Now

Stella put down her phone and turned to Daisy. "The newspaper editor wants the article," she said.

Daisy was shocked. "Okay," she answered. "So, what do we do?"

They stood in the kitchen, surrounded by the dwindling remains of the cake. Because Stella seemed fixated on the other matters at hand, Daisy began to do a cursory job of cleaning, placing a couple of empty bottles and paper plates in the recycling bin. It was easier not to sit still.

"Well, I have to write it!" Stella fluttered away from her, through the living room, onto a screened-in porch. Daisy followed her, surprised that, after a day's stay, there were still rooms in Stella and Bryson's house she hadn't seen. Daisy twitched. Stella seemed excited, a schoolkid given leeway to write an essay on a subject of her choice. Daisy wondered that Stella didn't realize what it had cost her not only to keep what she'd seen buried for over a decade, but to haul it up again now. "I use this as my office," Stella added. "When it's nice out." The porch was shaded with bamboo screens from the bright sun, cooled by a wide-paneled fan.

"I'll pull some public records online," Stella said, speaking almost to herself as she began to type. "But I want to talk to you, while you're here. How much can you tell me about exactly what happened?"

"What is this, an interview, or something?" Daisy's heart jumped in her chest and she instinctively crossed her arms.

"Well, no." Stella gave her charming smile, tilting her head. "But come on, it kind of is, right? This should be fun for you: this is what you never got to do. Tell your side."

"Fun?" Daisy's deadpan echo stopped Stella's laughter. "And, if you remember, I did talk about it. Nobody cared what I said—and I'm not sure why you think it would be any different now."

"Okay." Stella hit the backspace button several times with her index finger. "But I think people will listen. People around here know Bryson. That's a point of interest. And you can have more control over the narrative this time. Think, Daisy. What would you like for the article to say?"

"The truth," she countered.

"Fine—fine. What do you want me to say here? I feel like I'm getting this wrong."

"I don't know, to be honest," Daisy answered. "I was hoping that you'd act like what I went through mattered. That what I have to say matters. To you, not for the purposes of some article, or your marriage."

Stella closed her laptop and pushed it aside. "You're right," she said. "I'm sorry. I know it's pretty meaningless to apologize now, but I am. And it was a stupid way to bring all of this up. I shouldn't have been so thoughtless."

"Thanks."

"But I do think it's worth writing about. And it has to be now, if we're going to do it," Stella said. Daisy nodded her agreement. "I remember you telling me that you saw a girl dying. And that your father made you leave. And your mother didn't believe you, but..."

"Later, after she'd talked to my dad, she figured I'd hit my head or made it all up." She could almost remember the smell of smoke, chemical and sour, that clung to her hair and skin that night.

"What about before that, though? There were problems with the plant before then."

"Were there ever," Daisy laughed. "Fires every other year. Toxic chemical waste drained into the ground. Do you remember when all the fish washed up off the creek, that one year?"

Stella nodded her head. "I remember there being lots of dead wildlife, actually."

"Right."

"My folks lived further from the site, but your parents' property is right next to it." Stella opened her laptop again and typed for a few minutes, pursing her lips in concentration. She turned the computer so that Daisy could see it. "See, here's a map of the property lines. There are six families whose lands border the plant, and downstream of those, another seven. Do you remember those kids from school?" She pointed at the irregularly shaped outlines on the map. "This was the Henleys. This was Mr. and Mrs. Lovett. And this was—hm."

"Darlene Page," Daisy continued. "I think. I don't remember all of them."

"Do you remember any of them having little kids? Babies?"

"No." Daisy was focusing on the shaded patch in the middle of the map that outlined Zion Chemical. "Why?"

"Daisy, your mother."

"What about her?"

"All the pregnancy losses. Maybe she wasn't the only one."

"Oh. Right." Daisy nodded her head swiftly, as if this were an insignificant detail she'd forgotten. She watched Stella continuing to speak—hadn't she always been the brighter one, between the two of them? Maybe, Daisy wondered idly, her ability to distance herself from her subjects was an advantage here. One that she herself lacked. She couldn't quite make out what Stella had said, and now she'd gone on several sentences, and Daisy's ears may as well have been full of mud. All she could hear was the echo: *Maybe she wasn't the only one.* Stella was gesturing, smiling, eyebrows raised.

"So, I think the thing is to situate the dead girl as the biggest, and worst, unanswered question, in a long history of unanswered questions. If you see what I mean."

"They said there was nothing wrong with me."

"What?" Stella blinked.

Shit. Had she spoken that out loud? "With, uh, with my memory. I saw a doctor, back then. Completely lucid. No symptoms of psychosis. That's all."

"I see." Stella nodded her head slowly. "Okay. Well, look. I believe you, and I want to know what happened."

Daisy felt something shift between them. A bond opening, or a wound closing. The weight of shouldering the truth alone was finally lifting, but it left a bone-deep fatigue behind it.

"Actually, if you wouldn't mind, I think I'll take you up on the offer of that bed now," Daisy said. "Could you please point me to the spare room? I'm exhausted as it is, and this is a lot to take in."

"Of course," Stella answered, looking between Daisy and her computer. "Go up the staircase in the study—the guest room's the third door on the left."

"Thanks."

"I'll write the piece. We'll go over it when I'm done. I'll email it to my editor this evening."

Daisy was shaking her head. "No," she said. "I trust you. I don't want to read it. Just do your thing and send it in."

CHAPTER TWENTY-EIGHT

Now

Without a hangover to interfere, Daisy was up the next morning by sunrise. She spent the morning on a leisurely jog, then a long shower, both half-hearted attempts to distract herself from her thoughts. Finally, after a late lunch, she settled into the hammock on the porch with a book from Stella's study. The sun was bright, cutting through the midafternoon haze, when Stella finally woke. Daisy heard her stirring upstairs moments before her phone blinked, announcing a text message: *'Are you still here?'* She responded: *'Back porch.'*

The tap of footsteps approached and the door swung open.

"Thank goodness." Stella bumped the door open with one hip, holding two cups of coffee. "Here." She sat one cup on the table nearest the hammock. "I didn't see you in the guest room, and I guess it didn't occur to me you'd be out here. I was afraid you—well, I don't know."

"Afraid I'd lost my mind and wandered off?" Daisy laughed. "Really, Stella, I would at least have taken the car if I'd decided to leave."

"The article should be up," Stella said. "You have the website?"

"Yeah." Daisy sat up and swung her feet to the ground. "Have you looked at it?"

"Not yet."

"Okay." She opened her laptop and typed, waiting for the website to load. What did it mean, for this to be happening? She remembered her ill-fated visit to the police station. What would it feel like for people to take her seriously—people who could actually make a difference?

Daisy focused on the screen as she skimmed the article, then put her phone down and turned away, wondering why she had expected anything different. She had read the story Stella submitted, or she thought she had. The story featured was, as Stella had suggested, a retrospective on the fire. Where were the points of suspicion? The fact that police had never investigated it, or that it had taken emergency responders nearly an hour to even reach the site? There was a sentence tucked near the end of the one-page feature: *Reactions among locals affected vary widely. Daisy Ritter recalls her vision of an unknown girl at the site of the fire, although this was widely disputed among her immediate circle.*

"Well?" Stella asked, anxious.

Daisy held a hand up, requesting quiet. "I'm still reading."

"I'm going to make some breakfast," Stella announced, hand on the doorknob. "I'll be in the kitchen, okay?"

Daisy nodded silently, arms crawling. She reloaded the page as comments continued to populate the space beneath the article. The sensation recalled standing in the hallways of her high school again, or those unfortunate months she spent afterwards, except that instead of wondering whether she'd heard a whisper, and what exactly their words had been, she saw exactly what the words were, and continued reading and rereading them for as long as she could stand.

They're talking about Daisy Ritter. She's crazy.

That girl went to my high school. Lost her shit after the fire. Not sure what went down but she was spreading those rumors for months.

Daisy told herself that she should have expected this. If Zion held anything for her beyond humiliation and lies, she hadn't seen it in her thirty-five years of life. When that invitation had arrived, the first thing she'd thought was that it was some sort of a mean joke, and maybe she hadn't been very far from the truth. She could have been back in New Mexico at this moment, blissfully unaware of whatever Anderson was doing—ignorance seemed preferable to this, being alone and single. Or was she? Daisy realized that she didn't know. But she knew she couldn't stay here. As she walked back inside, she went straight to the guest room. Daisy collected the clothes she had unpacked and stuffed them back into her suitcase, sitting on top of it in order to close the zipper. The heavy bag thudded behind her as she went down the stairs.

When she walked into the kitchen, Stella poured another mug of coffee and turned to face her, handing it across the counter. "I guess I need to return some of these gifts, don't I?" she mused. "All of them, probably. What if we do decide to get married, after he's back in town? Do I still have to return them then? Daisy, what are you doing with your bag?" As ever, she was at her most pretty when concerned with the most trivial of problems.

"Stella, I read the article, and I—I think I need to leave," Daisy snapped, leaving Stella's hand midair with the coffee. "Let's just say it's not what I expected."

"You're leaving already?" Stella quavered.

"This was a mistake," Daisy said. "Staying here like this. Getting involved in any of this. I should go."

"But what am I supposed to do?"

"I have a feeling you'll figure it out," she said. "Those comments on the article… It's not the same for me as it is for you."

"What exactly did I do to deserve this?"

"Please," Daisy sighed. "You're only nice to people because you have nothing to worry about. You have never needed anything your whole life."

Stella was untouchable; she always had been. She wasn't the one who found herself stuck for something, be it patience, or a ride, or a place to stay, and she knew it. That was where her boundless kindness and good nature came from. She'd ask for forgiveness, but it wouldn't cost her if she didn't get it. Nothing would change. Maybe Daisy was right in the middle of what she'd feared, what she had dreaded.

"Aren't you going to stay for dinner?" Stella looked so innocent, as though she would cry.

"No," she said. "I'm not your fiancé, Stella."

Pulling the suitcase behind her, Daisy hurried out the front door to the rusty old car. *One more bridge burned*, she thought. What was it about this place that drew her to its heart, when all she could do was alienate every person she encountered? As Daisy let the engine warm up, looked out at the road in the sunset light, she realized she already knew. *It's the fire*, she thought. *I never squared with what happened there, and it's casting a shadow on the rest of my life*. Stella's revelation of the fifth body echoed in Daisy's mind. Did that mean she could finally expect some kind of confirmation, that what she'd seen that day was real? Her foot was heavy on the gas pedal, as if her body knew where she was going before her mind did. She needed to see the chemical plant again.

CHAPTER TWENTY-NINE

Before

Despite Daisy's unusual summer, the first day of school still brought a flutter of anticipation. Senior year meant that she was less than a year from being finished with high school. Ten months stood between her and moving out of her parents' home. She imagined herself finding a job, or perhaps an apartment she could rent with people her own age, an escape from the pressing quiet of home.

She knew that Stella would not be one of those roommates. Both of Stella's parents had attended college, and whether or not Stella would do the same had never been a question. She had set her sights on a career in journalism while they were in the seventh grade, and Daisy knew that she would move away for school. This placed Stella in the minority in Zion, though.

For as long as Daisy could remember, she had wanted more than anything to feel that she was one of the regular kids, which she imagined as being able to go to parties, or disagree with her parents, or do something foolish, without feeling paralyzed by guilt. In Daisy's mind, the first day of her last year of high school marked one step closer to being able to breathe.

The morning passed without consequence. Daisy sent texts to Stella inquiring about her classes, although she knew that Stella never checked her phone in class and wouldn't answer until lunch period. When the bell rang for lunch, she took her usual shortcut through the gym to her locker in the front hallway of the school building. Ducking through a crowd of students who were seemingly oblivious to all but their conversations, she approached her locker, then stopped short. A tall and square-shouldered blonde girl that Daisy recognized from church slouched against the wall of lockers, her back squarely blocking Daisy's. *What was her name, again?* Daisy had seen the girl once before, at the Fourth of July picnic Tracker's boss had held the previous summer.

"Excuse me." Daisy stepped up to her locker, and, unnerved by the girl's cold stare, stammered a series of interruptions, trying to get her attention. "Sorry. Hi. Could I just—Excuse me, please," she said, huffing a sigh. "Can I get to my locker?"

In response, the girl fixed her with a look that almost threw Daisy backwards, a shocking response from someone Daisy had never spoken to. The girl's eyes were taut with a deep-set anger that Daisy had no defense against.

She realized that the girl had returned to her conversation, nodding her chin in a drawn-out gesture of comfort and disdain. "It burned down," she was saying. "The main garage fell clear over."

"I heard they locked it up the next day and no one ever went back in," another student replied.

"That's right," the girl answered. "I know all about it." She shifted her weight from one hip to the other, occupying her space with a belligerent ease.

"How'd you know anything about it?" one of the boys asked.

"My dad is the manager there. He does all the hiring," she said. "*And* firing. When they figure out whose fault that fire was…"

Beginning to feel invisible where she stood, Daisy listened skeptically, though the small crowd of listeners seemed to accept what she said on the credit of her confidence.

"People died there," added a boy in a hoodie and black jeans. "They said on the news the company settled out of court."

"Yeah, four people died," the blonde girl answered, her voice earthy and low, as if she were telling a ghost story, as if they sat around a campfire. "And they're lucky if they died fast. Doesn't stop some people from spreading rumors. My pastor says some people are meant to be lessons to others." She put her hand on Daisy's arm, startling her, and put an arm around her shoulder, holding on too tight for her to move away. "Daisy Ritter's dad was there. One of the survivors. But she's been running around, telling people made-up stories about a fifth person who got killed. Someone who didn't even work there. You are Daisy, aren't you?"

"Y-yes, I'm…"

"One of the survivors said she was watching in the forest, and she didn't even do anything to help. Went home covered in ashes from the explosion."

"I-I did try to—"

"Quit stammering," the blonde girl laughed. "What, can't get your words out, fire girl?"

Daisy was stunned into silence, shocked that a stranger could dislike her so violently. She felt her limbs tense, stuck to the ground. *No one except for Jesse*, she thought. *But that was different.*

"You're not gonna answer me, of course." The blonde girl let go of Daisy's shoulder with a gentle, almost invisible hip check that made her stumble. "Her own parents don't believe her. Everyone at church says she probably got too close to the fire, inhaled something bad. You know they live right by the place," she said, lowering her voice. "Land's cheaper there."

A warning bell rang, alerting the students that ten minutes remained for lunch period, and the small crowd began to disperse. Daisy eyed her locker, still blocked from reach. She looked into the girl's eyes.

"Who even are you?" she whispered, confused before anything else. "You don't know me."

"Maybe I don't want to know you." The girl turned around and walked away, rounding the corner of the hallway to disappear from Daisy's sight. That was about the only prompting Daisy needed to take the rest of the day off. She opened her locker, removed her backpack, and put her phone in the pocket of her jeans, then slammed the locker door closed with her elbow. During class hours, there would be teachers watching the various exits of the building, but nobody would notice a student walking out during lunch, even if they didn't plan to return. As Daisy turned to leave, she saw Stella approaching her.

"Hey," Daisy called, her voice betraying her upset. "Did you just see…" Stella's expression, halfway between guilt and dismay, told Daisy that she had seen the entire exchange.

"Sorry, Daisy." Stella reached out to her.

"Why don't you get going?" Daisy pulled back from Stella's hand with a forced smile. "You don't want to be late for class."

"What about you?" Stella asked. "Where are you going? You know I'm not okay with you skipping school."

"I'll tell them we were on vacation or something. That my schedule got mixed up. Nothing happens on the first day, anyway."

And, although it wasn't untrue, Daisy felt her heart drop at the loss as she walked out of the building: for herself, for the distance between her and all of her classmates, who were beginning a normal first day of their last year of high school.

CHAPTER THIRTY

Now

Although Daisy had rarely driven to the old chemical plant site, she found her way to it in the dark. The drive leading there was overgrown, tall grasses crowding around the chain that blocked the gravel road. She pulled the rental car off to the side of the road among the trees, mostly, she hoped, out of sight. The dark was new, and the periodic zips of blue light around her legs did nothing to show her the way. Daisy stepped over the chain that blocked the driveway and walked the remaining hundred yards to the yard. She considered again the word *panic*, connecting it to the myriad sounds that grew loud against her presence, the rustling grass, her own footsteps, evening birds and insect song. And the other, half-heard, whispered noises from among the trees, and the looming shapes of the yard ahead, whether real or not, perhaps only remembered, sharpened its meaning.

She scanned the sky for any moon but saw only a thin cloud cover and a few stars. The building was blocked off by the same old chain-link fence, its gate wrapped around with a length of rusted chain. The fence was six feet high, perhaps a hand's length above her own head, and she climbed up, her toes finding a pinching hold in the wire, swinging over with a dreadfully loud, rusty squeak, then dropping to the ground on the other side. She instinctively looked around to see if she'd been heard or followed—as if she could have seen anyone in the dark. The old building was laced around with caution tape, which she crossed over as well, drawing close to the gaping mouth of the side of the structure. There, she thought, she had seen the girl run out, and there she had fallen down. Daisy looked and saw where the men had been sitting, their shouts calling her back.

More than anything, she wished she had refused to leave. She felt a deep spring of rage and sorrow for the unnamed girl, wherever her body might be. How could she have hoped to learn anything by being here? All she could do was revisit her own failure. If she had stayed with her, the girl—a child, really, as she was, too—might at least have had someone to watch her.

All the times she had disobeyed her father, and she chose that one, that most crucial time, to do as he said and turn away.

Daisy sat on the ground cross-legged, just where the girl had fallen, and tried to remember everything she could. This time, not of the events, of Daisy's own experience, but of the girl herself. How had she lain here? How had she felt? What had it looked like, to see a burning building fall on top of your body? What had she been doing here? With her hands braced on the cool, damp earth behind her, Daisy looked up at the dark, uncertain sky and felt a shiver trickle down her spine. In Daisy's imagination, the nocturnal noises of the forest became phantoms and spirits that surrounded her, blocking any escape. She realized suddenly that this was, perhaps, the finest reason she had for refusing to let herself linger in a room. Sit there long enough and the ghosts, the half-impressions that reached through time, the leftover bits of energy, became more real to her than whatever it was she saw around her. More real than the panic. The rustle of the trees at night, the backdrop, the skip in her pulse that came from being alone in the dark, all melted away, less real than the figures and voices of ghosts and the questions they asked.

That was what she thought, until she saw the flashlight beam, heard the definitive crunch of shoes on gravel.

CHAPTER THIRTY-ONE
Before

The distance to Daisy's house from the school was less than three miles, though a combination of the warm afternoon and her racing heart made it feel shorter, made her steps feel light, as if her fast walking pace raced against the worries that clouded her mind: who knew? How? Had someone else seen her that day in the forest?

For the first time, a cold idea sank heavy in her mind. Only Jesse was there. She was almost certain they had been there alone. Would Jesse have told someone? All of the unknowable, almost unreasonable trust that had sprung up between them turned into shame as her insecurity spoke: of course, it wouldn't make anything but sense for Jesse to find her odd, dangerous, embarrassing, stupid. What if he had seen something happen that she hadn't? What if she really had hallucinated it? What if Tracker was right? She walked faster and faster, felt the air cool the beads of sweat that misted her forehead. Daisy stopped at the bottom of her family's driveway, out of sight of the house. She knew Ellen was at home, likely working in the garden, and she couldn't be seen arriving home early without an excuse.

Daisy cut through the woods to the far end of the clearing, where she was able to see Ellen deadheading the calendula blossoms. She waited until her mother stood up, brushed her hands off on her apron, pale and birdlike even from here, and walked inside. Daisy darted across the yard, staying near the perimeter, behind bushes where she was able to, until she crossed into the woods on the other side, and made her way with a surer foot to Jesse's house, and sat in the shade in the old gazebo, its roof halfway fallen in. With doubt now cast on everything, she was half afraid she would find some kind of ambush there, and watched from several yards off, trying to see if anyone had followed her. But, although she had grown up playing in the woods, that was where it stopped. She was not a tracker or a hunter, and she had little practical talent for the outdoors.

When Jesse finally arrived home from school, she waved her hand to catch his eye.

"You shouldn't sit in here," he said. "The roof isn't really stable."

But he walked up the old steps, took a seat on the bench next to her. Somehow always half a step too formal, Jesse wore blue jeans, but a buttoned shirt and a belt. To observe this, then to notice that she thought he looked nice, spurred her defensiveness, almost making her angry.

"How was your first day?"

"It… wasn't great. How was yours?" *Say something else, stupid*, she told herself. Instead, her self-doubt spiraled.

"It was fine. I didn't see you," he said, acting friendly, as if he didn't know anything had happened. "Where were you all day?"

"I left after lunch period," Daisy answered.

"You left?" He studied her more closely.

"Yes." Again, she turned and looked over her shoulder. Had anyone followed her here? Was anyone following him? "You didn't hear? Are you being dumb on purpose?" She took a step back from him, her eyes sparkling with emotion.

"What's this about?" he asked.

"Don't pretend you don't know!" As she spoke, she could hear the words, sounding distant, a stranger's voice. She was almost in tears.

"I can't help with anything if you won't tell me about it, Daisy."

She scuffed her shoe in the dried leaves and dust at her feet. Jesse held his hand out, reaching toward her. She did not react. "Jesse, did you... Have you told anyone about what happened? At the fire?"

"Not a soul. I swear to God."

"Somebody else knows."

"Why do you think that?"

Daisy gulped. "There was a girl at school today. She knew what we saw. She knew all about it and she was telling people I made it up." She raised her eyes to look at him hopelessly. "And if you didn't tell anyone, who else could it be? How could anyone know?" She felt her tears spill over and drip onto her hands. "I don't know what to think. Did I even see what I thought I did?"

Jesse inhaled slowly, his fingers tapping the wood beneath them. "I believe you."

"But you didn't see her?" Daisy asked. "Are you sure?"

"I couldn't see anything."

Daisy sighed and covered her eyes again in dismay.

"But you did. I know you did." As if saying it made him braver, he put his hand over hers.

"How?" She wondered where his certainty came from, wished she could feel it too.

"Because you said so, Daisy." He touched her cheek and softly turned her face toward his. "And I don't think you're a liar."

Daisy leaned forward and threw her arms around his shoulders. "I thought you had said something to someone. I thought I was crazy. That you were making fun of me somehow, or..."

"What? No. Absolutely not," he said, squeezing her closer. "Never. I'm..."

As he spoke, she pulled back, looked up at him. What was he about to say? After a moment, he abandoned the thought and leaned in to kiss her. She inhaled with surprise, then leaned in, pressing her lips to his, at once relieved and frightened, her hands trembling, wishing there were nothing else but him. Finally, she pulled away.

"I should go home before my mom misses me."

"I don't want you to go," he said. "I don't know what's going on here."

"I don't want to, either." Daisy squeezed Jesse's hands until her knuckles whitened, leaned up to kiss him again. "I have to, though."

Jesse walked back with her, taking the path that cut through the forest. With the leaves so thick and dark, it felt again like a land of stories, a fabled forest, deep and anonymous. She stifled an instinct to look over her shoulder, checking for strangers, ghosts following. When Jesse hugged her, she turned her chin up and let her hand rest over his shoulder, taking this small space between them, this small awkwardness, holding it so they both could see it, until he leaned near and kissed her goodbye.

As she approached the house, Daisy prepared a story in her mind to tell Ellen, something to excuse her being late. But instead of her mother waiting for her, she found her father sitting in his rocker on the porch. Caught sneaking in, she walked up the steps without hesitation, still half giddy.

"Where've you been, Daisy?"

This was the moment when she was supposed to have an answer. Daisy knew that people often gave themselves away just by acting guilty. If she'd been able to come up with an excuse and rattle it off on the spot, she could have walked right inside. As she searched for a suitable answer, she realized she had given herself away with her silence.

"Never mind." Tracker pushed his rocking chair back with a creak and looked up at her, his eyes cold and bright in the dark. "You think you're anything but obvious? You don't know men, Daisy. Hell, you don't know people. You think you know that boy?"

She folded her arms as if preparing for a fight, and Tracker laughed. "He'll drop you the minute you're inconvenient. If he even waits for a reason. Just you wait." Tracker seemed to have put himself in a good humor with his little tirade; Daisy sensed he didn't care whether she came home late, or at all.

"Someone knows, Dad," she whispered. "Someone at school knows what happened."

He said nothing, but halfway turned his face to look at her.

"I didn't say anything," she said. "I swear I didn't. But I'm not sorry, either. Even if everyone thinks I'm a liar."

"Daisy, I don't know why trouble seems to follow you around." Tracker sighed, running a hand across his brow. "Your mother talked to the pastor about a boarding school. Kind of place that wouldn't give you an opportunity to get yourself into trouble. Or anyone else."

For a moment, Daisy held his stare in the half-dark of the front porch. "Whatever," Daisy scoffed, heading for the door.

As Daisy lay in bed that night, her thoughts volleyed between Jesse and the girl in the forest, numbing her of the dread of returning to school the next day. She gave little thought to her father's vague threats of boarding school. True, Tracker had sounded dead serious when he said it. But he was always serious when he was drunk. Daisy rolled over and sighed, thinking again of Jesse, and fell asleep.

CHAPTER THIRTY-TWO

Now

Daisy froze for a moment, readjusting her senses, seeing what was in front of her, or what little of it she could see. There was dark, textured dark, like moth's wings. A white beam of light that cut through, waving back and forth. How had she missed the sounds of a car approaching? Her heart lurched in her chest. Had a car approached? Had someone wandered out of the trees? She inched further into the shadows of the decrepit structure, lowering herself against the corner of the wall, waiting for the light-holder to call out, to announce themselves. Was it even someone who knew she was here, or some other wanderer? She closed her eyes and willed her shoulders to weaken, to sink inwards, making herself smaller. Through her closed eyes, she sensed the light flickering near, a blood-vessel-red illumination against the backs of her eyelids. She lowered her chin and looked up to see, in flashes, an impossibly pale face suspended in the dark. Dark eyes, but pale hair that reflected the moonlight. Daisy felt her body tense involuntarily and recalled that she could not trust her impressions, not ever, but especially not here.

"Hello?" She pushed her voice out through the dark, rose to her feet, and felt the beam of light hit her face, a warm, blinding sense of relief.

"Police." The woman stepped forward and Daisy saw the face above the dark blue jacket. "You know you're trespassing, right?"

Daisy froze. She had, again, deceived herself. She had stepped up to meet a ghost, an otherworldly messenger, and met with the least otherworldly messenger she could have hoped for.

"I'd like for you to step closer. Hands where I can see them, please." Tall and almost wiry, she had a pleasantly boyish southern accent, a clear alto voice. Daisy stood up, feeling the cold in her knees and legs, wondering where she knew her from. "Can I ask what you're doing here?"

"Nothing," Daisy answered. "Just looking around."

The cold edge in the woman's voice jogged Daisy's memory, reminding her of something—she could not place it.

"Answer the question."

"I, ah." Daisy crossed her arms and rubbed her elbows, feeling a sudden chill. Though it was dark, she could see the woman's features well enough now to trigger an unpleasant jolt of memory. It was the girl who had blocked her locker that day in senior year, who had seemed inexplicably to know so much about her. The memory of that day sent an additional chill of foreboding down her arms. "I know I shouldn't be here. I live nearby, and this place is kind of…"

"Special for you?" came the almost amused reply. "Lots of memories?"

"In a way," Daisy said. "Exactly."

"Yeah, well, you shouldn't be here. Someone who drove by saw your car, called in a wreck. This isn't a safe place—not for anyone. Not alone at night." Their eyes met and they shared a moment of understanding. *Not a safe place for anyone, but especially not for a woman.* Daisy wondered if the officer could sense her quiet gratefulness that she was a woman, too. "We went to high school together, right?"

"Yeah. How could I forget?" Daisy let out a quiet, annoyed groan. This embarrassment, at least, was comforting.

"Who else could you be, right? Well, listen, I have to take you to the station. I wasn't the only person who got the call that you were here. You promise not to come back, there won't be any issue." She had an almost apologetic, kind tone to her voice. Daisy hesitated, as if she had any real option. "Come on." The woman extended a hand. "Officer Hanson. You can call me Kate."

When Kate softened her voice and began to speak, the panic seemed to tame itself. Daisy's fear dissipated, the sounds of the forest becoming pleasant, musical. She felt a weird sense of relief as she followed Kate to the lights of the patrol car, despite some distant signal in her head telling her she ought to have been ill at ease sitting in the back of a police car. It was the same kind of comfort from being near your mother, or picking up a favorite book—but from a stranger. Daisy figured she must have been disoriented from the night, from the location, that something so out of place could bring any comfort.

"So, what brought you back into town? And landed you in the local paper the same week? It's like you just can't resist the public eye." Though Daisy found that she was eager to talk, she stopped herself from sharing too much. "Just visiting friends."

"I didn't expect to see you back here," Kate said, almost under her breath. "Figured you'd left for good. And then I saw that article." In the dim light, her eyes seemed to spark with amusement.

"An old friend of mine wrote it," Daisy admitted. She so enjoyed having someone listening to her that it was difficult not to speak. "You know—with the place getting sold, and everything. It just felt worth taking a last shot at figuring out what happened."

"Stella, right? So, what was the real story—according to you?" Kate's pale eyes caught hers in the rearview as the car wound down the hillside. "What did happen here, Daisy?"

"I seem to remember you knowing everything about that."

"Humor me."

Daisy sighed. "I saw the fire, you know. Ran up to see if my dad was okay. I found a girl there, dead. Well, almost. Someone who wasn't supposed to be there. My dad told me to get lost, and after that? It was like she never existed. She was never there. Nobody was interested—the police definitely weren't interested."

"You have to admit," Kate said, "it sounds more than a little crazy."

As the car pulled back onto the main highway, Daisy remembered, distantly, that her car was sitting abandoned by the roadside up in the woods. "All it took was a rumor at school, and I was basically a spectacle. You know how kids are."

"How people are."

"Right," Daisy said. "As if adults are any better."

"Agreed."

Sitting at a red light as they turned back into town, Daisy studied the driver in the car adjacent and wondered if she could be recognized, if she even cared.

Kate parked the car outside the police station. The building hadn't changed at all since Daisy's last visit there. She opened the door and Daisy stepped out, then felt a shock as Kate turned her shoulder and flipped open a set of cuffs.

"What?"

"I can't bring you in like we're friends," she said. "You were trespassing." She leaned just close enough to close the other cuff. "After all this time," she said quietly, "haven't you ever considered just dropping it?"

CHAPTER THIRTY-THREE

Now

This kind of surprise didn't turn her heart into ice, the way people liked to say. It vaporized it. Her body felt empty. Just another stranger who already knew her story, already knew what was wrong with her. She followed Kate inside wordlessly, wondering why she felt so hurt. A stranger who knew exactly what to say to her to draw her out. Just past the desk, Kate removed the handcuffs, then led Daisy into a holding cell. After Stella's brilliant flop of a retrospective, she would be lucky if she didn't wind up in the papers again the next morning.

"Hey, don't I know you?"

She turned to see a diminutive, disheveled brunette with wispy features. The woman looked vaguely familiar, but Daisy wasn't in the mood for more bullshit. "I don't think so. No offense, but I don't feel like talking." Daisy folded her elbows over her knees and tried to find a sitting position on the hard bench that was only mildly uncomfortable. She could sense Kate watching her from the doorway, propped open with a dirty mop bucket.

"Daisy, I have to confess, I do know who you are."

Daisy braced herself for an unkind joke. *Fire girl*, she thought. *Or—wait. This woman had been at Stella's wedding.*

"Ugh. Saturday, right?" She rested her forehead in her hand. "I kind of remember seeing you there."

The woman lowered her eyes. "I don't really remember anything about that."

"Thanks." Daisy took another look at her cellmate. "But I know I was a mess."

"Everyone's a mess. Look at me: I'm thirty-four, divorced, single, and here for the third time this year."

"I'm sorry."

At this, her cellmate began to laugh. Daisy almost asked how the woman had found herself here tonight, but it was clear enough: late night, smeared makeup, the ease with which she wore her buzz. Whoever Daisy's cellmate was, she had been too drunk on a weeknight many times before now.

"What's your name?"

"I'm Harlow."

"You're Jesse's wife."

"Ex-wife."

A moment of embarrassment settled between them, quickly dissolving into pointless laughter, under an empty, melodious influence. Daisy smiled sadly at Harlow.

"Wait, you *are* his ex?"

"Oh, yeah. If you saw us together at the wedding, that's because we're friends. That was easy enough," she said, "since we weren't really in love."

"What happened?"

"We got married really young, and not for the right reasons."

"What reasons? Sorry," Daisy added. "I'm not usually this nosy."

"Me? I was finishing college and I thought I was meant to get married. It turned out we didn't really like living together, and we didn't want to do the same things. I mean, I don't want children, for instance. But we like each other perfectly fine."

"Uh-huh." Daisy nodded, wondering what Jesse's reasons had been.

Harlow didn't know, she could see, how much that would hurt him, a casual loss like that. She knew the weight, the care Jesse put into his plans.

"Plus, if I'm being honest, there was someone he never really forgot about. That didn't help things between us."

"Oh? Who was that?" Daisy asked.

But Harlow didn't have a chance to answer, because at that moment, one of the other officers pushed the door open. He approached with a set of keys.

"Mrs. Lopez? Your mother's here."

"Business as usual, huh?" Harlow laughed and stood up. "And it's Ms. Matthews now, not Mrs. Lopez."

"I'll remember next time," the man said, gruff but not unkindly.

"There will not be a next time," Harlow's mother snapped, her eyes tired. "Harlow, you're thirty-four. The next time someone calls me, I'm letting you stay here all night."

"I know, Mom." Harlow wrapped her mother in a clumsy embrace. The door fell closed with a metallic clap and the officer turned the key on the cell again. Hearing the noise, Harlow turned to wave at her. "You going to be okay in here?"

"Sure." Daisy managed a brave scowl. "I've spent nights in worse places."

As the room emptied, leaving Daisy alone, she realized that might not have been the truth. The boarding school—though she shuddered to think of it—had probably been on par with her current lodging. Had it not been for Anderson, who could say what her life might have been like? *Anderson.* She felt a pang in her chest, wondering what he was doing.

Daisy crossed her legs underneath her, brushing at the accumulated dust and bits of leaves from her walk through the trees. Each time she thought she had reached the center of what this place wanted with her, she was wrong again. She craned her neck to try to look through the door, but with the mop bucket on the other side, it was closed, leaving her alone. The room began to feel chilly, the way an air-conditioned room does on a warm, humid evening, her body somehow feeling the vast difference between the climate outside and in. That uncanny air seemed to call to something of its own self in the space that had opened up in her chest.

Maybe that should have been a sign that Daisy ought to have stayed away, keep the native weirdness in her bones in hibernation for as much of her life as she could. The things that happen in a place keep on living there. Daisy settled back against the bench, then against the wall, wondering whether the sticky dampness on her shoulder blades was from some residue on the concrete or her own cold sweat. She thought of the bed she shared with Anderson, the costly linen sheets and the wide window that looked out over the desert. Would the curtains be drawn in the morning, she wondered, or would they be open to let the sunlight in, birds cracking their beaks against the glass and dropping to the ground below? She wanted desperately to call him and ask him to leave the curtains shut.

Her chest prickled and her throat squeezed in. *No way*, she thought, *crying is the only thing that could make this horrible night worse.*

Somehow, she could not have explained how, Daisy felt her eyes begin to close, her limbs growing heavier with sleep. She leaned against the wall. The lingering cool of the deserted chemical plant, the memories there that seemed to glow with their own light, whispered to her. She had never forgotten this. The haunting had never ceased. It was the part that came after, stumbling across Jesse and breathing him in as if he were air and she were being buried alive, how much she had loved him. Until now, she had forgotten that part.

Daisy opened her eyes, blinking away the sleep, and remembered trying to stretch, to find her agility after a full night of sitting cross-legged on a tree branch. A night spent waiting for him. Had she ever been so stupid, to imagine someone would drive across two states to help her, pick her up in the middle of the night? This was what she had forgotten: being left on her own, by the last person she trusted.

The rush in her ears and her ragged breath muddled with the door clattering open, the rattle of keys. Daisy looked up to find Kate unlocking the door. In the narrow windows that bordered the ceiling, she saw daylight.

"No crying in the drunk tank," she chuckled.

"I'm not," Daisy spat.

"Sit up. You ready to go?"

"What?" She pushed herself upright, rubbing her sore elbows.

"Not gonna say it twice," Kate answered, waving her toward the open door. "If you'd rather sleep it off here a little longer, that's up to you."

Daisy's feet flashed with pins and needles as she shuffled out of the room.

"Can I use a phone?" she asked.

"If you need a ride," Kate said, "I'll take you to your car. My shift's ending."

"I don't know." She had a sense that Kate wanted something from her, but she couldn't tell what. Ordinarily, this would have been a reason to walk away, but she knew she couldn't leave the rental car sitting roadside.

"Come on," Kate said, pouring coffee into a Styrofoam cup. "It's no problem. I don't live too far from there."

"You don't?" Daisy wondered aloud. "I didn't know that."

Kate's response was to push the coffee cup into her hand. "Your ride's leaving now," she said.

Being driven somewhere, especially with a stranger, imbued the moment with a vulnerability Daisy did not enjoy. She stared out the window and let her eyes lose focus, blending the greens and yellows against the milky blue of the early morning sky. Kate glanced at her every few minutes, saying nothing. Daisy grew increasingly uncomfortable. When Kate finally pulled over, revealing the rental car at the side of the road, any trace of sleepiness had disappeared from Daisy's head.

"Thanks, I guess," she said.

"I should say, don't let me see you up here again," Kate said. "But..."

"I should go." Daisy opened the door and Kate stopped her with a hand on her wrist.

"Just so you know," Kate said, speaking almost in a whisper, "all the files from that fire are destroyed or sealed. This town has moved past what happened."

Daisy listened with a raised eyebrow, lips pursed. What was it about Kate's words, her manner, that gave Daisy an impression that she knew her so intimately? She flashed a suspicious stare at the coffee Kate had given her. Her need for caffeine, though, outweighed her discomfort with Kate. Daisy held the coffee cup in one hand and opened the car door with the other.

"Did you hear me?" Kate asked.

"Yes. I remember," Daisy answered finally. "Everyone moved past it as soon as it happened."

CHAPTER THIRTY-FOUR

Before

One weekend when the weather was still warm but the leaves were just beginning to turn, Daisy followed Tracker out on one of his excursions. She had covered herself as best she could: informing Ellen that she would be busy, leaving her room clean, even behaving especially well over the previous few days. She had no plans to confront him, or even to be seen, but she knew, somehow, that observing her father away from his family would be a piece of what she couldn't otherwise explain.

It was Saturday, usually a short workday. Daisy walked to the chemical plant after breakfast, snuck through the parking lot, and hid under the covered truck bed of her father's pickup. Tracker had let Ellen know that he planned to go hunting after work, that he might be home for dinner, or not. Daisy knew it was a risk, that she would have no possible excuse if she were caught, but she knew too that her father was a creature of habit, that he wouldn't check any compartment he did not need to. And, besides, she found no hunting gear in the truck. Something was up. In the dusty heat, she had almost fallen asleep when she felt the truck rock as Tracker got into the driver's seat and started the engine.

He had never said anything, not that she could remember, about where he went hunting. She tried to keep track of where he was going as the truck turned down their road and onto the larger highway, but the heat and the dark clouded her sense of place. As the truck made one stop after the other, she heard other cars around them, realized they were somewhere with traffic lights. The truck whined and squeaked to a stop, the tired brakes groaning. Daisy heard her father get out of the truck, walk around to the gas tank. Her heart began to race and she felt the delirium of the heat, suddenly regretting her decision. She squeaked behind a tool case, although her legs were exposed, like a child who knows only to hide their face. She sucked her breath in as she heard the gas tank open, smelled its fumes as her father fueled the car.

Daisy had to concede that this might have been a mistake. Once again, her courage had outdone her abilities. She felt sick and hot, trying to curl onto her side to get her knees against her stomach. But when her shins bumped the edge of the tool case in the dark, it screeched across the metal truck bed with a groan, its weight wobbling the old vehicle. Daisy was still trying to catch up to what had happened when the truck cover opened and the light hit her face.

A moment dragged for hours, then: the hot sun, the fresh air, her nausea, the gasoline fumes and the squeak of the pump, Tracker's cold blue stare cutting right through to her guts. He lifted her by the elbows and hauled her to the ground, let her wobbly knees and the open edge of the truck deal out punishment for him. Daisy imagined that if father had ever failed to kill a deer on the first shot, he would have worked with this kind of efficiency, this kind of cold anger. Daisy looked up at him with a hand at her temple, stood up on the third try, one hand on the truck.

"Where are you going?" she asked. "Why can't you talk to me? I want to know who she was. I…"

Daisy hadn't had a proper wound since she was a child with summertime scraped knees. She felt a drop of blood on her cheek, let the pain clear her head as she looked at her father. She looked like a homeless girl, a tagalong, sweaty and dirty, someone who had snuck into his car or approached him for money. It occurred to her that he didn't hit her like a parent disciplining a child. He had a different look on his face, a different sharpness in his body. He hit her like a man hits a woman that he hates. With that one second, in which he demanded an answer, she turned the same disdainful stare back on him. Tracker locked the bed of the truck and muttered something with a warning tone, then drove away, leaving her there in the parking lot.

Daisy dug in her pocket for some change and went to the payphone outside the convenience store. She dialed Stella's number, then remembered that she wasn't there. Stella was away at a yearly family reunion, somewhere on a lake in the Northeast, and would not return until late that evening. It wasn't fair, she reasoned, to involve Stella in this. That wasn't within her scope.

Daisy looked around at the intersection. They hadn't driven more than half an hour, but she was in a part of town she didn't recognize. She walked half a block, looking for a public restroom, a place to hide, a place to sit down. The nearest intersection read Maple and Curtis. A car horn blared at her, and she realized the vulnerability of her position. Daisy walked back to the gas station, counting nickels and dimes from the bottom of her pocket, and found she had just enough for one more call.

CHAPTER THIRTY-FIVE

Before

"Hello?" Jesse answered with the put-on deep voice of someone who knows who's calling, but wants to sound as if they don't.

"It's me."

"I know."

Another car whizzed by and Daisy stepped back from the road. "What, um. What are you doing?"

"Right now? Nothing."

She waited, hoping for any improbable thing to break the silence, the added embarrassment of asking for help proving almost too much. Another passing car honked at her.

"Where are you?" Jesse asked.

"I actually don't know. I…"

"Can you tell me?" She heard the tone in his voice shift and imagined his eyes widening.

"I don't know. The street signs say Maple and Curtis, but I don't have any idea where I am." Daisy took another look at her surroundings and sat down miserably at a bus stop near the crossing. She spat on the hem of her shirt and wiped at her forehead, the cotton knit coming away rust-brown where it stretched over her fingers.

"Stay where you are," Jesse was saying. "Okay? I'll be there as soon as I can."

Daisy didn't know how much time passed, but the wait was more restorative than she expected. Despite her disheveled appearance and the shock of what had just happened, the air she breathed was clearer, and though she felt fear reverberating from her father's stare, she knew herself stronger for having stood up to him, even if it meant failing at finding the information she wanted. She had what was important: confirmation that he knew something. Something wrong, something unspoken.

When Daisy saw Jesse's car pull up, she was suddenly conscious of a sticky film of dust and sweat from the day on her skin, but a rush of energy lifted her to her feet like a cool breeze and buoyed her as she walked to the car.

"Hey." She dropped into the seat. "Don't ask me anything. Not yet."

Jesse complied, no words crossing his lips, though she saw his eyes flash, communicating all the feelings she had hoped to silence. "Please," she said, "just drive."

As Jesse began to drive, the car's alarm tone sounded, alerting them that the passenger seatbelt was unfastened. Again, he gave her a pleading look. Self-conscious, she turned away.

"It'll be fine," she said. "And you're a good driver, right?" The fact was, she hated wearing seatbelts; the faintest bad mood was enough for her to disregard wearing one, and today she didn't need an excuse.

"That's not fair," he said. "Daisy, please." He reached for the seatbelt, his hand wavering. "I don't know what to do here."

She reached for his hand, her fingers grimy from the back of the truck, and streaked with dried blood. But something pulled her nearer; her fingers twined around his, she reached for his other hand with hers, squeezing them both between her own. She anticipated what he would say, what she was afraid Stella would have said: *Don't worry. Everything will be fine. Don't cry.* Blanket statements of faith, of positivity, from someone who only saw the surface. By way of comforting him, she clipped her seatbelt.

"Me either."

"That's okay," he answered.

"What is?"

"That we don't know," Jesse answered. Looking into his eyes, she noticed, for the first time, their weight, their gravity. Something heavy, separate from herself, but an anchor. "If you let me, I will find a way to help, whatever it is I can do."

She took a long breath, felt the oxygen in all of her body, the sweat on her back, the stinging on her forehead, the energy of being near him that ran down her legs to her toes and back into her chest, felt a gentle weight of relief. "Okay."

"Where are we going?"

"I told Mom I'd be with friends until later," Daisy said. "So I can't go home for a few hours. But I need to clean my clothes and straighten up. I can't be like this when I go back."

*

Half an hour later found her in the renovated wing at Teresa's home. Jesse showed her to the guest room and shower. It struck Daisy as absurd that, at this moment, she should want anything but space, anything but a closed door. The thought of being left alone to her thoughts terrified her.

"Can you stay here for a minute?" she breathed. "Don't—don't look at me. Stay over there. Just don't leave."

"I won't." He sat on the counter by the sink, looked away while she slipped out of her clothes and behind the shower curtain. Daisy started the shower, let the water run cold while she scrubbed her face with soap. As the water grew hot, she sank to her knees, felt that her body was still steady and strong.

"Can I ask now?"

"Yes," Daisy answered. But the noise between her ears, the pictures, the questions—those she could not begin to unravel. "I snuck out in the back of Dad's truck. I know he's lying about where he goes, but I don't know why."

"Did you fall out or something?"

Suddenly, it seemed like a mistake to tell him too much. Jesse trusted the adults in his life. What if he insisted on telling someone, on complicating things in ways she couldn't control? She lifted her hands to the sides of her head, palms pressing in tight. "Yes, Jesse, for God's sake. I fell out. You and your obvious questions, again."

Whatever word was coming next got caught in her throat, rolled out in a ragged sob. Daisy pushed her hair back from her face and pulled the shower curtain aside just a few inches, her exposed stare a sort of apology. But she saw something different in him: the breadth of his shoulders, the straight line of his forearms where his arms were crossed in thought. His chest rose with a deep breath, then he shook his head, let out a sharp breath. She could see what he would look like as an adult, as a man. But that look in his eye was the same. A closeness, despite whatever distance was between them, and something tender. Finally, Daisy realized what that look had meant all this time. She pulled the shower curtain back across and ducked under the hot water.

"Are you okay in there?"

Sitting still like this began to feel like a distinctly bad idea. Before Daisy's heartbeat ran away from her, she stood up again, began to scrub under her arms and then at the dirt under her fingernails, letting the water fall in her eyes.

"Yes." She shut the water off and reached a hand out from the curtain. "Could you pass me a towel?"

"Here." He placed a dry towel in her fingers, let his other hand rest on hers for a moment. "I'm going to go put your clothes in the wash. I'll leave a change outside the door."

"Thanks."

Wrapped in a towel, she clicked the bathroom door open with hesitation, checked that the room was empty, half wishing she would see him there, not knowing exactly why, and found a stack of folded clothes at her feet: flannel pajama pants, two t-shirts.

She rolled up the pants at the waistband until the hem no longer dragged the floor, combed her hair with her fingers, and hung the towels on hooks. Once cleaned, she saw that she could cover the scrapes on her elbows and forehead easily enough, with clothing, or her hair. Daisy heard a cough and footsteps, Jesse letting her know that he was there, before he opened the door of the guest room.

"Feel better?"

"Yes. Thanks."

Standing at opposite doorways, they looked across at each other, then at their feet, then back up. Daisy spotted a smudge of dust on the floor and poked at it with her toe.

"We could watch TV," he said.

"Sure," she answered, relieved. "That sounds good."

"What do you want to watch?" he asked at the same time.

"Um, anything." She gladly followed him downstairs, past the sheet-covered doorways, into the finished living room. Television was only an excuse for her to sit next to him, to feel his arms around her and be still. As he clicked through channels, she enjoyed the air conditioning, the clean smell of the house, the smell of age but fresh paint, the quiet hum of the fans. Beyond the window, she saw the expanse of the yard, summer's dull, deep green reaching to the decrepit gazebo, dropping off at the creek line, then darkening into forest. From here, it looked as if it would go on forever, like she was in a fairy tale, or somewhere imaginary. After changing the channel several times, Jesse let it play a black and white movie, something he seemed familiar with, and she lay still, let her eyes fall shut. It wasn't that she felt safe here; she simply carried the quiet chaos she'd grown up with in her heart wherever she went. But she felt sure of Jesse, who was maybe the only person she knew who had no stake in her saying or doing one thing or another. Daisy realized that she trusted him.

"Jesse, my parents are going to send me away," Daisy said. "To some Christian reformatory boarding school."

"How'd you know?"

"My dad said he was looking at it already. That was before all this nonsense today."

"Where is it?"

"South Carolina," Daisy said. "I think. Nobody's allowed to leave. No phone calls. I'm not a criminal," she said. "I didn't mean to do anything wrong."

"You won't go," Jesse said, more decisive than she had ever seen him. His arm tightened around her shoulder. "I promise."

"What are you going to do?" She hugged her knees. "And besides, I don't know if I can stand to stay at home."

"I wouldn't want you to," he said, touching the mark on her forehead. It stung under his hand, but Daisy didn't flinch. "All we need to do is find somewhere you can stay until I go to college. Then you can stay with me. It has to be somewhere safe," he said. "You're not going to run away and be homeless. My dad's girlfriend in the city has kids a couple of years older than us, in college. You can stay with her daughter. I'll talk to her."

"Do you really think—"

"She has a second bedroom in her apartment. I think she's even looking for a roommate. Listen," he said. "I'll figure something out. Whatever's going on here, it isn't going to get any better."

"That's all I want," she said.

"We'll start planning it tonight," Jesse promised. "You just need to be careful. Don't tell anyone. Don't say anything." For Daisy, this suggestion was a godsend; for Jesse, it was reckless. Putting himself at risk of trouble for no good reason. Unless she, Daisy, were a good reason.

"I won't," she promised, kissing him.

CHAPTER THIRTY-SIX

Before

All the latent nervousness in her limbs seized up as she heard a car on the gravel outside.

"Maybe my mom's home early." Jesse leaned back and looked out the window. "That's not her car."

Daisy glanced outside, then turned to Jesse, eyes wide. "It's my mother." At that moment, she heard three sharp knocks on the door.

"Don't answer it," he said. "Don't go home. It's not safe."

Daisy rolled her eyes. "It's safe if I don't do anything out of line." When she saw the shock on his face, she softened, pulling him into a hug. "I have to. It's just going to be more unpleasant if I don't go now."

Hearing another rap at the door, Jesse stood up, walked down the hallway. "I'll tell her you're not here," he said.

That isn't going to work, Daisy thought. She shuddered inwardly at the thought of Ellen seeing her there in Jesse's clothes. To Ellen, sex outside of marriage, or, Daisy imagined, any sex that was just to make you happy, was an insult to God. And as far as what had or hadn't happened, she wouldn't believe a word out of Daisy's mouth. Ellen was mild-mannered, until she sensed something trying to get between her and Him. Then, she was unmovable.

Daisy heard the door swing open. "Can I help you?" Jesse said.

"I know she's here." Ellen's calm tone was deceiving. This was the bedrock of Ellen's personality, where others might betray fight or cowardice when pressed beyond reason. "If she doesn't come to the door, I will find her and bring her home." When Daisy heard the cool and unfriendly tone of her mother's voice, she knew she was speaking the truth. Daisy walked barefoot to the front door, Jesse's clothes hanging loose on her. She lingered, sizing up Ellen's expression from behind Jesse's shoulder, until her mother grabbed her arm and pulled her across the threshold.

"Can't I go get my clothes? I—"

"Not a word." Ellen said goodbye to Jesse with a blank, cold nod of her head, pushed the door shut, and led Daisy to the car.

The drive back to their house passed in silence. Ellen opened Daisy's door and looked toward the front steps. Daisy got up and walked inside a few steps ahead of her.

"Sit down."

Daisy sat at the kitchen table and waited. Ellen sat across from her, her mouth creased with what looked like grief. "Have you slept with him, Daisy?"

Daisy resented that look of pain, hated Ellen trying to make her feel bad for being a human being with something she wanted to keep secret. "Of course not."

"Shame on you." Ellen reached across the table and slapped her hand with such speed that Daisy flinched, sliding her chair back a few inches.

"I haven't."

"Your father told me you had gotten into trouble." She leaned forward, swept Daisy's hair off her forehead with a soft touch. Her eyes swept over Daisy's scraped arms.

"He wasn't going hunting," Daisy said. "He was somewhere in town. He found me when he stopped at a gas station on Curtis Avenue."

Ellen's lack of response shocked Daisy into anger. "You knew, Mama. You already knew. What's going on?"

"Take it from somebody who knows." Ellen's eyebrows drew close together, as if Daisy had hurt her. "I do the very best I can for you. Don't ask questions you don't want the answers to."

"I need to know the truth," Daisy insisted.

"*Know ye not that your body is the temple of the Holy Ghost in you, which ye have of God, and ye are not your own?*" Ellen recited. Her stony expression began to melt into fear. "Daisy, don't you understand? Your body is not your own. You'll be punished." Ellen slid into the chair next to Daisy's and hugged her. Daisy could feel the sadness in her trembling voice. "Avoid the works of the flesh. God will punish you, just like me, Daisy."

"Mom. Come on, listen." Daisy squeezed Ellen cautiously, then inched away from her. "You know that you haven't suffered miscarriages because you slept with Dad before you were married. You know what the reason for that is, don't you?" In the warm, dimly lit kitchen, Ellen looked young and breakable. Daisy had never been more conscious of her own stronger, fuller figure, existing in her body with a comfort she suspected Ellen had never had. "You know that, right, Mama? It's not your fault."

When a few moments had passed, Daisy rose from her chair. Ellen stood up silent and quickly, backing Daisy against the wall with one long, extended finger. "Your body is the temple of the Holy Ghost," she repeated. "Your father is at the end of his rope with you. If he decides to send you away, I can't do anything more to help you."

"You can't?" Daisy echoed, whispering. Surely, Ellen wouldn't ever do nothing to help her. She didn't mean that.

"Your father is under a lot of stress and that's all there is to it," she added in a furious whisper. "You can hate him all you want, it won't make any improvement."

Gladly, Daisy thought, though she said nothing.

"If you're doing anything stupid," Ellen said, "and you know what I mean, you'd better be smart about it. I left a plate in your room. Now go."

Daisy went to her room and turned the lights off, ignoring the plate of cold food on the dresser. The house grew quiet and still, and Daisy heard her parents go upstairs to sleep. She could have run back to Jesse's house right then. Or into the woods, though the thought of sleeping among all those noises made her shiver. But what Daisy wanted, and what seemed the most impossible, was for a simpler frame of mind, to feel like a child again, unworried.

She listened for her mother, heard her gentle snore from upstairs, and inched open her window, then shimmied out. She crept swiftly through the yard, keeping near the edge of the forest, where she could easily duck and hide in the bushes if she needed to.

Daisy reached up and rattled the windchime that hung from the tree, its bells singing, and hoped Stella would hear. She stood by the wire fence, looking anxiously toward the yellow-lit windows of the Whittens' house until she saw Stella's slim figure approaching her, dark against the twilight sky.

"What's up?" Daisy whispered. "How are your classes?"

"Fine," Stella sighed. "It's going to be a busy year." Once again, Daisy felt lonely, seeing Stella so perfectly in her element. "How's Jesse? You like him, don't you?"

Daisy nodded. *Like* was there somewhere. Whatever that meant. Only an imprecise, shifting word like that stood a chance at describing the whirlwind of feelings she had for him: giddiness, fear, something *else* that kept her awake nights. There was so much in addition to those feelings, though, that she didn't know how to explain it all, not even to Stella.

Daisy hugged her across the fence, minding not to pull Stella too close to the barbs on the wire. "Everything's a mess. My parents are saying they'll send me away to some stupid boarding school. I don't know what to do."

Stella returned her hug, then inched back, and Daisy saw that she was fussing with her hair. "What happened?"

"I got in trouble with my dad. I know there's something he isn't telling me. I don't want to leave you. I don't want to leave Jesse," Daisy said. She realized that words were tumbling from her mouth, that she hadn't spoken with Stella in days, that she missed her. But also that her upset and her eagerness to catch up were making her sound incoherent. "I can't explain it all right now. Why can't you stay?"

"I'm going to a party," Stella answered. Daisy saw that she was wearing tight blue jeans and a pretty top. "My friend's picking me up. I'm sorry," she added. "Maybe we can hang out soon."

"I don't know how much longer I'll even be around," Daisy said, wiping at her eyes angrily. She leaned in, desperate to close the distance between them. "I'm going to run away, Stella. I'm not going to that place. I'm going to stay with someone until Jesse starts college, then we can live together."

"Are you okay, Daisy?" Stella asked. Daisy could sense her disapproving look even in the dark. "You seem a little…" Headlights pulled into the drive behind her. Without warning, Daisy had an unshakable feeling that she might not see Stella again. It was the same foreboding, the same shadow that had passed between them in the auditorium, visible only to Daisy, who had learned to sense shadows even in the dark. She held onto the wire of the fence with one hand, held it steady as she pressed a fingertip against a barb, held it out for Stella to see. In the blue-lit evening, the blood that welled up looked violet, almost shimmering.

"Blood sisters?"

"Daisy, don't!" Stella winced. "I just told you I'm about to leave." From the car that waited, a horn beeped. "We're blood sisters," Stella assured her. "Always. Just—I can't right now. And Daisy?" she said as she turned to leave. "Don't do anything stupid."

Pressing her smarting fingertip against her t-shirt, Daisy retreated a few yards, then watched as Stella approached the car and got in. Daisy crossed the yard in the moonlight and climbed back in through her open window.

CHAPTER THIRTY-SEVEN

Now

Daisy sat behind the steering wheel, watching Kate's police car until it disappeared around the bend. She sighed and squeezed her hands to her temples, a sleepless night battling the storm of thoughts and memories in her mind. She drove down the familiar road with the comfort of habit, unsure where she planned to go next.

She passed by her parents' driveway without slowing down. They had been clear enough that they didn't want her around there, and she wasn't sure she had enjoyed visiting, either. As she passed Teresa's house, she remembered how Jesse's mother had told her: *You'd never know he only lives five minutes away.* She sipped the coffee and kept driving.

Jesse's house was only two miles down the road from Ellen and Tracker's graying-white rancher. As she parked, Daisy glanced at the dashboard clock with a wince: half past eight. Suddenly, she didn't care that it was early, that her visit was unexpected. It had been even earlier when she had woken up by herself to climb out of that window so long ago. She remembered how she had waited long into the day, the blood and dirt drying on her hands, before she realized the inevitable, what she had already witnessed between her own parents: that, one way or another, a lover would always let you down.

Crossing the yard to the front door, she didn't care that she was in her old jeans and t-shirt from the night before, eyes hollow from sleeplessness, her hair uncombed. She climbed the porch stairs and knocked at the door, then rang the doorbell, then knocked again. Only after waiting for a few minutes did she notice the office building, a converted guest house, beyond a row of crape myrtles blooming with red flowers. A sign by the front door read *Jesse Lopez, Doctor of Veterinary Medicine.* Daisy walked closer and saw that the small parking lot outside the office was full; it must be a busy morning. As she approached, a woman stepped out of a car, then opened the passenger door and lifted out a small crate from which Daisy heard an indignant meowing.

"Are you looking for the vet's office?" the woman asked, kindly bustling past her. "It's right here. You must be picking up; I see you don't have an animal with you." She smiled and held the door open. "Here, go ahead."

"Thanks." Daisy walked in and observed the waiting room: a tiled floor, a row of chairs. She sat on an empty chair, somewhat uncertainly, and waited. A vet technician in a green scrub jacket called each patient by name—*Mr. Meow? Ranger?*—and greeted the pet's owners with a knowing smile as they walked up. Daisy saw the joke in this gesture, how it disarmed the pet owner's anxiety.

"Ma'am?" the technician asked. "Did you have an appointment?"

"No," Daisy said. "I'm here to see Jesse. I mean, Dr. Lopez. Please, don't interrupt whatever he's doing."

The technician nodded. "I'll let him know. He's booked with patients until lunchtime."

The technician assessed the pets on a metal countertop before showing them to a back room where, Daisy assumed, they waited for Jesse. *Dr. Lopez will see you shortly*, she heard. She found she enjoyed the wait, seeing that he took walk-in appointments. With the clock ticking toward mid-morning, Daisy grew tired, feeling the exhaustion of the night before and the argument with Stella weighing on her mind. By eleven, only one person remained in the waiting room with her, accompanied by a leashed spaniel. The idea of sleep began to seem more important than whatever Daisy had wanted to ask Jesse. That morning of betrayal, waiting for him, years and hundreds of miles away, was so distant now, and the morning light that slipped through the blinds felt warm on her shoulders like a blanket.

The door swung open and a man walked in, accompanying a girl who looked to be about ten years old. The girl's eyes were puffy from crying. She held a shoebox in both hands as carefully as one might hold a tea tray.

The man approached the counter and rang the bell. "Hello?"

Half a minute passed in silence. Daisy saw the strain of worry on the man's face, heard his daughter crying quietly. When the vet technician returned, she sighed with relief.

"Can I help you?" she asked.

The girl reached up to place the box on the counter. "It's my cat," she said. "He needs the vet. We came as fast as we could."

"He was hit by a car," the father added, wrapping an arm around the girl's shoulders. "I don't think they can do anything for him now, Nora."

"He's just sleeping," the girl insisted.

Daisy glanced at the woman holding the spaniel, sharing a wince. The technician looked into the shoebox, her face blank, then called down the hallway: "Jesse, can you come out here, please?"

Wearing glasses and a white coat, unbuttoned over his t-shirt, Jesse approached the counter. Daisy saw the quick glance he exchanged with the technician, then the girl's father.

Jesse closed the lid of the shoebox. He bent down to meet the girl's expectant stare.

"I'm Dr. Lopez. What's your name?"

"Nora," she answered. "Can you help my cat? He's asleep right now."

"Hi, Nora," Jesse answered. "Can you tell me what happened?"

"He ran in front of a car." The girl's hand reached for the lid of the shoebox; Jesse held it closed. Nora's face fell with realization. "I wasn't there until after. I didn't get to tell him I love him."

Jesse was silent for a moment, waiting for the girl to catch her breath. As he stared over her shoulder, his eyes found Daisy's. She nodded an encouragement then looked away.

"Can I tell you something, Nora? I'm only a veterinarian, but I know that your cat knows you love him. He wouldn't blame you for missing him, but he wouldn't want you to be sorry for something like that."

The girl nodded and walked outside, clutching the box with both arms. "I didn't know what to do," the father said with an apologetic shrug.

"It's alright," Jesse said. "I'm sorry about your cat."

"Thank you." The man nodded, shook his hand, and walked after his daughter.

Daisy resisted the temptation to look outside at the girl and her father, tried not to imagine the small body inside the box.

"Daisy," she heard Jesse say. "I just have one more patient."

"Take your time."

After the last patient left, Jesse walked out, scrubbing his hands at the sink.

"Done already?" Daisy asked.

"Lunchtime," Jesse said. "We open for patients again in two hours."

"I see."

Jesse held the door open and Daisy walked outside. He paused, seeming to study her unkempt appearance. Daisy was wearing her clothes from the night before, her face unwashed, her hair no doubt a disaster. "You look tired," he said. "Everything alright?"

"Thanks. I am." Daisy laughed. She glanced down at the wrinkles in her shirt, but could only guess at what kind of state her hair was in. "It was a long night."

Daisy followed Jesse toward the house. *Remember why you came here*, she told herself. *This is the same Jesse who said he would be there to pick you up. Who wasn't there when you needed him the most.* But she was distracted with how tired she felt, and by how strange it was to see Jesse. When she looked at him, it was hard to remember that he was the same person she had been so angry with for so many years. He was just Jesse.

CHAPTER THIRTY-EIGHT

Now

He opened the curtains of his living room to let the light in, then offered Daisy a chair at a small table facing the window. "Anything to eat?"

"No, thanks. It's too hot to eat. And I'm too tired."

Jesse poured two glasses of iced tea from a pitcher in the fridge and sat down across from her.

"I saw Stella's article."

"Don't remind me." Daisy frowned. "I was dumb enough to think we could be friends again. I guess nothing's changed. Including my poor decision-making skills."

"Why do you say that?"

"Last night, after the article went up, I left Stella's and went up to the old chemical plant. I don't know why," she said, sipping her tea. "Just to—look at it, I guess. I thought maybe I would remember something new."

"At night?" Jesse looked at her with surprise, then broke into a grin. "Why am I still surprised? You've never been afraid of doing anything by yourself."

Except being alone, Daisy wanted to say.

"Turns out, the police in this town actually care about trespassing now. I spent all night in the drunk tank. Although I was mostly sober," she added, half smiling.

"What, last night? Why didn't you call me?"

"Call you?"

"Yes," he said. "Didn't I say you could call me if you needed anything?"

Daisy shook her head. He knew why. This was too easy, Daisy thought, too natural.

"You know who else was there? Your ex-wife."

"Harlow? Oh." Daisy saw the combination of annoyance and regret cross his features.

"She seems kind," Daisy said, finishing her tea. "She said you got married young. Sorry that didn't work out for you."

"Yeah. Not much to discuss." Jesse finished his iced tea and sat the glass down on the table. "We started dating senior year in high school, got married before we finished undergrad. And split up a few years later."

"You forgot about me in a hurry," Daisy murmured sharply.

"Is that what you think?" Jesse stretched and stood up. "Do you want to take a walk, see the rest of the place?"

"Sure." Daisy followed him outside. "How long have you been here?"

"Since I finished my bachelor's degree," he said. "I had the guest house turned into an office. Fixed up the old barn for the horses."

"Are they your horses?" she asked, with some surprise.

"No," he scoffed. "They're boarded, mostly. Some in hospice care, you could say."

On such little sleep, the sun on the meadow, still dewy, was surreal, like another dimension she'd dropped into, peaceful and distant. In the restored barn, she followed Jesse as he opened each paddock, dispensing feed, releasing several into a grazing area. At the end of the row, he came to a stall where a gray-nosed, sleepy-looking horse awaited him with his nose over the bars. "This one, his owners couldn't afford to pay for his care. And I didn't want to put him down. So there you have it," he said. "My one horse."

"He's…" She tried to compliment the horse: sweet, friendly, something. But he shook his head when she moved to touch the broad nose.

"He's a cranky old man, is what he is. I call it character."

"Guess you still like things that seem broken."

He looked back at her without smiling. "I guess they don't seem broken to me."

"That sounds like something you would say." When they left the barn, she followed Jesse to the kennel, where several dogs were boarded while their owners vacationed. Two were there for medical supervision. Daisy sat on a bench in the brightening morning sun, sleep deprivation making her nearly dizzy, while he tended to the dogs.

"That isn't true, what you said about forgetting you."

Daisy smiled. That was a pleasant sentiment, but one that did her little good. "I'm not sure what I should say."

"Sometimes I think everything I've done since has been about us," he said. "Harlow, the wedding. The divorce. Staying here in this town," he repeated, looking up at the little roof above them. "You got into my head somehow, maybe into my bones."

"Yeah? Me too," Daisy said. *About getting away from it. As far away as I could.*

"Why'd you come?" Jesse tilted his head and smiled, just the same smile, despite the more solid jaw, the stubble that darkened his cheek. He extended a hand and pulled her to her feet. They laughed, either embarrassed or something else, as she stumbled, stopped short of touching him.

"I don't know, Jesse." Daisy saw her car sitting in the driveway. She had come here with a question and fallen into this strange morning of light, this quiet, almost unchanged world where he seemed to reside. Daisy followed Jesse back toward the door, paused on the shaded patio. She sat in a wooden rocking chair, let her eyes close for a moment, then looked up at him.

"It isn't easy for you to be back here, is it?" Jesse asked.

"Here, Zion, or here with you?" She brushed her hair away from her face, feeling just sleepy enough to answer honestly. "It's good to see you. But yeah, being here is kind of tough."

When he saw the look on Daisy's face, he went on: "You're thinking about her, aren't you?"

She crossed her legs and leaned back in the rocker. "The girl who died? Yes, more often than not, especially the last few days. But don't you have to go back to work soon?"

"Yes. Where are you staying?"

"At a hotel in town," Daisy lied. She hoped he hadn't noticed the suitcase on the back seat of the car.

"Are you free for dinner?" he asked, and paused. "We'll finish up in the clinic around five." Daisy nodded her head. "You could even take a nap until then."

"I might close my eyes right here," she said. "Maybe just for a few minutes."

CHAPTER THIRTY-NINE

Before

While the end of September crept closer, Daisy's effort in school dwindled to a minimum. She clung tightly to her diminishing routine with Stella: their morning talks by the lockers, occasional meetings by the fence.

Ellen had stopped asking her where she was going, or where she had been. Tracker took almost no interest in Daisy, to the degree, lately, that he seemed almost warm to her for the first time in months. After his recent violent episode, this had the strange effect of keeping Daisy especially nervous and yet more hopeful than usual that things could be repaired. Maybe things were okay with her family. But then she remembered the rumors. Someone was out there who knew something about her. Something was here, in the connective tissue of her own home, that was poisoned by the ground beneath it, and if she didn't want it to poison her too, all she could do was to leave.

Ellen went so far in her permissiveness to allow Daisy to go to the fall dance at school. Her condition was that Stella, whom she trusted, was to act as Daisy's chaperone. Before they left, Ellen took Stella's hands while Daisy waited by the door, addressing her in a low, serious voice. "You're a good girl, Stella. Don't let her do anything you wouldn't do. No dancing. No boys. Especially not—"

She jerked her head in the direction of Teresa's house. "She's been spending too much time with him lately."

"Oh, not to worry, Mrs. R. Jesse won't be there," Stella said. "He never goes to dances."

"They shouldn't even hold these events." Ellen turned away and took a washcloth to the stained edge of the kitchen sink, scrubbing with determination.

"We'll be back early. If the dance is boring, we might go to a movie with some of my friends."

"They're nice kids, right? Like you?"

"Of course they are."

"Alright, then." Ellen tucked the washcloth into her apron and squeezed Daisy's shoulders. "I'll see you in a few hours."

"Okay, Mama."

The gymnasium at school had been decorated for the dance, with large fans arranged to blow orange and yellow streamers in an impression of falling leaves. The pumpkins, hay bales, and even a lone scarecrow that adorned corners of the room and the refreshment table stood in contrast to the attire of the students. The majority of the young women made the most of a rare opportunity to be seen in formalwear, while most of the male students wore t-shirts, or, at best, a button-up shirt and slacks. Daisy had borrowed a dress from Stella, red with a white ribbon at her waist that tied in the back. A tea-length gown on Stella, the hem just reached Daisy's knees.

"Are you sure you don't mind me coming with you?" Daisy whispered, taking in the scene from the doorway.

"Of course not," Stella answered, scanning the crowd as she looked for her friends. She looked to Daisy with a smirk. "No dancing, though. Look, there's Harlow. Come on."

"Stella," one of them shouted. "We're over here!"

"Oh." Daisy heard a low voice as she approached. "She brought the fire girl."

The girl's voice was quickly shushed, but hearing it at all was enough.

An hour passed while Daisy watched Stella move through the crowded room, dancing in a circle with Harlow and several other girls. As it turned out, Ellen needn't have worried that Daisy would dance, or talk to boys, or do anything other than sit still by herself, which is precisely what she would have done had she been at home.

"What are you doing over here?" Stella called. "Just staring into space?"

Daisy smiled as her friend approached. "I guess."

"We're going to catch a movie. Are you coming?"

"I don't know. My mom wouldn't want me to stay out late."

"You're with me," Stella reminded her. "She won't worry."

The group traveled to the theater in two cars, Daisy squeezed into the middle seat in the back of Stella's. She looked at the girls on either side of her, wondering who had made the comment earlier: *She brought the fire girl.* Was it one of them? Would they laugh later on, cringing at how they'd had to squeeze in next to her? Worse, would they ostracize Stella for toting her along? Daisy sat as still as she could, squeezing her knees together to take up as little space as possible. She was the last out of the car, aiming to walk at Stella's side but instead following along behind her.

Daisy was the last in the group to walk into the darkened theater. She saw Stella and the rest of her friends, backlit by the lights and the sound of the movie trailers, filing into a row near the front. With a hand on the back of the seat, she stumbled to keep pace. *Why do they have to keep these places so damn dark?* She couldn't even see her own feet. Suddenly, her foot met an obstacle, large, unmoving. Daisy squinted down, and finally made out a face, eye sockets obscured in the dark, a pair of folded arms.

"Help me," it whispered. Her stomach curdled.

"Stella?" Daisy called. "There's…" It didn't make sense for there to be a body here. Not where a half dozen others had just walked past. *They're all right about me*, she thought. *I'm losing my mind. Seeing dead people where they can't possibly be.* Her throat squeezed and her knees locked.

Then, the dead body sat up. Daisy heard giggles, soft laughter sharpening into a crow-like chorus.

"Hey, relax, fire girl," the girl said. "I was just playing." The girl rose to her feet, brushing popcorn crumbs from her back.

But it didn't feel like playing. Daisy smelled smoke, heard shouts and flames rushing. The noise they made was like breathing, sucking all the oxygen from the air around her, leaving her to gasp dumbly like a hooked fish. She ought to have laughed; she could feel it, this was a moment to play off, absorb the joke. But instead, she froze, caught between two places at once.

"Come on," the girl said, sitting down. "I said I was playing. If you'd seen a real body, anyway, you'd know the difference, right?"

"Yeah, Daisy," another girl echoed. "Did you or not?"

"Stella, tell her." Daisy's voice was a scratchy whisper. "You think I'd lie to you? I told you what I saw."

The chorus of whispers hushed as six sets of eyes rested on Stella. She shifted in her seat, glancing up at the big screen as if it annoyed her to look away. "Daisy, come on. The movie's starting. Sit down."

Daisy felt the group's attention return to her. A few voices further back in the theater called out, annoyed, for them to sit, be quiet.

"She made it up," the girl whispered, "and now she's afraid to back down."

"Who knows," the other one echoed. "She looks crazy enough to me. She doesn't know what she saw out there."

A wishful notion crossed Daisy's mind, that these girls liked her, that they accepted her as Stella's friend, and that this was a friendly ritual, picking on the new kid. That if she could laugh along with them, they'd let it be, that she could seem normal.

"Sit down, fire girl, or you're going to get us thrown out."

Daisy glanced helplessly at Stella, whose eyes were glued to the screen. This was not in fun. She wasn't one of their friends. She was the fire girl. Her knees wobbled as she hurried up the aisle and ducked toward the nearest exit.

CHAPTER FORTY

Now

Daisy opened her eyes to the waning orange light and faint chill of evening air. She looked to either side, remembering where she was. From the kitchen, she could smell food cooking. The rocking chair looked out toward the forest; the foliage was backlit with gold from the sunset. Daisy's initial shock from waking up somewhere new faded into comfort, taking in the peaceful view and sounds, a wistful reminder of the things that she had missed about this place. She reached for her phone and realized there was a blanket draped over her legs.

"Jesse?"

"Morning, Daisy." As he answered, she saw that he was seated on the steps, then looked around again and realized that there was only one chair on the patio.

"Don't you mean evening? What time is it, anyway?"

"A little past six."

"I didn't mean to sleep so long." Daisy stretched her arms, reaching above her head, and settled back into the chair. "This is a beautiful view." She swiveled the rocking chair to face him and saw that he was reading a book.

"I like it," he answered, putting the book aside. "Kind of soothing, you know? It doesn't feel lonely."

"Even though it is," she said. "Only one chair? I guess you don't get a lot of company out here, do you?"

"No," he admitted, smiling. "That's okay with me."

Daisy pictured Jesse sitting in this same rocking chair, alone each evening, after he had finished caring for the animals. If he only had one chair, maybe he didn't want any company. She crossed her legs under her and pulled the blanket around her knees. Sensing that he preferred quiet, Daisy opened her phone and scrolled through the notifications she had ignored a few minutes earlier. One message from Stella, offering an apology and repeating the offer to stay with her. Finally, Daisy returned to the article Stella had written. As she read through it again, she noticed that certain sentences were written in a different style from the rest. She suspected that the piece had been edited without her knowledge. It was some other reason, then, that kept Daisy from calling her back. The fact that she still felt a bond of friendship with Stella frightened her.

"Daisy, you've got to be hungry by now." Jesse closed the book and stood up.

"A little," she said. "The last meal I had was cake and champagne."

"Again," Jesse laughed. "Why am I still surprised?"

"Well, it was the most practical option," Daisy said. "After Stella left Bryson at the altar, there was quite a lot of leftover cake and champagne. Someone had to deal with that before it all went bad." She laughed. "Anyway, I'm starved."

"Dinner's almost done," he said. "Baked chicken, beans and rice. Nothing special."

Jesse disappeared into the kitchen, leaving Daisy alone.

He was right: the view from the rocking chair was soothing, the yellow-green of the meadow receding into the deeper hues of the forest, the layers of mountains blue and violet beyond. She could hear tree frogs, the whispering breeze in the grass, mourning doves calling. Daisy began to feel how someone could bask in this, let the melody of evening wash over what ailed you, until it seemed small by comparison. This was home.

This isn't why I came here, she thought, rubbing her eyes. *This is a siren song*. Dishes clattering in the kitchen, the smell of food, the mountain air. Jesse's smile when she woke. Things like this could make a person forget why they were there. But why was that? The fire. Everything that went wrong. Back then, Ellen and Tracker had outright silenced her. Going to school every day had felt like walking through a minefield, and Stella, the last person she'd trusted not to let her down, had always been somewhere else when she'd needed a friend. But, unexpectedly, Jesse had been there. He had never made her feel strange, or self-conscious. With him there, she was somehow less alone.

Until that one day. Then, she had been alone.

"I hope you're hungry." Jesse walked back outside, holding a plate in each hand, and handed one to her. "What's the matter?"

Daisy took the plate from him, fragrant roasted chicken next to rice and beans cooked with herbs. She sat on the floor next to him. "You really ought to get another chair, you know?"

"Right," he grinned. "One day, maybe I will."

Daisy hadn't eaten in hours. And suddenly, it seemed to have been much longer since she'd spoken with someone who was really listening to her. *Tempting. No, no. Stay focused*. "Jesse, you asked why I came to see you."

"Yes." He looked up from his plate, a fork in one hand. "I asked you, but don't we both know the answer?" Daisy nodded her chin, toying with her food.

She shifted, imagining her past as if she were far from it, as if she were researching an article. "That whole year, nobody believed what I saw. The dead girl. Why did you believe me?"

"Why did I?" Jesse set his plate aside and rested his chin on his fist. "I think the better question is, why didn't everybody else? We know the answer, of course—they all had something to lose. Even

Stella. She didn't want to lose her friends. Believing you would have meant everybody else had to change their life, in some way."

As Daisy listened, she sensed that he had rehearsed this answer many times over, that it was something he had thought about at length.

"But you didn't stand to gain anything by lying about it. And you certainly could have made things easier for yourself by going back on what you said you saw. But you didn't."

"No."

"You were brave."

"I guess I was, back then." Maybe that was one thing the old Daisy had going for her. She could have used some of that right now. "I don't even know where all of that went. I have my life together now—or, I thought I did."

He ate quietly, waiting for her to speak. He was too polite to bring it up, how he and all of his friends at Stella's wedding had overheard her argument with Anderson, that she'd lost a baby.

"After I left, I put myself through school," she said. "I worked really hard. I'm good at my job. I thought I had a good life. Now, nothing makes sense."

"You're still brave," he said. "You're still here, in town."

"I don't know if I'd call it that," Daisy said. "This place has something over me. If they sell the plant, nobody will ever know what really happened." She shrugged her shoulders. "I couldn't stay away, Jesse. The truth is, sometimes I don't even know if I believe what I saw."

"Why's that?"

"It's not that implausible," she said, "that I could have halluci-nated it. Is it? In all that smoke? Or—or passed out, and dreamed it? Who can say?" Even then, as she spoke of it, Daisy could see the girl, the features so similar to her own.

"Come on, that's not you talking." Jesse leaned forward, shaking his head. "You gave up so much to stand by what you saw. You're tough."

Daisy took another mouthful of rice, then pushed the plate aside. The memory of the fire, that smoke and its awful smell, was still enough to kill her appetite. The clouds above drifted, casting a golden-orange sunset light over the porch. How was it possible, Daisy wondered, that after all this time, he could be real, be right here, just inches from her? She sighed, let her arm brush against his, then propped her chin on his shoulder.

"This is silly, isn't it?" she sighed.

Daisy reached up to touch his hair: dark, almost black, a few threads of gray at his temple. She let her hand slip to caress his cheek, then brought him close, pressed her lips to his.

"There," she whispered. "I never got to kiss you goodbye."

"Even if I'd doubted you," Jesse said, "I cared about you, Daisy. You could have told me you had wings, and I would have believed you."

"This doesn't seem real," she said. "That we could be here, after all the times I wondered."

"Wondered how you were," he added. "Or where."

When she remembered, the moment seemed to break into pieces in the air, to fall around their feet. Daisy stood up, walked sharply down the steps.

"Where was I, Jesse? How about where were *you*?" She pressed her hands together, felt the sting of broken glass on her palms, though they were long healed. "I was alone. You never showed up."

CHAPTER FORTY-ONE
Before

While Daisy waited for Jesse to make arrangements for her to live with his friends, which took longer than she had expected, she was on a knife's edge, hoping for one plan to work out before the other.

One night when she noticed Ellen secretively packing a suitcase, Daisy was on alert. She placed a few items into a small bag: her driver's license, a few dollars. She didn't have anything of value, and looking through her room, she didn't see much that she thought would be any comfort to her.

Close to two in the morning, Daisy heard footsteps down the stairs, the gentle patter of Ellen's slippers, then saw her pale hand sweeping the curtain aside.

"I know you're awake, Daisy. Get out of bed." Her voice always took on this soft, removed tone when she was truly beyond changing her mind. "We're leaving in an hour."

No, Daisy thought. *Not now*. "Leaving for where?"

"You know."

"No, Mom, you said it wasn't until the end of the month."

"One hour."

Despite her anger, Daisy found herself unexpectedly calm, ready to act. She did not answer her mother, but stood up and pulled a suitcase from beneath her bed.

"Don't bother packing," Ellen said. "You're not going to be allowed to bring anything in with you."

"Then what do you want me to do?"

"Comb your hair and wash your face. Get something to eat. It's a long drive."

"Mom—" Daisy trailed off. She saw that she had Ellen's attention only for a moment, that her mother was distant from whatever discomfort the situation might offer. "Why?"

"Daisy, it's for your own good. Your father and I can't control you anymore."

"But I'm not even doing anything," Daisy said. "I'm not a criminal. I'm not in any kind of trouble. I…"

"Because," Ellen finally snapped. "Because Stella told me about your plans to run away."

"Stella?"

Shocked into silence, Daisy looked down at the scratch on her finger, still healing from a few days ago. *Blood sisters, my ass*, she thought.

*

The Chevrolet sedan, at eight years old, was the Ritter family's newest and most reliable vehicle, and the one of choice for the drive to the boarding school. Driving at nighttime lulled her already strange mood into silence, a calm settling over her nerves, perhaps the calm of paralysis, of the knowledge that she was stuck. The rural landscape seemed to become more alien as they went further south, and though it was autumn, warmer. Ghostly Spanish moss hung from trees either side of the interstate, and the bugs were larger with each county line they crossed, as if they thrived on the humidity and heat, their wet, crunchy bodies smacking against the windshield.

Tracker drove quickly, and because the registration on the Chevy was expired, he stayed off the interstate highways, using a combination of maps and what he called 'sense of direction' to keep moving south. Using the printer at the church office, Ellen had quietly printed directions from Mapquest.com, to which she referred silently, almost angrily, without ever insisting that Tracker actually use them. Daisy rolled up the sleeves of her t-shirt and leaned across the back seat, intermittently checking her phone and staring idly out the window. Time almost seemed not to pass at all. Daisy tried to think about nothing, even though it meant pretending that she was alone, that her parents weren't sitting two feet away, Ellen with her inscrutable but unhappy silence, Tracker's quiet chaos occasionally bubbling over into a curse word at a missed turn or another driver.

After sunrise, when the morning had turned yellow and charming, the roads narrowed, in the way that roads do when you're getting closer to where you're going. No small dirt road, leading to a smaller, graveled road, leads to anywhere but the end of somebody's trip. Daisy was drowsy from lack of sleep, from the hum of the engine against the roads. When the car passed a hand-painted sign that read 'Blessed Savior School for Girls', her eyes opened wide, and she had never been more awake. There was nothing else at the end of this road. Just as she had seen in the brochure, the border was marked by a tall fence, the entryway a locking metal gate that stood near two tall trees.

"This is a prison," she whispered, hoping her parents could hear the anger imbued in each word. Unsatisfied with their lack of response, she repeated: "This place is a damn prison. It's not a school. Shame on both of you. I don't deserve this."

"She's not going to be happy," Ellen whispered. "But God knows this is the only thing left we can do."

"She'll survive," Tracker grunted, using a tone of voice that very much suggested he didn't care whether Daisy did or didn't.

Daisy felt a dull shock of surprise, then realized there was little enough reason for it. This explained everything. She couldn't even find it in her tired limbs to fight, or to feel angry. There was nowhere to go, nobody to call.

"Do I even get to take my clothes?"

Tracker's silence was careless, but she felt shame in Ellen's lack of response.

She was processed in like an inmate. The three-story brick building was surrounded by a tall fence, flanked in the back by another gray building dotted with small windows. When Daisy was allowed a few minutes alone with her parents, she looked right through her father. He had made it clear enough how he felt.

Daisy stood up as tall as she could and stared Ellen coldly in the eyes. "This is wrong."

Ellen tried to embrace her and began to recite. "*Children, obey your parents in the Lord, for this is right. Honor thy...*"

"Ephesians," Daisy whispered. She felt a shadow pass over her, wondered why she even remembered that phrase, when she made so much effort not to soak up any of Ellen's Bible enthusiasm. "I don't love you anymore," she said.

"I've done my best," Ellen said. "All your life, I've done the best I could to take care of you, and now I think this is the best I can do." Daisy understood distantly that Ellen was in crisis mode, that she had chosen flight over fight and was only inhabiting her body out of necessity, but she found she felt no pity for her, not as she usually did, not even when she imagined Ellen grieving her lost pregnancies. "You're in over your head with this boy. Don't think I don't know what you're up to. You're unbalanced and ungodly. This is the right place for you."

"With dropouts? And criminals? And teen mothers?" Daisy's protests were meaningless. She pictured Stella, who was surely, by now, arriving at school, looking forward to her last months at home before she prepared to leave for university.

"I'll see you at Christmas."

Daisy dodged her mother's embrace. "I don't think you will."

Ellen retreated into silence. Daisy returned it, turning to face the gray wall until the woman from the desk came back to take her away. As she did, she looked at the partly healed score mark on her finger. Blood sisters. She felt her cheeks burn with muted shame. She had worried so much that someone was going to betray her. That Jesse would. She could have believed that Jesse would turn on her. But never Stella.

CHAPTER FORTY-TWO

Before

As Daisy was checked in, she saw that she would have to use her wits to keep the belongings she had brought with her. She was asked to undress, give up any personal items, and then change into the school uniform, a plain gray dress. When nobody was looking, she pulled two hairpins from her hair. Long and curly, it took more than several pins to contain it in any fashion, especially in this kind of warmth. She had worn it in a long, messy braid, which she now pulled up and wrapped into a large bun. Its volume was sufficient to conceal the driver's license and the twenty dollars she'd brought, which she slid into a bobby pin pushed through her hair.

Although Daisy had known that places like this existed, unregulated Christian private schools, usually of the reformatory variety, what she could not have imagined was the boredom. She was more grateful, when they came, for the moments of being shouted at, singled out for not knowing a prayer or a hymn, for the small disruption in the endless boredom. Students received the same letter grades she was familiar with, though she would be graded in categories of behavior and spiritual development, rather than anything that resembled a familiar class subject. For once, Daisy thought longingly of algebra.

After dinner, the girls retired to the dormitory, where they were split into bedrooms that held six bunk beds apiece. Daisy's bed was on the bottom bunk, in the corner. When the lights went out at night, the room was perfectly dark. As she tossed in her bed on the first night there, she heard the scratch of a lighter and saw a face illuminated in the air across from her.

"Hey," a voice whispered. Daisy's heart began to race, imagining all things in the pitch black around her. "I saw you in class this morning. I'm Sammy."

Sammy was friendly, with short-cropped hair, which she had to conceal under a cap until it grew out. She had kept it cut short, she explained, before her parents sent her in because she asked another girl to prom. "Just follow the rules and try not to attract any attention," Sammy said. "And if you see me during the day when we're in school, remember to call me my full name." She rolled her eyes and added: "*Samantha*."

And Daisy hadn't intended to attract any attention. But on the third day there, she had her hands hit with a ruler for singing in the bathroom. It was easy, Daisy thought, even when it hurt, and when she began to flinch, she imagined her mother, who was so practiced at removing herself from discomfort. How badly might it have hurt Ellen to leave her here? From her composure, Daisy had no way of knowing. After that incident, the teachers seemed to regard her as a troublemaker. On the fifth day, having forgotten the words to a prayer, she was instructed to kneel and pray for several hours on the cement floor in the solitary room. This was harder, she found, when her own resolve began to fail, her legs burning with exhaustion. Daisy told herself that she was strong, and she could tough her way through it just like she had with the ruler. But, finally, she fell asleep in a heap on the floor. Her punishment for this was to be assigned to a solitary dorm room. Without even a stranger to whisper to in the dark, a reminder that there was a world outside here, the boring hours began to feel as though they could stretch into infinity.

Two more days passed before she found a chance to use a phone unattended, and took it without question. A hall monitor left her door unlocked and she walked straight out, down the darkened hallway, and found the only-for-emergencies landline on the wall by the main door. She dialed Jesse's number from memory. She didn't know the time, only that it was late.

"Hello?"

"Jesse," she whispered. "I didn't think you'd answer."

"Daisy, what happened?"

"Stella told my parents everything. I can't talk long," she said.

"Tell me where you are."

"What do you mean?"

"I said I would help you, Daisy. I meant it."

At this, her eyes began to water. She forced it back, squeezing her lips together tight and breathing in through her nose. She had to stay alert.

"I'll come pick you up. You can sneak out. Mom's going to be out of town on the nineteenth," he said. "That's in ten days."

"That's my birthday."

"How do I get there?"

Daisy heard footsteps at the opposite end of the corridor. She whispered the name of the school, the highway, told him about the lone entrance, the gate by the tall trees.

"I'll be there," he said. "I promise."

As Daisy heard the footsteps of the hall matron returning, she hung up the phone slowly and silently, crouching in the dark. After the footsteps had passed by, she snuck back to the door of her room and crept in. Once safe in her bed, she closed her eyes and tried to sleep, found that she wept beyond her control.

But she had only a few days to pass before her escape. She told herself it should have been easy, holding her breath for ten days. An end was in sight. She only had to believe it was coming. Soon, she would be living with Jesse's friends, able to see him on weekends, to live somewhere she felt safe, away from her family and whatever buried secrets they had. And soon after that, Jesse would leave home for college, and they could live together, be together. On her birthday, she would be eighteen, in just ten days, old enough to legally and freely live away from her parents. Away from this place.

With her escape growing nearer, the days that followed passed with a kind of grace. As it turned out, having one person in the world that she could trust made enough difference. She could feel that it wasn't much, that it somehow put an unnatural pressure on whatever bond was between them, but it was enough to survive. There was one person who trusted her, who believed her, whose existence reminded her that she wasn't crazy, that she was able to trust herself.

Daisy gave absolutely no thought to where they would go. He needed to go back home; she knew that. He needed to finish school and go to college. His life was different. She could hide somewhere nearby, as long as she wasn't somewhere her mother and father could find her. She could stay near Jesse, or find a way to pass the next few months until he moved for college. The only thing she knew for sure was Jesse.

On the morning of her eighteenth birthday, Daisy didn't bother waiting, or trying to make a delicate escape. Doing so would only have wasted time. Unable to sleep, she got out of bed and dressed before dawn, while the sky was still dark. She didn't try to unlock her window. Instead, she looked to the cheaply made metal bedframe. It was bolted to the wall, as if some former inhabitant had used it to blockade the door. Who would want to block themselves in, in a place like this?

Daisy made quick work of loosening the screws, using the edge of a hairpin, and soon removed a length of metal tubing from the foot of the bed. She took a deep breath and hit the window as hard as she could. The glass cracked but did not shatter. Daisy took off her shoe and beat the rest of the shards loose. She had no option but to move quickly now, no time to think about her palms and the bits of glass as she pulled herself over the window frame, or the not-quite-right twinge in her legs as she dropped to the ground and started running.

No alarm sounded, and if anyone heard the glass break, she would already be at the gate before they began to look for her. Daisy remembered as she ran, bracing through the pain in one ankle, that she had used to steal her father's beers not because she liked them, but for the joy of stealing them, before she began to enjoy the feeling of being drunk. There was a part of her, too, that enjoyed the act of escape for its own sake, and she wondered if this might lead to freedom, if she might come to enjoy that one day as well.

She raced through the field, taking a circuitous path to the end of the long gravel drive. She climbed up a tree, low-hanging branches decked with ghostly Spanish moss, and, finding a good vantage point, settled in to wait.

Even the hours that passed didn't trouble her: not the way her limbs grew numb, forcing her to painstakingly shift without moving the branches. Not the occasional watch that came down the drive, the car that she assumed was sent out looking for her. As the sun rose, the cool of the night settled into a pleasant warmth, then a building heat that ignited the thrill in her limbs. Daisy found that she was shivering, and refused to look at her stinging hands or to focus any energy on her sore ankle.

Later in the morning, she saw one of the matrons come out in a car and meet a police cruiser. Another car showed up, and soon there were ten people, walking in evenly spaced rows across the fenced ground. She knew that if they brought dogs, she was finished. She watched the cars, waiting for a dog to spring out, for one of the hall matrons to offer a piece of her clothing, stolen from her bed, as scent. Daisy might have prayed then, for the first time in her life, keeping perfectly still, holding her breath, wishing for any ounce of the good luck that had eluded her for her entire life. But no search dogs appeared. Half an hour passed before the officers left and the school officials went back inside.

Finally, she let herself feel the excitement: of seeing Jesse, of escaping into the open, of the beginning of her freedom. Soon, the sun was bright and hot overhead, the shadow of the old tree directly below her feet. For the first time she allowed her imagination to explore what she might do, how she might live, who she would become. Finally, in spite of the fire that had left her life in ashes, the world brimmed with possibilities.

CHAPTER FORTY-THREE

Before

It was noon before Daisy realized she couldn't wait any more. Jesse was not coming. She knew every hour that she waited was tempting her luck.

She knew that she needed to get distance between her and the school, and quickly. Around here, in this dress, she would be instantly identified as a runaway. She tried and failed to remember the route her father had taken when they dropped her off. A month of the same walls, the same hallways and windows, seemed to have washed her sense of direction clean with numbness. She remembered only the roads growing narrower and narrower, and tried to visualize them in reverse, the gravel path giving way to something with pavement, then something with lanes, vehicles, that would lead to civilization. But she had no way to tell time, other than the gray morning merging into midday, lighting up all the anxious nerves beneath her skin.

If any locals around here so much as spotted her, they would likely call the police; for this reason, she followed parallel to the road, but stayed far enough from it to duck when she heard a vehicle approach. But straying too far into the wilderness was another gamble. From the looks of it, there might not be a place to eat or sleep for a week. As Daisy made this calculation, she realized the immediacy of her predicament: she was already, right now, without a place to eat, sleep, bathe. Once again, it was the kind of game where she might see one good chance, and if she did, could not afford to miss it. She promised herself that she would starve before she returned to that place. Let everyone else think she had succeeded in running away; let it make no difference to them. Either way, to this place, she was dead and gone.

That chance came at some point during the afternoon, the sun slow on its long climb downward. Where the gravel road joined a road with pavement, Daisy saw a delivery truck approaching. She hung back at first; a local truck, if it were one of the companies that brought the bottled water or food service to the school, or the postman, would have known her for a runaway. But the truck was colored with a brand name she didn't know, taking up most of the two-lane road. Heart pounding, though she felt she had no other choice, she stood up as tall as she could, got as close to the road as she was able, and waved one hand. She hoped that smiling would make her look friendly, but also serious, not too friendly. Getting into a truck with a stranger was the last thing she wanted to do, next to wandering this area on foot for days on end.

The truck pulled over, slowed to a stop. She climbed into the seat.

"Where you headed, miss?"

"I—" Daisy paused, kept her fingers wrapped tight on the door handle. "I'm not sure. Away from here."

"What's your name?"

"Stella."

The man smiled as he drove without facing her, clicked his tongue. "No offense, but you don't look like a Stella."

"I—"

"Listen," he said. "I have children at home. I can tell you're in a bad spot. Getting in a car with someone you don't know should always be your last option."

"It is," Daisy admitted.

The man asked a polite question every few miles: where was she from? Where was she hoping to be eventually?

"And there's nobody," he asked, "absolutely nobody that you can call?" Sitting down, feeling the cool air from the vents, Daisy realized that she was tired. Too tired to lie.

"No." Daisy looked straight out the windshield, unashamedly wiping tears from her eyes. "There was one person I thought I could call no matter what, but it turns out that wasn't true."

CHAPTER FORTY-FOUR

Before

Though she barely took a breath through the whole drive, Daisy never felt that her safety was threatened. The truck driver let her out at the first stop off the highway. Daisy, who had been expecting all the worst possible things from the situation, almost began to cry. She had to choose carefully, though, when it came to spending. The large truck stop had clothing—that she knew she needed—also pay-per-use shower stalls, which she would have liked, but chose against. She wanted a beer, but with no identification, she would have had to steal one, but also with no bag, she had to make another choice. After some deliberation, she purchased a touristy-looking t-shirt dress, a flimsy plastic purse, and a jar of peanut butter and crackers, as well as a bottle of water. The water, she reasoned, could be refilled, and the peanut butter was the most calories for the amount she could afford.

Daisy changed in a bathroom, stuffing the sweaty gray dress and stockings into a wastebasket, and splashing cold tap water over her frizzy hair and neck. After weeks away from her home, her own clothes and makeup, Daisy expected some change in her reflection, but found with a sense of disappointment the same face staring back at her. The same girl. If anything, she looked distilled, more herself than before. She counted the leftover money into a zippered pocket in the purse: six dollars and some change. As she put the peanut butter into the purse, it occurred to her that the nights might begin to get chilly, that she might have found some useful reason to keep the gray dress, that she didn't know where she was going to sleep. Still, the symbolic weight of leaving it in the garbage gave her too much relief to consider fishing it back out.

She sat at a plastic-topped, sticky table in the dining area, which smelled of old fried food and cigarette smoke. Unless she was able to sneak onto a truck somehow, this would be her last stop. She considered approaching someone else for help, but she had a sense she'd used up all her luck on the first driver who'd picked her up. She unfolded a napkin from a wobbly metal dispenser and began to eat the crackers and peanut butter.

Suddenly, she spotted a payphone in the corner of the dining area. The shifting clouds outside revealed a sunbeam as the bell on the door jingled. She remembered Stella, leaning near to her, the blood from their wrists tracing together, and how she had said, *I always believe you first. You can always tell me first.* Daisy began to count the change in her pocket. Stella would know what to do. She might even be able to help. But then Ellen's voice phoned in: *It was Stella who told us you were planning to run away.* Even if Jesse had to fail her, she always half expected that from a boy. He could never have truly disappointed her—not like this. She was cold, all by herself, with nowhere to sleep. She even wondered if she should try to phone the school, see if they would take her back in. Maybe there really was nowhere for her to go. Not alone.

Trying to eat felt ridiculous. Daisy sat the half-eaten cracker on the table and turned toward the window. She was already enough of a spectacle here, a girl, all by herself, and she didn't want anyone to see her crying. She reached for a napkin, but found the dispenser was empty. *This is how kids end up homeless. Without anywhere to go. This is my fault. If I died right now, nobody would notice I was gone.*

Reflected light danced as the door swung open. Daisy raised her head, hoping against hope Jesse would walk in, but he did not.

"Hey." The man in the booth behind hers, who had been sitting with his back to her, folded his elbow over the shared seat back and turned around with a conversational eye. "You okay?"

"Yes," she answered, folding her arms in a pathetic attempt to be assertive.

"My name's Anderson. What's yours?"

She glanced over him with suspicion and found that he looked young, interested, not unkind. Still, it didn't seem safe to get acquainted with anyone. Not that Daisy had a better move planned. Her voice scraped in her throat when she tried to talk. "Thanks for asking, but I'm fine."

She braced for whatever comment or, inevitably, question might follow. Had he noticed that she'd changed into a new dress? Was she found out? But he turned back to his table and sat in silence. Daisy sniffed and blinked back tears. The young man turned around and placed the napkin dispenser from his table in front of her. She looked up gratefully, then used napkins to dab first at her eyes, then at the cuts on her hands, which had begun to ooze again. Daisy threw a furtive, wordless glance back at Anderson. He left his table, walked outside. Through the smudged windows, she saw him light a cigarette, the smoke drifting in the air around him.

She could call home. Call collect, maybe, and hope they answered. Stella and Jesse had made it plenty clear they couldn't be relied on. Daisy knew if she went back to the boarding school, she'd be punished: in a solitary room for weeks, or worse. She was weighing that option against this one, of being here with nowhere else to go, when a pair of scuffed tennis shoes came into her line of sight. She looked up to see a pudgy man wearing a collared uniform shirt. A plastic nametag on his chest read 'NATE: Shift Manager'.

"Hey, Goldilocks. You can't work in here." He spoke with a Southern accent and the brusque delivery of a statement repeated once too many times. "God damn, if I had a nickel for every time I've said this."

"What? I'm not *working.*"

"I don't care what goes on out there, but our rule is, if I can see you from the counter, you're too close. Get out back, in the truck parking lot. Or wherever."

"Oh—okay." She spoke hurriedly, praying to escape notice. "I'll go."

"Now, missy." Nate shuffled her to the door, one hand on her shoulder. She could see her reflection in the backlit window, a shadow stumbling past. On the other side of the glass, the man from the other table—*was it Andrew?* she thought. *No, Anderson.* He was putting out his cigarette, checking the time on his watch. "Don't let me see you in here again." Nate held the door open and waited for Daisy to exit. "Damn lizards." Daisy hesitated.

"Hey, there you are." Anderson threw an arm around her. "I've been looking all over for you, Jane. I came as soon as I got your message."

Daisy lifted her eyes to meet his. He was playing a game, but the smile they shared was genuine.

"How long have you been here?" he asked. "I hope not long. Car trouble?"

"Ages," she said. "I was on the highway, and the engine kept overheating. It's parked over there."

Nate stammered a half-assed apology. "Misunderstanding. A place like this, we see a lot of… you know."

Anderson stood in between her and the shift manager. "Say one more word to her, and I'll get you fired for harassing her." Nate rolled his eyes, gave an exaggerated sigh, and walked back inside. Anderson loosened his hug, gave her some distance.

Outside, the sparse yellow lights permeated the hazy air, a smattering of moths batting themselves at the door. Beyond that, only dark, and the low, almost orchestral drone of the highway in the distance.

"You shouldn't stay here," he said, lighting another cigarette. "Damn, I need to quit smoking."

Anderson offered Daisy a smoke. Her hand wavered. Why not? She'd never cared much for it before, but maybe it would calm her nerves. No, she decided. She didn't want to accept another favor.

"You don't have to tell me anything," Anderson said. "But you shouldn't hang out here."

Daisy refused to speak, blinking at tears.

"You're far from home, aren't you?"

"No."

Though it was an obvious lie, Anderson nodded his acceptance of her response. He had chestnut-brown hair, eyes that could have been blue or green. He was older than her, but, she thought, glancing at his reflection, not by that much.

"I'm on my way back to New Mexico," he said, letting his low, easygoing voice fill the tense silence. "I was visiting my family in Florida, but my flight got rescheduled, so now I have to drive to Baltimore, catch another plane there." He laughed, and when he tilted his head, the streetlights made his hair shine almost golden. "The highways out here are spooky if you're driving alone. And boring, too. I'll be glad to get back home."

"What's it like there?"

"The air's not as heavy."

"My name's Daisy." She was trying to remember her manners when she offered to shake his hand.

"What happened to your hands?"

In the rush of adrenaline, Daisy had forgotten. She looked down at her palms with dismay, felt her knees grow weak. "I don't have anywhere to go," she whispered. "And I've hardly got anything to go back to."

"Okay, Daisy."

"It doesn't seem okay from here."

"Well, look. When my flights got rescheduled, the airline gave me some hotel vouchers. I'll get you your own room, something to eat. Nobody can think on an empty stomach."

"You would do that?" she asked. "For someone you don't even know?"

"Didn't you ever feel like the world put you somewhere, in a certain place and time, for a reason?"

Anderson unlocked his car and opened the passenger side door. Although he seemed kind, Daisy hung back. But wasn't he, too, taking a risk, inviting strangers into his car?

"You've got the strangest look about you," he said. "Like you don't belong here. If I turned around for a moment, I'm pretty sure you'd disappear."

"A ghost." The image of the dead girl rose again to Daisy's thoughts.

"I hope not." He smiled, started the engine.

She leaned back against the headrest, let herself breathe out slowly, then in again. The car smelled clean. For the first time in weeks, she felt a comparative sense of calm, of no longer being exposed. She hesitated to even think the word 'safe', but it was better than being at the side of the road, or alone in a truck stop, or locked up in a prison masquerading as a school. She let herself cry quietly without trying to hide it.

"Thank you," she whispered.

CHAPTER FORTY-FIVE

Now

"Daisy?" Jesse caught up with her, reaching for her arm as she stormed away. She took half a step backward, but found her hands reaching for him, resting on either shoulder.

"I waited for you for hours." Her lips pursed, as if they would hold all her words back, but continued to tremble. "All by myself, in the middle of nowhere. Why weren't you there?"

Short of breath, she paused, looking out at the trees, the blue sparks of fireflies that dotted between them. "How can you act like you cared about me? You left me alone."

"I know." Even now, he had a calm that radiated from his smallest movement, his quietest breath, that came from some kind of confidence in himself she couldn't touch. It made the animals like him, animals and children. "I deserve it. Go ahead."

"I trusted you. You said you'd be there." Daisy felt her anger deflating, the tension in her limbs melting into tears. The feeling of being alone and exposed was still there, just below the surface, same as it had been all those years earlier.

"Daisy, you don't get it. I was there. I waited for you all night."

"What?" Daisy remembered the cuts on her palms, the twisted ankle, the static that had settled in her limbs from hiding up that tree for hours. "What is that supposed to mean?"

"You said there was only one driveway in, and one out. Well—"

"Oh, no." She closed her eyes and began to shake her head.

"There were two," Jesse continued. "I snuck away for the weekend, drove out there. I waited all night. Into the next morning, until the cops started showing up. Daisy, I was there. I couldn't find you. I had to drive back by myself. I had flowers and a card for your birthday."

"You did?"

"After what we went through? You really thought I would just leave you?"

Daisy's eyes stung with shame. "I didn't know what else to think." She felt a wave of exhaustion, physical or otherwise, sink over her body. "I didn't have anything to make me think otherwise."

"I loved you, Daisy." He spoke the words quietly, but with determination, as if he were still hurt she didn't believe him.

"Well, I…" She began to say it, but the words were lost. The whisper of the ghosts seemed to call from the trees, pulling on some thread attached to her very ribs, pulling her close to him. "I loved you, too, Jesse," she said.

She didn't know which one of them moved first, or if the cool breeze off the forest just pushed them together, pulled her hands around his shoulders, twined his fingers in her tangled hair. His lips brushed hers, hesitated, then he brought her closer. There was something different here, someone more self-confident. Daisy wondered if she had gained anything of the same, but quickly forgot her thoughts, her breaths lifting her closer to him as they kissed. This was how they had always been, even if he was different: how she fell into him, how he softened when he held her, her hands tracing over the firmness of his shoulders, slim but strong.

"Wait." She pulled away, drew a breath, and wrapped her arms tight around him, squeezing herself against his shoulders.

"Sorry," he whispered.

"Don't be. It was both of us."

"I'm sorry I wasn't there," he said. "I'm sorry I didn't find you."

She smiled at him without trying to conceal her nostalgia, the hint of sadness. "You were really there?"

"Probably not even a mile from you." Jesse stared out at the sunset, laid his arm over her shoulders. "Maybe even close enough to hear if you'd called me."

"Yeah?" she whispered, covering her eyes. "Well, I wish I had. Who knows how different things could have been?"

Her hand found his, the other arm wrapping him close to her. It was the same as it had always been: she wanted to stay close, to stay next to him. To feel like she could go anywhere she wanted, drive away to somewhere new, somewhere they could lay together forever. The little sounds of the forest swelled nearby: crickets, bullfrogs, evening birdsong, a distant screech owl. Daisy pressed her face against Jesse's chest, wishing that her legs could grow roots, solidify her life here in this moment. The haunting face of the girl in the forest startled her in the dark and she lifted her head, eyes snapping open. Her daydreams weren't safe, either.

"Kiss me," she whispered.

*

Daisy woke up in the witching time of night, the crossing point that can be both late and early. Jesse slept soundly, chin tucked down, his left arm stretched beneath his head. She heard an echo in her mind of the old songs they used to listen to, about love buried and preserved. Maybe being dead was to finally give up worrying about things. Maybe she could do that, she thought, for at least a couple more hours. She exhaled softly and slipped under his arm, stretched her legs out next to his, and closed her eyes.

When she woke again, morning had dawned. Jesse was awake. He whispered a greeting and pulled her against his chest. She rested there, still half sleepy, blinking her eyes.

"It's nice waking up here," Daisy said.

"Nice having you here."

Daisy stretched and yawned, listening to him breathe as he laced his fingers in her hair. In the quiet minutes that followed, she wondered what it might have been like if they had never been separated. Odds were good that they would have split up in a youthful argument. Most young couples did. *But maybe*, she thought, *maybe not*. When she heard cars passing by on the road outside, she began to remember the outside world, the rest of the things she needed to worry about.

She lifted her chin, letting her lips brush against his in a lazy kiss. "We were really in love, weren't we? It wasn't just about the fire, was it?"

"No," he said. "It was more than that."

"Are you sure?"

Jesse leaned away, reached into the top drawer of the nightstand by the bed. He returned to her side, one arm wrapped around her back. In his hand, he held a tarnished penny, years old, flattened on the rails of a train track. "Do you remember this?"

"I remember."

"That was the day I knew I liked you," he said. "Today, it feels almost like you were never gone," he said. "Do you ever wonder?"

She traced his hand, touched the penny. "I can't help wondering."

Yet she had been gone, for nearly half her life. For seventeen years now, she'd loved someone else. Could she allow Jesse back into her thoughts without letting the past pull her too deep into its orbit, swallow her whole? And what if she were to stay here? Daisy wondered. Would that mean leaving the last half of her life on the other side of the country, and with it, another set of what ifs? What if she and Anderson had never decided to go to Stella's wedding? What if she had decided to try to forgive him? Unbidden, another what if rose to the surface: what if she hadn't lost the baby? How might that have changed things? Daisy pictured the spare bedroom at her house with Anderson. She closed her eyes and saw the half-done paint job finished, the furniture they'd ordered assembled and arranged: the crib with the farm animal mobile hanging above it, the rocking chair. And the version of herself who sat smiling in the chair, swaying gently back and forth, holding a baby. Could that have been real?

"What's wrong?"

Daisy sat up on her elbows. She looked back to Jesse with a faint smile, drew close to kiss him again. "Jesse, you're the only thing that's not wrong with me right now." With a long sigh, she pulled herself away and got out of the bed.

"That was a dumb question," Jesse said.

"What do you mean?" She paused, then turned away. "Of course. I keep forgetting you overheard."

Daisy found her shirt at the foot of the bed, tugged it over her head. "I was hoping you wouldn't mention it." She could feel him watching her, looked away to preserve the distance between them.

"I'm sorry," he said.

"I'm fine," she said, catching the defensive note in her voice a moment too late. The ever-present impulse to keep moving wrestled with the quiet morning light, the way it made his eyes shine. If she stared at him too long, she could have forgotten how she'd come here, how she needed to leave.

Jesse sat up in bed, stretched his arms out in front of him. "You're stronger than you think, okay? It's been a long time, but that's still true."

Her eyes flashed a quiet warning. "If you knew me better, you might not say that. Have you seen my jeans?"

"Yeah, over here." He leaned down to pick them up from the floor by the side of the bed. "Catch?"

"Thanks." She caught them, smiling, and finished getting dressed.

"Are you going to stay in town?"

"Honestly? I'm not sure."

"Think about it, Daisy. Call me if you do."

As she moved toward the door, Daisy turned, hurried back, and gave him a last kiss. "Goodbye, Jesse."

CHAPTER FORTY-SIX

Now

Morning air swept through the open windows of the borrowed car. Daisy watched Jesse's house recede in the rearview mirror. She touched a hand to her hair, remembered his fingers tangled there. *What am I doing? This is reckless. You can't jump back in time, pick out the pieces of the past you like, leave the rest behind. Or can you?*

No, she thought. *Not possible.* With each day, she could feel past versions of herself materializing, recognizing and claiming bits of the person she'd become. She was still someone who could laugh at Stella's jokes, get lost in Jesse's eyes. Despite the years that had passed, Daisy's mother still knew how to ease her aches and pains, even before she did herself. But the trouble with that was that *this* Daisy, the one she'd left here in Zion, was the one who got herself into trouble. Got herself lost beyond repair. But she needed this Daisy, too. Needed to remember how she'd navigated such a forest of questions and come out mostly in one piece. From here, Ellen's ability to move silently through her days, every few months burying another pregnancy, looked almost mythical.

And it was a good thing that it was Sunday morning. Daisy didn't have any stomach for talking to her father, and she knew Ellen would be at church. The t-shirt and jeans she'd been wearing for two days now wouldn't do, and all of the other clothes she'd packed were wrinkled in her suitcase. The nearest Wal-Mart obliged, where she bought a polka-dotted jersey dress with elbow-length sleeves, that hung almost to her calves. She added a gray hat and a pair of pink flats, then changed in the bathroom on her way out. The Tucker Swamp Baptist Church had always held their Sunday service at nine, and latecomers were called out.

Daisy sat in her borrowed car in the parking lot until she saw Ellen file in, murmuring greetings and hellos to acquaintances, though she had no close friends. She was a fixture, there for Jesus, not the community. When most of the crowd had already made their way into the church, but with just enough time before nine that she would not in fact be late, Daisy walked in. She kept her felt hat pulled low over her eyes and sat in one of the pews at the back. The hum of chatter, of music, of whispered voices, shuffling Bibles, and the preacher's voice like a dull bassline, always conspired to make her tired. Daisy hadn't attended church with Ellen since she was twelve, when she started her period. *You're a woman now*, Ellen said, with something like disappointment and worry and affection all at once. *There is no good without freedom of choice*. Daisy had, of course, made the wrong choice. Tracker had never attended church with them, which Ellen allowed, due to the stresses of his job, or perhaps because he didn't have a period to worry about.

Daisy nodded off and opened her eyes several times, at ease in the familiar location. Ellen had used to pinch her hand, or, on a kinder day, slip her a peppermint to help keep awake. Daisy didn't mind drifting off: she knew the organ music would wake her when it was time to leave. That was the overall design of the church, allowing for your neighbors to judge you but protecting you from the out-and-out embarrassment of sleeping through the service ending, unless you were so drunk you deserved it. When the service finally finished, Daisy sat up straight and refreshed. She slid to the end of the pew and lifted her head, making eye contact with Ellen as she walked down the aisle. Ellen looked almost to be in a trance, her lips still murmuring silently, her own mother's Bible held against her ribcage. Daisy could not have echoed a word of what the sermon was about, but Ellen seemed to have soaked in the stale, vaguely threatening atmosphere of the room entirely. Like the air before a thunderstorm, but where a thunderstorm never came.

"Mama." Daisy put her hand on Ellen's elbow as she walked past, seeing that she would easily go unnoticed. Ellen's eyes flashed down to meet hers. She tilted her chin, and Daisy saw her nostrils flare briefly. "Would you sit down?"

Ellen dropped onto the bench next to her. "What are you doing here?"

"I came to talk to you."

Ellen smelled like dried flowers as she hugged her daughter, of baby powder and slightly of acetone. "I know you aren't here for the Lord," she murmured, "but I hope you let it wash over you nonetheless."

"I just wanted to talk, I guess." Daisy breathed in Ellen's hazel stare, felt she was holding her in her gaze. "We didn't really get to catch up when I was there the other day. Can I buy you lunch?"

They agreed on a chain-owned diner that was relatively nearby, meaning it was halfway to the next almost-town, a yellow-and-cream plastic facade set over cement bricks just off the two-lane highway. Ellen ordered ice water with lemon and hot tea, as well as one over-easy egg from the à la carte menu.

"Mama," Daisy sighed. "I see you're still eating like a bird."

"You've probably noticed," Ellen answered, "it's more difficult to keep your figure as you get older."

Daisy raised an eyebrow and smirked. "Yeah, if having a figure means not having much of one. I, for one, think my hips are one of my best features." She ordered a bacon and cheese omelet, and home fries.

"Have you talked to him?" Ellen clasped her spider fingers around her ice water.

"Talked to who?" Daisy instantly thought of Jesse, probably awake by now, probably sitting with a cup of coffee in the rocking chair out back.

"Your—boyfriend, right? You told me you'd learned he had someone else."

"Oh."

In the pause that followed, the waitress returned with their food. While Ellen glanced upward in a silent prayer, Daisy stabbed a few bites of potato with her fork and ate.

"I haven't talked to him," she said. "He left a few messages at first, but nothing in the last day or so."

"You didn't answer?"

"No, Mama, I didn't," Daisy replied. "The truth is, I don't know what to believe. If he's lying, that's a problem. And if I accused him of lying, that's also bad. I don't know where to start." A sharp stab of guilt ran through Daisy at the thought that Anderson might be telling the truth.

"And why's that?"

"We've been together for a long time," Daisy said. "We've been through a lot. I was…"

She leaned over, lowered her voice as if it hurt to say it. "I was pregnant. Until a few months back."

"What happened?" Ellen's eyes creased at the corners, her mouth pursing in question. "Oh, Daisy."

In response, she held her hands up, shook her head. "It just happens, sometimes. I've been so focused on moving past it, maybe I didn't notice if he was acting different."

Daisy took a big bite of omelet, something to make herself stop talking. She was sure Ellen would point out that she was unmarried, that maybe it was for the best.

"The what ifs really stay with you." Ellen sipped her tea. "I guess you remember what I went through."

"I remember not talking about it." Daisy lifted her eyes from her food, studied her mother's reaction. This had always been the forbidden thing, to speak a problem aloud. "It always seemed like pointing out a problem meant that I was the problem."

"Being a parent doesn't mean you all of a sudden have understanding that you didn't before."

"What happened to us, after the fire? Dad was different after." Ellen opened her mouth, but Daisy interrupted, warning. "I know he was, and you can't just say it was trauma or whatever. He was different. All of us were."

"You could never forgive him, could you?" Ellen smiled. "You couldn't forgive him for being human."

"Why didn't we ever talk about it?"

"I don't think you understand men from his era."

"I think you forgive too much." Daisy laid her fork down on her plate.

"They taught us to put our husbands first. That the rest would follow."

Daisy picked up her orange juice then set it down again. She was too angry. If she wanted this conversation to get her anything, she needed a different angle. "I know you wanted more children," she said. The idea of the big family Ellen was supposed to have, when she was a child, had been a source of fear. She had prayed for a loud, happy house full of children. Daisy saw it on Ellen's face now, revisiting the miscarriages, year after year. "Did Dad?"

Ellen picked up the lemon wedge to squeeze it into her tea, dropping it into the now-lukewarm cup. As she fished in after it with bare fingers, she cursed, splashing tea over the saucer. "Of course he did, Daisy," she said. "What Christian man wouldn't?"

"But he never said anything about it," Daisy said. "Otherwise, why would you have talked to me about it?"

"It's a thing for women to know," she said. "Women bear the weight. Your father knew there were… deficiencies in me. That God didn't want us to have another. We know that now, at least." She looked toward the fluorescent light above her. "Thy will be done," she murmured.

"Do you think Dad was unhappy with us?"

"He had every right to be."

"Talking like that ruins my appetite, Mama. What did he ever do, that you felt so beholden to him?"

Ellen batted her eyelids, as if she thought that might not be such a bad thing. "You don't know where I came from. Before I met your father, I thought my life was a lost cause."

"He *is* a lost cause."

"He's a good man," Ellen answered. "You know, he's stopped drinking."

"That would have mattered to me fifteen years ago," Daisy spat.

"Leaving him would have meant walking away from my entire life. And for something like that…"

"Like that? What do you mean?"

Finally, Ellen looked clear into her eyes. "Is it so hard to understand?" she said, traces of shame showing in the little lines around her eyes and mouth. "Your father was engaged to another woman when I met him."

"What? I never knew that. What happened?" Daisy asked.

"It was so long ago, Daisy," Ellen sighed. "Years ago. Now, you may not have loved your upbringing, but that was the best I could provide for you. There have been worse childhoods."

"I know, Mama," Daisy answered, drawing the words out as she squeezed her mother's hand lightly. "I'm not here to make you feel bad. I want to talk about the girl."

Ellen stared into her tea.

"I'd tell you not to make the same mistake I did," she said. "That you should forget about your boyfriend. Even if it means starting over. But you never know what goes into people's choices. Where was I going to go? I was just happy to be able to be a mother. Your mother, Daisy. But at least *you* have a degree. And you don't have children. Daisy, God always knows what he's doing."

"You're onto something there," Daisy sighed. "It's good to be able to work. But when bad things happen, you know, it's never felt like God to me. Just—" She trembled a little, trying not to lose her composure. "Just messed-up humans and bad luck."

With her baby powder and dried flower fragrance, Ellen seemed almost doll-like. For her to have stayed with a man out of pure lack of choices somehow seemed less inconceivable now.

"Trust, Daisy," Ellen said. "You wouldn't have lost a baby he wanted you to keep."

Daisy pointedly ignored this sentiment, which didn't seem to remove any of the sting of loss. If that made it easier for Ellen to survive losing her pregnancies, then Daisy could stand to bite her tongue.

"You changed the subject. Mama, who was the girl in the fire?"

Ellen's face turned stony. "There wasn't a girl. Four men died. That's bad enough without you insisting on something you half dreamed."

Tracker had always, always pushed her to work there. Anywhere. Daisy remembered the feeling that her youth, her time, anything that could be classed as potential income, was subject to his greedy gaze. *Why have children?* she wondered. *So you can eat them?* It didn't matter. Whatever his tendencies were, Ellen was the one between them with half a brain, and Ellen was the one who had let it all happen.

"Mama, do you remember how bad he used to want me to work there?"

"He mentioned it a few times. I remember that."

"For a while, though," Daisy drew her voice out, trying to soften her thoughts like taffy. "For a while, he had his mind set on it. And then he stopped bringing it up." The thought occurred to her as suddenly as she saw the change come over Ellen's face. Tracker had found someone else. *What if he'd had another kid he put to work, too?*

"I don't remember that." Ellen had never looked so small, so protected in her mist of religion and denial. "And as for whatever you believe you saw in the fire, I think God sent you a vision of yourself to protect you, to set your path right."

"And would you say that it worked?"

"Would he get it wrong?" Ellen's face threatened to collapse again.

"But everything's falling apart." What did Ellen's God know about Daisy?

"Maybe you're still on your way."

"I don't know, Mama. Maybe you're right."

When they said goodbye, Daisy hugged Ellen, though she still felt angry, very angry, but there was no point unleashing it on Ellen, not here, not now. *Maybe the one thing you've never had is the thing you value above all else, even when it's wrong.* Ellen's very bones believed that stability, the predictability of her home was the best she could hope for, that it was worth any price she might have paid. Daisy sensed a tangle of strings, something she didn't need to bother unraveling, not now that she knew.

Wouldn't it be easier to buy a plane ticket and leave? Daisy walked to the car and started the ignition. She took out her phone and browsed for airfares, pictured herself getting off a plane, arriving at the house, leaving behind the tangled mess that was Zion. Anderson would be in his favorite seat on the couch, a forgotten cup of tea on the coffee table. *I'm ready to talk*, she would say. Or maybe she would walk in asking for his forgiveness for not trusting him. She would promise that she'd been more hung up on the past than she realized, that she was going to really put it away and move forward now. In her daydream, he leapt to his feet, couldn't wait to hold her: *Thank God you're home.* They were a team, just like they'd always been. Nothing could break that unless they allowed it to.

Daisy hesitated. The phone rang in her hand and Stella's number appeared on the screen. *Thank goodness*, Daisy thought, though she wasn't sure why. She answered straight away.

"Hey, Stella."

"It's me."

"I know."

A moment passed as Daisy wondered whether she should apologize, or whether she was waiting for Stella to do the same.

"Daisy, can you come by the house? Are you still in town?"

"Yes," Daisy said. "Yes, to both."

CHAPTER FORTY-SEVEN

Now

When Daisy arrived, Stella pulled the door open with one hand, throwing the other around her in an embrace. "I'm sorry," she said. "I acted like such an ass."

"I'm sorry, too," Daisy said. She stepped inside. Stella wore an oversized white button-up and black leggings, her gleaming hair in a neat ponytail. "It's so strange being back here, I couldn't see past what happened before. And I know the article wasn't your fault."

"I was afraid I'd never see you again," Stella said. "When you left the other day, where'd you go?"

Daisy sat heavily on the sofa and began to laugh. "You will not *believe* how I've spent the last two days."

"Go on," Stella said. "Do tell."

"Well, I—" Daisy opened her mouth to speak, eager to tell Stella the whole whirlwind: her visit to the chemical plant, the night in jail, spending the next night with Jesse. But instead, she found her eyes watering, words spilling out faster than she could keep track. "I talked to my mom. You know, we really talked. We never did much of that before."

"I remember."

"My father was engaged to someone else when he met my mother. I never knew that—had you ever heard anyone mention that before?" Daisy sniffed and Stella pushed a box of tissues toward her. "Thanks. She said—she thinks God wanted me to have a miscarriage. She said I wouldn't have lost a baby he wanted me to keep."

"Oh, Daisy, I didn't know you…"

"Well, shit." She laughed weakly. "Now you do. I'm healthy— I'm okay. It just sucks. And that's always her answer: God wants it to be that way. Ugh." Daisy blew her nose. "For some reason, it just doesn't help when something hurts you and people tell you that God has his reasons."

"Of course not."

"And I asked her again—who the girl was. What she knows."

"What'd she say?"

"Absolutely nothing." Daisy took a new tissue from the box and dabbed at her eyes. "Not a damn thing. I feel as though she knows more than she'll ever tell me."

"I'm sorry, Daisy."

"Thanks."

"Ellen has her own reasons." Stella turned to face Daisy and crossed her legs. "If she listens to you, she's open to another set of questions that she knows she can't answer."

"I guess."

"On that subject, you know, I talked to Bryson. He's canceling the trip and flying home early."

"That's good news, right?"

"He says he's spoken with the board of his real estate company. He's putting the land purchase on hold. Says we can have full access to whatever materials they got from Zion Chemical."

"Where are they?" Daisy asked. "How soon can we see them?"

"He'll be back tomorrow morning," Stella answered. "I think the offices are locked up while he's away. Sorry—I know you'd probably love to get going today."

"I'm not sure about that," Daisy said. "My last couple of days have been pretty full. If you don't have any other plans, maybe we could stay in and just talk."

Stella beamed. "I'd love that."

In the years since she had left home, Daisy had mostly given up on having good friends. Anderson was her one and only. She knew people: she had friends who were acquaintances, people she'd met in college, others she knew from work. But Anderson had been her best friend as well as her boyfriend. Nobody, not even a lover, could hurt her like a best friend could. She had learned that lesson, and didn't need a refresher.

But avoiding close friendships had also meant a kind of loneliness. Daisy had thought that she and Anderson added up to a perfect whole. With him, she always had a sense of holding up her end of the bargain, of doing her part to make their life work. Conversation with Stella was different; they were each whole on their own. Stella ordered pizza, while Daisy painted her short, bitten fingernails.

"What should we watch?" Stella stretched her legs across the sofa and picked up a remote control. "How about this one? No," she said, scrolling past the title. "I've seen that a million times."

"I haven't seen that, actually."

"You haven't?"

"No," Daisy said. "I remember hearing about it. That came out a few years after I stopped going out to movies."

"Wait." Stella looked to Daisy with disbelief. "You don't watch movies? Why?"

"I watch movies," Daisy scoffed. "I don't go to theaters. I don't go out to movies."

"Why?"

"I don't know." Daisy crossed her knees, pulled a cable-knit blanket from the back of the sofa and tucked it around her legs. "I stopped after the fall dance, senior year. And I guess I just never did, after that."

"It's my fault," Stella said. "I'm sorry. I was such a stupid, scared kid."

"Kids are often stupid and scared," Daisy answered. "It's not who you are."

"Let's go to a movie now." She sat up, excited. "I'll lend you a dress. We can go to dinner, too. It'll be like a date."

"No, no." Daisy shook her head. "I appreciate it, Stella. But to be honest, the idea of it still kind of gives me the creeps. It's ridiculous, I know." *Just because you broke it doesn't mean you can fix it*, she thought.

Stella cheerily acquiesced, but the mood was dampened. When the doorbell rang, Stella jumped up to get the pizza, both of them relieved for a change of subject. Daisy was glad when Stella started the movie. They could be friends, she thought. Maybe she could have a friend. But she would never be normal. Part of her was still the fire girl, as much as she had wanted for that not to be true.

CHAPTER FORTY-EIGHT

Now

When the movie ended, Stella went to bed, but Daisy was sleepless. The cool, fragrant guest room was still and quiet, and the window showed only a little of the night sky. She walked back downstairs, poured a glass of wine, and found her way to the hammock on the back porch. The late-summer sounds of tree frogs and crickets was better than silence. She wasn't so alone with her thoughts outside. With Bryson returning, she realized Stella was likely to marry him. Daisy wondered if Anderson would have walked away from a sizable business investment for her. She pictured Ellen, safe in her routine, alone with her regrets: at least Ellen had never been alone. And here Daisy was, thirty-five years old, and afraid to walk into a movie theater. She didn't have to try to remember the fire. She could step into that memory as easily as opening a door. She could see the girl, feel their hands touching. *But what if I was wrong, somehow? What if it just wasn't real?* Daisy picked up her phone and dialed the only number she knew by heart.

"Hello?"

The sound of his voice sent her heart thudding into her feet.

"Anderson, it's me."

"Daisy. I didn't think I'd hear from you."

"Really?"

She could hear noise in the background. "Sorry—hold on. I'm at a restaurant." She waited, listening to the buzz of background noises, then a door swinging shut. "I'm surprised you called."

"Why?"

"I don't know," he said. "When I didn't hear from you for a few days, I just... Gave up, I guess."

That didn't take long, she thought.

"I was hoping we could talk. I hated how we left things," she said. "I'm so sorry I made a scene. It was my fault that..." *That you left,* she started to say. *But wait,* she thought. *Was it really, entirely, my fault?* "I saw the message on your phone. I know something's off. Can you just level with me?"

Anderson gave an exaggerated sigh.

"Please," she said. "I'm thousands of miles away. It's not like I can raise hell and embarrass you from here."

"Fine," he said. "Okay. There's somebody else."

Some small part of Daisy realized that she had been expecting this. Yet, the rest of her stung with shock, as if the wind had been knocked from her lungs.

"How long has it been going on?"

"Well, I..."

"When was the first time you two..."

"Seven months ago."

"Seven *months?*" Daisy sucked her breath in, felt her eyes prickling.

The day the bleeding had started, she'd driven herself to the hospital, waited over an hour for an ultrasound, unable to reach Anderson on his work or cell phone. When she'd gotten home later, he had just stepped out of the shower, seemed surprised, as if he hadn't gotten any of her messages or voicemails.

"No wonder things haven't felt right."

"Of course they haven't." He said these words as if he were opening a checkbook or sitting down to a business meeting.

"Daisy, I'm so sorry. I hate that I was dishonest with you. You deserve so much better."

"I always thought we were in this for the long haul."

"Yes," he said. "Absolutely. We were."

"Were…" This wasn't quite what she had expected.

"You didn't think so?"

"No, it's just that you said *were*. I guess that's not what I was expecting to hear."

There was a long pause, and she could tell that he was refusing to say something, something that was becoming clear. Somehow, it hadn't occurred to her that he would want to leave her. That he wouldn't fight to win her back. That was why he was apologizing, right? Heart sinking, she decided to put that off for a few minutes. "Tell me about Charlotte."

"Daisy…"

"I'd like to know the truth. Who is she? How'd you meet her?" She swung her legs to the ground, reached for her wine glass.

"We work together," he said. "She's one of the new junior assistants."

"How junior?"

"That's insignificant."

She sipped the wine, twirled the stem between her fingers. "You're right. We need to move forward. It doesn't matter," she continued, keeping her voice low and calm. "Look, we obviously need to talk in person." She heard his sigh but pressed on, though she already knew the answer. "Are we really ready to toss out the last seventeen years over a mistake?"

Once again, long seconds passed while she waited for his voice. She remembered the time difference, that it was dinnertime there, imagined the brightly painted colors of the sunset.

"Daisy, I always feel like you know what I'm about to say."

"Pretend I don't."

"Maybe the affair was a mistake—going about it this way. God, I never wanted to do this over the phone. I should have *told* you, way before it got to this point."

Daisy let out a long, silent breath, raised a hand to her temple.

"Okay," she said. "You can stop there. I get it."

"I'm sorry it happened like this."

"Me too." Daisy felt as if her skin were crawling with ants. She only had a few moments of calm left in her. "Can I ask why?"

"Of course." He answered, again, with the official, curtailed tone of someone laying out a spreadsheet or pointing to a chart. "You know, it's exhausting to feel like I always have to look out for you. And that whole story about the dead girl—"

"Story?"

"Come on, Daisy, it was obviously made up. I don't want to always feel like I'm taking care of you. The miscarriage only made it harder."

"Taking care of me?" she laughed, feeling distant. "As hard as I tried to keep the past where it was."

"You okay?"

"You don't get to ask me that now," she said, her voice rising almost to a shout. Daisy quickly adjusted her tone; after all, she didn't live here. And she wasn't about to let a cheater goad her into making another dramatic scene when she least wanted it. "I really thought you were above something like this. I wouldn't have been with you otherwise."

"This wasn't what I intended."

"And yet, it's what you did," Daisy answered. "I'm not coming back. You can have all my stuff shipped."

"To where?"

She finished her wine and furiously brushed a flyaway hair into place. "I'll get in touch about that later."

As soon as the line went dead, Daisy got to her feet. She walked through the darkened house and tiptoed up the stairs, brushing tears from her cheeks only to rediscover them there moments later. She rinsed her face with cold water, reached for her toothbrush. Maybe lovers couldn't hurt you like a best friend could. But Anderson had been both of those. *Without him, all I have is loose ends. Hang-ups over a past that shouldn't matter anymore. I had to start my life over at eighteen and now I have to start over from zero again.* She sat on the edge of the bed, willing herself to stop crying, and found that it did no good.

Sitting still only made her feel worse. She changed into running clothes, leggings and a tank top. She was tying her shoes when Stella walked past the open door, rubbing her eyes.

"Are you still awake? Why?"

"I'm going for a run," she sniffed.

"Daisy, it's eleven at night."

"Stella, I'm a wreck. I don't care if it's late. I want some fresh air, and I'm going out for a run."

"You're not a wreck." Stella sat on the floor next to her and, thankfully, stopped short of hugging. "Daisy, what's going on?"

"Anderson broke up with me. It turns out he's been cheating, for seven months." She tilted her chin back and squeezed her eyes shut. "God damn, I can't stop crying. He says I'm too much to deal with. When the number one thing I've tried to do, all these years, was to keep the past in the past. To let it not matter. Instead I've let it control me, because I don't know how to deal with it."

Stella placed her hands on Daisy's shoulders. "We can do it, though. Now we can. I'm going to help you."

"How?"

"People are gonna listen to you now. We'll find something tomorrow in Bryson's files."

"I don't have anything without him," Daisy said. "He's my whole life."

"That's not true," Stella answered. "You earned your degree. You're good at what you do. Do you think anyone could have done all that, far from home, with no family behind them, after what you went through?"

"It was hard." Daisy leaned her head on her knees. "I don't *want* to start over again."

"No." Now, Daisy let Stella hug her, smooth her unruly hair out of her face. "But you can. You can do it."

"I guess we'll find out."

"Come on." Stella stood up, took Daisy's hands, and pulled her to her feet, leaning back on her heels to balance Daisy's weight, like when they were little and held hands to spin in circles. "If you want to go for a run, I'm going with you."

CHAPTER FORTY-NINE

Now

Bryson's office sat on the corner of a quiet street, a stately, two-story house that had been remodeled into offices. With Stella driving, they arrived fifteen minutes early.

"His flight landed an hour ago," Stella whispered. "He ought to be here by now."

Daisy eyed the building with something like fear.

"What if we don't find anything?" Daisy asked.

"Then we'll know," Stella answered. She checked her watch against the clock on the dashboard. "He's definitely late."

"Flights get delayed all the time. You seem anxious."

"Daisy, I haven't seen him since I left him at the altar."

"Of course." Daisy focused on Stella. "Sorry. I've got a bit of tunnel vision here."

"I can't blame you." Stella twirled a lock of hair around her finger. She had put on her engagement ring again, a sizable rock that kept tangling in her hair. "When I called him, he answered right away. It was three in the morning over there."

"What'd you tell him?"

"To come home. That you were here, that you knew things that could help us." She craned her neck as they heard the sound of a car pulling into the drive behind them. "Oh, finally. He's here."

Daisy saw Stella's face brighten at the sight of his car. She recognized Stella's expression. When a person looks at someone they care about, the pupils dilate just slightly—it was something she had read somewhere. Almost as if to let in more light, more of the vision they beheld.

"I'll wait here for a bit," Daisy said. "Give you two a few minutes."

Though Daisy had every intention of giving Stella her privacy, she couldn't help but hear her friend's footsteps, practically at a run as she hurried to meet him. And though she didn't look directly at them, she saw that Bryson left his car door open in his rush to reach Stella. They would be okay. This would work out, somehow. For Stella, it already had. She let the time pass while they talked, examining the blue rings under her eyes, the unkempt look of someone who hasn't slept well in a few days. Yet, she was awake. Single. If all she had to her name was a forest of trauma and some small-town infamy, she was all the more determined to find a way to make it work.

When Stella tapped on the window, Daisy opened the door and stepped out, pulling sunglasses on in the bright morning.

"Daisy, this is Bryson Crane."

"Morning." Daisy shook his hand. Bryson wore a suit wrinkled from travel. "You look almost as tired as I feel."

"Combination of jet lag," he said, "and good old lack of sleep." He held onto her hand for a moment. "I feel like I need to thank you for something, but I'm not sure what it is exactly."

"Come on," Stella said, standing on the tips of her toes, full of anticipation. "Let's go inside."

Bryson greeted the receptionist as they followed him into the building and up an oak staircase to the second floor. "My office is right there," he indicated. Daisy was surprised to see that he seemed nervous. "Not that that matters. You're not here for a tour." He opened a door that led into a room lined with heavy wooden cabinets, then unlocked the cabinet nearest to the door.

"Weird," he said, shuffling through a pile of cardboard boxes. "I was sure it was in here." Daisy gave Stella a worried look as

Bryson closed it, then unlocked the next door. "Here," he said. "Right here. Like I said, jet lag."

He handed Stella a brittle, aged manila envelope with the words 'ZION CHEM' scrawled in marker on the front.

"This is it?" Stella turned it over, looking at it front and back, then promptly handed it over to Daisy.

"When we met the former owners about buying the site, they gave us some files—property boundaries, zoning information. What you could or couldn't legally use the land for, things like that." Bryson yawned as he spoke and Stella moved closer to him, wrapped a hand around his arm. "This envelope was stuck in the middle of it. Handwritten, all of it. Notes from police interviews at the site."

Daisy looked down at the packet in her hands, then back at Bryson. "Are you serious?"

"This wasn't supposed to be there." He paused. "Have you ever hidden something important, somewhere you thought it would be safe, so well you forgot where it was?" He pointed at the envelope. "Somebody hid that, a long time ago. They only handed it over by accident."

"Oh, my God," Stella breathed.

"If you two don't mind, I'm going to my office to catch up on emails. I'll be right down the hall."

Stella followed him to the doorway, squeezing his hands, kissing him as though he were leaving for a year, but Daisy hardly noticed.

"Well, you two certainly act like newlyweds," she murmured.

"Oh, I—"

"Don't apologize," she scolded, smiling.

The storage room had neither tables nor chairs, so she sat down on the floor, waving for Stella to do the same. "Alright," Stella whispered. "Open it."

CHAPTER FIFTY

Now

As Bryson parked his car outside the police station, Daisy eyed the building.

"Wow," she said. "Funny to see it by daylight."

"Hm?" Stella turned around from the passenger seat, raising an eyebrow.

"Oh, I might not have told you," Daisy said. "I was here the other night. I'll explain later."

The station hadn't changed a bit, not since she had left town all those years ago. She'd missed seeing that, arriving in the dark with Kate for her night in the cells. Its faded brick walls appeared to be receding into the dusty, midday sun. Daisy climbed out of the car with an icy glare. *As if it wants to escape notice*, she thought. *We'll see if that's changed.*

"Would you like for us to come in with you?" Stella asked. Bryson nodded his agreement. Daisy thought that he still looked jet-lagged. She suspected, though, that Bryson and Stella hadn't slept much between them the previous night.

"No, thanks," Daisy said. "I'd like to do this on my own."

"Let me know if they give you any trouble," Bryson said. "I'm sure they know how much money is on the line with this deal. If they don't listen to you—"

"They will." She stood up straight, tucked the folder of papers under her arm. "This time, I think they will."

But as Daisy pushed the door open and approached the counter, she felt a chill: of anticipation, nerves, memory. The interior hadn't seen any renovation, either. Years ago, that kind of sensation—the tingling nerves, the quickened breath—would have frozen her in her tracks. Now, she felt ready.

"Can I help you?" A young woman looked up from a paperback, one hand holding her place in the pages.

"Yes, thanks. I'd like to talk to one of the detectives."

The receptionist looked up. "You're not with the media, are you?"

"No," Daisy said. "Not right now, at least. It's about an old case."

"Hm." She dog-eared her page and tucked the book away, then picked up the phone. "Sergeant, could you come out here, please?"

Daisy didn't recognize the officer who came out to greet her, though she hadn't exactly expected that many of the same people would still be working there seventeen years later.

"Morning, ma'am. I'm—"

But as he stuck out his hand to introduce himself, the detective faltered momentarily. He quickly recovered, shook her hand. "Rob Powers. Sandra said you're here about a cold case?"

"Yes."

"Okay," he said, something dismissive in his tone. "That's what I thought. Right this way."

As Daisy followed him down the corridor, she asked, "That's what you thought? Why?"

She followed him into an open office space with a few desks, sat down across from him.

"This isn't a joke or something, is it?"

Daisy paused. Until now, the morning had moved forward with an easiness that raised her suspicion. But this—the moment he recognized her, the dismissal in his tone—had a way of setting her at ease.

"I saw the news. You're Daisy Ritter, aren't you?" Powers leaned back in his chair. "Look, I'm new here. I have seen my share of pranks. Please don't make a fool of me over this."

Daisy did not smile. She pulled her chair a few inches closer to the desk.

"So you already know what this is about."

"I think so, yeah."

"How about you tell me, then," she offered. The man began to stammer. "That's okay—I mean it. Tell me what you know, and I'll jump in and correct you if you get anything wrong."

"Well, wasn't it ninety-nine? June or July?"

"It was June seventeen," Daisy said. "Firefly season."

"Zion Chem caught fire. Few men died."

"Okay," she said. "Go on."

"The plant shut down," he answered. "They paid damages to the families that were affected. Everyone says it was an open and shut case."

"Okay, let's break there," Daisy said. "A lot of what you said isn't wrong. Four employees were killed. The thing is, there was another person killed there. A young woman."

"And this isn't something you invented or, I don't know, dreamed up somehow?"

"I know, Rob, because I was there. I was as close to her as I am to you right now." He nodded his head, clicked the computer mouse, and began typing. "Did you ever make a report?"

"I did," she answered, surprised to find the memory jump readily to her lips. "I came in and told two people what happened."

He sighed and shook his head. "Nothing on the books."

"They didn't seem that interested."

"Okay, well, I understand, it was years ago." He didn't seem to have any idea how grateful she was to have a chance to be listened to. "Just tell me everything you remember, as clearly as you can. If there are memory gaps, don't worry about it."

"There aren't," Daisy said. "No memory gaps. It was July seventeen. I was sitting in the woods in a hunting blind with my—well, he wasn't my boyfriend then. Just a kid from school, helping me study for an algebra test."

"In the summer?"

"Summer school," she said with a rueful shrug. "I failed during the school year."

"Okay. Go on."

"It was evening. It was just starting to get a little darker, but we were in the woods, so I don't think it was sunset yet. The fireflies were just coming out."

"Say, between six and seven."

"I think so. We heard a noise, which didn't frighten me, because Zion Chem blew up all the time. I don't know when they finally closed it, but there were fires every year. I listened a little, kept working. Then we started to smell the smoke, heard the explosion. I knew my dad was there, so…"

"Why was he there?"

She looked up at Powers. "He worked there. I got up to the entrance, saw the fire, but couldn't make anything out. I went in to look for him. I wanted to see if he was okay."

"And?"

"What happened was, I walked into it, and I kind of got distracted. I saw people who got hurt, the building on fire. Then the girl. She came running out—she was already hurt really bad. Then a beam collapsed on her. Right across her middle. She was dying."

"And you left?"

"My dad came up to me and told me to leave right away. He said he couldn't see any girl. I was scared," she said, feeling at a loss. "So I left." She wasn't sure why, but she wanted to apologize.

"Did you raise the issue with him later?"

"Yeah. I told both my parents and just got more of the same. I lived at home another few months, but they put me in a boarding school and then I ran away. Nothing happened. That was their line. And when the news reports came out, nothing there, either."

"Okay, so assuming that happened, why didn't anyone find out about it? Why wasn't there an investigation?"

She found the familiar images replaying before her mind's eye, watching, unable to look away, until Jesse's hand pulled her back. There was no knowing where the body could have gone, what might have happened. She wondered if chemical fires could burn hot enough to incinerate bones.

"That part," Daisy said, placing the folder on his desk, "is your job. I can only guess that she wasn't really supposed to be there, so it follows that there was some kind of cover-up. That'll be more interesting to someone else." She held his gaze, felt her heart twist in her chest as she remembered. Though he typed with his index fingers, he seemed to be surprisingly efficient, tapping away on the keyboard. "The thing is, I've spent so long trying to find out who she was. If you had seen her, you would understand."

"And what brings you here now, seventeen years later?"

"Well, you heard they were about to sell the land," Daisy said. "Any evidence, anything that's still there, could be lost."

"And what's this?" He indicated the folder.

"Read it yourself," Daisy said. "Whoever hid these did not intend for them to be found."

"It might take me a minute to get through these," he said, opening the folder.

"I'll wait," she said. "And just in case you get any ideas, those are photocopies. I still have the originals."

Daisy watched his face as he read the first page, then the second. She drew in a deep breath and looked out the doorway. Just down the hall was the room where she had sat as a teenager, when she'd been dismissed almost just the same. She glanced at Officer Powers, who was absorbed in the papers she'd brought.

"Ms. Ritter." He spoke softly, laid the file back down on his desk. "Could you excuse me while I make a quick phone call? I think this is something my boss will want to hear about."

As Daisy waited in the hallway, she watched the second hand on the wall clock tick. Each second seemed to stretch into an hour; by the time two minutes had passed she was nearly biting her fingernails. Finally, the door opened.

"Sorry for the wait," Powers said. "Do you mind if I keep that file?"

"So—"

"I had to call my captain." He closed the door of his office behind him. "He's on his way in now. Would you mind coming out this way? I just need you to sign something."

Back by the reception desk, he took a sheet of paper from the printer and handed it over.

"What's this?"

"Witness statement. Just a record of what you told me in there."

"Oh, my God. Really?"

"Yes, ma'am," he said. "Why?"

"It's just that no one's ever taken me seriously before," she said. "Let me read over this real quick, then I'll sign it."

"Excuse me."

Kate brushed past Daisy's shoulder, stood to face Powers. "What's she doing here?"

"What do you mean?"

This time, she directed her smirk to Daisy. "Trespassing again? Really?"

"No." Powers turned from Daisy to Kate, uncertain. "She's here because she's a witness to a crime."

Kate laughed sharply in response. "Spend too much time around her and you might end up in the news, too. Or maybe the drunk tank." She returned to her office, her caustic laughter lingering in the corridor.

"Funny," Daisy said. "We went to the same high school. One day I didn't know who she was. The next, she hated my guts. I guess some things never change." She reviewed the paper in her hands and signed it, then handed the clipboard back to Officer Powers.

"Thanks. Kate's good at her job," he answered. He hesitated. Daisy sensed there was more to say, a silent *but* following the initial statement, though it went unsaid. "Nothing else for now, but expect a phone call in the next few days. They'll be sending a forensics team to the site. Probably ask you to come along, just to point things out."

"Wait. Me?"

"I'm not certain there's anyone here who knows the area," he went on. "If you'd be willing to show up and just describe what you saw, where she was."

"I don't know." She crossed her arms, pictured it again. Imagined her midsection underneath a singed beam of wood. Then she heard Anderson's voice: *Come on, Daisy, it was obviously made up.* "Yeah, I can do it. Just tell me when to be there."

When Daisy returned to Bryson's car, Bryson was asleep. Stella rested her head on his shoulder, holding his hand in both of hers. Daisy tapped softly on Stella's window, then opened the back door and sat down.

"How was it?" she asked.

Daisy met Stella's eyes in the rearview mirror. "They're reopening the investigation."

"Oh, Daisy," Stella breathed. "You did it."

"Not yet. They want me to go to the plant with them soon, show them where it happened, I guess."

"I'd give you a hug," she said, "but I don't want to move."

"He did the right thing," Daisy said. "You seem really happy together."

"I think I knew he would come around to the right choice," Stella answered. "But I had to be sure. I missed him so much."

"I have a feeling you two would appreciate having your house back to yourselves tonight," Daisy laughed. "I'll pack up when we get back."

CHAPTER FIFTY-ONE

Now

"You know you don't have to leave," Stella said, helping Daisy pull her heavy suitcase down the front steps.

"You're a married couple," Daisy laughed. "And you didn't even get your honeymoon. You at least deserve some nuptial privacy."

"Well, technically we're still unmarried," Stella said. "But hopefully not for too long."

"Oh?" Daisy opened the trunk of Ellen's car and hoisted the suitcase up. "What's your plan?"

"Something quiet," Stella said. She adjusted her sunglasses, a hint of regret showing in her face. "I can't believe how much we spent on the wedding, honestly. I'm happy to sign my name and let that be it."

"Can I ask you something?" Daisy asked. She opened the door and leaned back against it.

"Sure."

"Why'd you really invite me? You didn't need me here to figure any of this out."

"Truthfully? I always missed you," Stella said. "When I was walking down the aisle, I thought I'd made my choice. I guess it seemed like the easier of the two evils, at that point. But when I saw you, I remembered all the stuff I used to like about myself. I decided I was going to find a better way, whatever it was."

Daisy felt her eyes watering. "I needed to do this. Maybe you knew that. Still, being here, going over the details again, I keep asking myself why I didn't stay. Maybe she could have lived."

"It's not your fault," Stella said. "You've got to forgive yourself for that, Daisy. You were a child in the middle of a traumatic—dangerous—event, with people you trusted telling you to…"

"I knew it was wrong to walk away," Daisy said. "I didn't speak up for her as well as I could have."

"Everyone was against you."

"I know," Daisy answered.

"I was the worst of them all. I should have helped you."

"You were young. You weren't supposed to know what to do."

"Then admit it," Stella said. "You did the best you knew how to."

Daisy reached over to hold Stella's hand. "I hope we can be friends again."

"Me, too," Stella said. "Where are you going to go?"

"I don't know. I can work from anywhere, so that doesn't help me decide. I'll probably find a short-term rental, maybe a storage unit so I can at least tell Anderson where to send my stuff."

"Well, you know where to find me."

*

As Daisy drove away from Stella's house, lazy Zion seemed quieter than it ever had. The narrow streets hugged the hillsides like ribbon. Even the flock of birds that moved across the sky seemed to do so with a sleepy relief. They looked as though they were almost home, she thought—wherever that might have been.

There were no real hotels in town, save the Holiday Inn just off the highway. She wanted to return Ellen's car, though; besides an obligation, it felt like a liability, as if it was always on the verge of breaking down. It would be a simple stop: drive home, sit with Ellen for a few minutes, call for a taxi to the hotel.

When Daisy left for her parents' house, she had no intention of seeing her father, nor even any thought of him. She pictured only Ellen at home, in her shawl, in the garden or the kitchen, filled with a sudden craving for her presence, a sudden certainty of what she needed to say to her. It wasn't about the details of the past, or any betrayed expectation, but only reassurance. That if Ellen, too, had to survive the unsavory facts Daisy had been shaped by, that she should know there was possibility in spite of it, that life could go on in whatever unexpected way it managed to, like water slipping downhill, that losing your idea of what your life could be was survivable. Daisy paused in thought as she turned into the familiar drive.

But it wasn't Ellen sitting on the front porch. Ellen's other car, the aged gold station wagon, wasn't even in the driveway. Daisy's father occupied his chair like a stone, the hunter's unmoving, all-noticing stance unchanged. Daisy's shoes pattered up the steps with long, definitive paces, trying to break her habit of dragging her feet, so that she sounded assertive, even before she spoke.

"Where's Mama?"

He lifted a coffee cup to his lips, sipped, and set it down. "Went to town. Shopping."

"Hm."

"You need something?"

"No. Mama lent me the extra car. Just dropping it off."

Tracker huffed his assent and nodded at the chair opposite his. Daisy pulled the chair a few feet away before sitting down, her purse balanced on her knees.

She swept her eyes over the yard, as if noticing, for the first time, Ellen's dogged hard work in trying to make it presentable. Maybe Ellen had never been hoping to make it a yard that it wasn't, not to imitate a more spacious, shaded, or lush lawn, but only to make it her own.

"I didn't expect to see you," she said.

"Don't know why," he answered. "It's my house."

"Very good point, Dad."

There's no point in attempting conversation. There never is. Still, she wanted him to hear it from her first. "I was at the police station this morning." She waited for him to react, half expecting a barb, but got only silence. "They're reopening the investigation into the fire. And they're looking for a body."

Tracker's chilly stare locked onto her, colder than she remembered.

Despite his age and his depleted strength, when her father straightened his shoulders and jabbed his chin forward, she drew in a quick breath of fear.

"I'm not liable," he said. "I can't be touched. Let me tell you something about how this relates to me: it doesn't." He seemed almost to be ranting, as if a lock had opened. Daisy noticed that his cup held only coffee, that he didn't smell of alcohol. Was his hand trembling? "I didn't put her there. I didn't hire her." She felt her chest grow cold with surprise. 'Her' was the person he had never before acknowledged, until this moment. "They find anything, I don't care. And as far as you're concerned, let me tell you how this relates to you."

"I don't—" She slid her chair a little further away. These false starts in conversation, impulses of words and sentences, he had always spoken over so effortlessly. Was that why she always faltered before speaking, before her sentence found its mark? Daisy looked down and noticed that her manicure had chipped to bits since she had arrived in town, that she was failing to keep herself together in every way imaginable.

"By the time you saw anything, she was good as buried. No way she was walking out of there."

"She was there."

Suddenly calm, he lifted the cup to his mouth again. Daisy noticed a definite tremble in his fingers.

"She was there," she repeated.

"I don't know what you're talking about."

Daisy stood up, feeling a cool shiver in her spine that might have been dread confirmed, or a new confidence. "You know, people say it takes a while for your consciousness to leave your body, even once your body's dead."

He spat off to his right. "Who says?"

"Nurses, doctors. People who've seen dying animals," she said. "You're not gone right away. Not all at once."

"Ivory tower bullshit," he laughed. "You can't prove that."

Maybe he's right, Daisy thought. *Maybe there's no point thinking about it. Wait.* She knew that voice, that cold part of her that always shouted the rest of her down. *He's an abyss. He's an empty quarry. Don't stand too close to the edge.*

"This was a good talk." Daisy stood up and started walking. She wasn't sure where to; she'd forgotten to call for a taxi. "You can tell Mama I was here. Or not. I'll see her around anyway."

She took her suitcase from the car and lifted it with both hands. It was heavier than she would have liked, but it felt good to carry something heavy. Out of old habit, she walked into the trees. If her father's cold, unchanging energy was a cliff's edge, one that would always exist in her psyche, the forest was there also, the refuge.

Daisy called the cab company, but the wait was longer than she wanted to stay in one place for. As she walked away, she remembered the day Tracker had caught her in the back of the truck. That moment she had picked out and clung to, filed away in the book of her memories, even when others might have chosen to let it float by, dismissed as a word spoken amiss, something she was reading too much into. Even when she had doubted it, she had held onto that moment—it gave her a reason to push back, because, in that moment of smallness, she had no choice but her courage and independence. Now, seeing the icy look in her father's eyes, seeing him undone by sobriety, she knew that she had been right. Those words had been no mistake. And she mouthed his scattered statement herself again as she started the car: *By the time you saw anything, she was as good as dead.* And, again, her own response: *She was there.*

She took the shortcut through the trees and, ten minutes later, stood in the driveway of Teresa's inn. For the second time in a week, she pulled her tired feet up the steps, across the airy front porch, and approached the door.

"Daisy." Teresa opened the door with her beautiful, enigmatic smile. "You're back. And alone?"

"Just me this time," she answered, letting the bag drop from her shoulder. "Do you have a room? Single?"

"I do." Teresa paused, making Daisy wonder how much Jesse had told her. "Come in."

"Please, don't tell Jesse I'm here just yet," she sighed. "I'll catch you up on everything, but right now I just need to rest."

CHAPTER FIFTY-TWO

Now

Close to a week had passed when Daisy met the police at the old Zion Chemical site. Her small room at the Blue Ghost was in a quiet, upstairs corner of the house, overlooking the meadow. Outside of meals and going for a run each morning, Daisy stayed in her room, working and reading; she wasn't ready to run into Jesse.

For a late-summer morning, it was unexpectedly cool as she walked up the familiar trail. Any number of people would have offered to drive her, but she preferred to go by herself: it meant she could leave whenever she wanted to. The sky was gray but bright, diffuse sunlight giving the woods a feeling of timelessness.

Daisy passed a row of police cars parked by the entrance to the plant and stopped by the chain-link fence, now open. She double-checked the time on her phone. She couldn't remember the name of the sergeant who'd called her, but she was certain he'd asked her to be there at nine. Never mentioned who to meet, who to ask for. Some of the cars were marked 'Forensics'. There were probably ten men and women there, a few preparing to put on hazmat suits. Suddenly, she felt that getting here had taken all the effort she had to give; how was she supposed to navigate the details of where to stand, who to talk to? Suddenly a car pulled in behind her, brakes protesting as gravel was tossed around the tires.

"I should have known you'd be here." Kate pushed the door shut behind her. She nearly walked past Daisy but reconsidered, turning to face her. Though her hair was combed and her clothes neat, something about Kate's demeanor gave a distinct impression of disarray.

"Did you wake up on the wrong side of the bed or something?" Daisy managed a smile, even though Kate's ire still made her feel like a cornered high schooler.

"Don't tell me our town crazy woman is taking up comedy." She rolled her eyes.

"Hey, Hanson."

Both Daisy and Kate turned to see Officer Powers calling her. "You're late," he said, then noticed Daisy. "Ms. Ritter, right? Wait right there. Hey, Captain? She's here."

A tall man about ten years Daisy's senior walked up to her. "Thanks for coming out. I'm—"

"Oh, I remember you."

All the years hadn't erased her memory of the young officer who'd brushed her aside. "You were there the first time I came in to make a report."

"You remember that?" He gave her a polite, skeptical half-smile. "People around here say you lost your mind. That you were committed somewhere."

"There's no shortage of rumors," Daisy said. "Of course, it didn't help that nobody listened to me to begin with."

He seemed to pretend not to have heard her, glancing over some papers on a clipboard. Daisy wondered again how that packet of interview transcripts had come to be misplaced. "Alright, then. I've got a copy of your witness statement here. Just need you to go through what happened, walk me through where you were."

Daisy took a bracing sigh. The smell of this place was still something less than normal.

"Okay, then," she said, taking a step ahead of him. "I was up there, in the woods, about a hundred yards off. When I heard the noise, I came down."

To walk through the plant with the officer felt like giving him a tour of a secret room in her mind, known by heart, but that had been kept locked for years. Parts of her memory seemed to shrink back, shocked by the light of day as she walked through the steps she'd taken as a girl. She pointed to the ground and told the officer: "Here is where I was standing when I realized something was really wrong, that it wasn't another little explosion." Where she saw the girl, the extent of her injuries plain. Where the building had collapsed—now, it sagged under its own weight, and the police officers cautioned her not to go too near.

"And then my dad found me," she said, "and he told me to leave, so I just…"

"You left?"

"I went home." She crossed her arms and held her head high, breathed through the tightness in her throat. "That's about all I can tell you. You don't mind if I go sit down, do you?"

"No. Of course not. They'll take a few hours, walk through the site. We're going to be thorough," he said. "This time, we are."

"Do you need me to stay the whole time?"

"No. You can head out whenever you want to."

That didn't sound like such a bad plan. Daisy thought maybe she would find some breakfast, then go back to her room at the inn and spend some time thinking about her next move. A town this small wouldn't have many options for short-term rentals. Maybe she'd head for a bigger city—not too far from here, but not too close either.

She watched as one of the men unleashed a dog, which Daisy realized was intended to follow the scent of human remains. For several minutes, she watched silently. She could have told them that anything they'd find would no longer bear much trace, that it would be consumed with toxic fumes or ashes. While the dog carried on its useless errand, the other officers walked the ground, planting small flags here and there. If they actually did find anything, she was pretty sure she didn't want to be here. She'd be perfectly happy to hear about it after the fact. Seeing the body once was enough. Daisy began to wave down Officer Powers to tell him she was leaving. But he was distracted, wearing a look of exasperation, talking to Kate.

"They're not going to find anything," she said, her voice rising, face flushed. "This is a waste of resources."

"Get it together, Kate," Powers hissed. "Now." He placed a hand on her shoulder and walked her away from the site, nearer to where the cars were parked. They stopped a few car lengths away from Daisy. "You've been erratic for the last month. Your job is gonna be on the line if this keeps up."

Kate threw a cold look in Daisy's direction. "She's been a joke for years. Everyone knows this is just—"

"If you need to get out of here, go calm down or something, I'll tell them you got sick. I'm not trying to get you in trouble."

Daisy could feel the uneven gravel through the soles of her shoes. Her long walks outdoors here wore the soles thin more quickly than city sidewalks. She looked up from her toes to see Kate, who had fallen silent, glancing between the plant yard and her police car. The way her eyes darted to and fro, the way she moved her weight from one foot to the other, Kate didn't look angry. She looked frightened.

"Officers?" Daisy ventured. "I'm heading out. Call me if you need anything."

She took a few steps toward the trail, along the outside of the chain-link fence that stretched around the perimeter. As she passed by, one of the men in the yard waved his arm, calling the others over: "Got something over here."

They retreated in a cluster out of her line of sight, into the half-ruined barn. "That's it," someone shouted.

Daisy felt it like an impact, like getting the breath knocked out of her. She froze, then crept silently to the fence, wrapped her fingers around the metal.

A few moments passed, though she thought it could have been hours. Daisy reminded herself to take a deep breath and felt how her arms and shoulders had squeezed tight around her ribcage with tension.

When two men came back into sight, carrying a small metal storage drum between them, she felt the air in her lungs grow hot, then cold, all her energy evaporating into sorrow.

"What is it?" one of the forensics officers called.

"Remains, skeletal. Can't say age or sex, but small. Adolescent, probably."

Daisy felt a sigh escape her lips and raised her eyes to the gently wavering treetops, feeling as if some part of herself had escaped, something she had been holding to her heart for years. She didn't breathe, trying to catch every word.

"How are we going to look into IDing them?"

"Missing persons, right? We'll see what kind of files we have from back then."

"Good luck. Kids disappear every day," Kate scoffed. "Every damn day, children go missing and no one takes notice."

"Kate, you seem awfully sure about that," the captain said. "Something about this case has you rattled. You sure you don't know anything you're not telling us?"

When Kate paused to breathe, she saw Daisy.

"Slow down, Hanson."

"Don't tell me to slow down." Her voice raised a notch. She approached Daisy, one finger pointing at her. "After everything I've done to keep you away, you return and within days, everything's ruined."

It occurred to Daisy that she might have been frightened, if she hadn't been so alert. There was a missing link here. Something that she ought to have considered long ago.

Seeing Kate's demeanor, one of the police officers moved after her, but Daisy held a hand out, motioning for him to let Kate come closer to her.

"What are you talking about, Kate?" she asked.

"Accidents happen every day." Kate's gaze began to wander, memory softening the set of her eyes. "Even terrible accidents, like the fire. They can happen anywhere, especially when you're working with volatile stuff."

"Sure," Daisy said, trying to draw her out. "That's right, they happen all the time."

"And just because one of the workers made a mistake and blew the place up—my family shouldn't have been liable for some girl who just happened to be there."

"But who is she?"

"Shut up, fire girl," Kate shouted, volleying between rage and nervous laughter. "How would I know?"

Suddenly it became clear. This was the reason for Kate's inexplicable anger with her.

"You were trying to protect your dad," Daisy whispered. "Of course—your father was the manager. He was the one who hid those interviews." Kate's father had worked for the family who owned the plant, Daisy realized. Not with his hands, not like Tracker worked. Not with the dangerous stuff. She remembered Kate in high school, who knew everything about the fire because her father was the hiring manager there.

"And nobody would ever have found them!" Kate stumbled over her words. "Finally—you got shipped off, and everything was fine, and then that bitch, Stella—"

"Watch your language." Daisy held Kate's glare. "Stella's my friend."

"No one is listening to me," Kate cried.

"I know what that's like. I'm listening to you," Daisy answered, trying to hold Kate's gaze, make a connection to keep her talking. "See? That's something we have in common."

"No, you aren't. I'm not interested in having anything in common with someone like you," Kate said. She lunged at her in a motion that was too disorganized to be threatening. Daisy took a deliberate step to one side and Kate stopped in her tracks, facing her with a cold stare. The captain approached her and held out his hands in an obvious gesture. Beginning to crumble, Kate handed over her weapon, pulled the badge from her jacket and clutched it in her hand.

"What do you mean, someone like me?" Daisy asked, again tuning into the mayhem behind Kate's voice, the half-crazed expression. Daisy could barely hear the ragged whisper as Kate spoke.

"My family lost enough in that fire. Someone like you wasn't supposed to be worth putting them through even more—legal trouble, criminal proceedings. I had to protect them. Why did you have to make it so difficult?" Kate began to cry openly, plopped down cross-legged on the ground. Daisy looked again at Kate and saw, behind her anxiety and erratic behavior, a deep well of fearfulness, a child who felt an unfair responsibility to protect her family at all costs.

"So, who was she?"

Kate shook her head. "They never told me anything about that."

"Kate, I'm sorry for what you went through," Daisy said. "It wasn't about you. I never had any intention of making things hard for your family."

"It wasn't your fault," Kate sniffed. "But it was so much easier when they finally sent you away. I admit, I really thought you made up the part about the dead girl."

"I've always had a knack for being in the wrong place at the wrong time." Daisy pursed her lips. This had always been true.

For the first time she could remember, Kate was listening to her with a curiosity that seemed genuine.

"Or maybe," Kate said, "you were in the wrong place at the right time."

"You know, I wasn't really supposed to be here at all," Daisy admitted. "My mother never thought she'd be able to have kids. I was a—"

Kate wobbled to her feet and took several broad, uneven steps away from the group of people and collapsed against the side of her car. In a pattering of feet and a flurry of voices, the other police officers hurried after her. Daisy lifted her eyes to the scene by the car, one officer pulling Kate to her feet, the other looking on with a combination of disdain and concern.

I was an accident, she might have said. Ellen had said, *a blessing*.

Daisy didn't know which answer she would have given. But one thing she knew for sure: this was still a story with missing pieces, question marks. And something told her Ellen might have answers.

CHAPTER FIFTY-THREE

Now

Daisy walked through the woods to her parents' house. As she crossed the yard, she saw her mother walk down the steps of the porch with silent footsteps, heading in the direction of her garden. She picked up her pace and caught up.

"Daisy, I wasn't expecting to see you."

"I'm staying nearby," Daisy said. "Thought I'd drop by. Sorry to frighten you. Have you listened to the news today?"

When Ellen smiled, she didn't quite look her age, but more like someone who was both very young and very tired. "I never watch the news."

As she continued on her way to the garden, Daisy stepped in front of her. "Mama, they found her."

Finally, Ellen paused, her eyes widening.

"They found her," Daisy repeated. Ellen recoiled as if she'd been slapped. She nodded her head and began to walk around, but Daisy threw her arms out and hugged her close. "Wait," she said. "We need to talk about this."

"Okay, Daisy," Ellen said. "I've been afraid of what you'd think of me, if you knew the truth. But there's no putting it off any longer."

Daisy took a close, remembering look at her mother, at the graying-white house behind her. This would always be the place that had let her down, but it didn't have to be only that.

"It rained last night," Ellen observed, nodding at the mist on the grass. "Good morning for pulling weeds in the garden. The soil will be soft."

"I'll help you," Daisy said. "But you have to talk to me."

"I don't have a pair of gloves for you to borrow."

"That's fine." Daisy held her hands out, displaying her short, ragged fingernails. "Nothing to show off here, anyway."

"Very well," Ellen answered. "She was your sister. Her name was Eden. Your father got her the job there."

"My sister?" Daisy's throat squeezed in suddenly, pinching her voice to a whisper.

She walked at her mother's side through the grass. The hollow at the edge of the yard where Ellen planted her garden was overgrown with wisteria, its vines wrapped around the trees, a canopy of blossoms overhead. At their feet, the small herb garden stood carefully tended.

"Every year you don't pull the new growth down, it takes over a little more." Ellen stood in the shade of the trees. The blossoms, a creamy shade reminiscent of seashells, were almost as numerous as leaves around them, obscuring Daisy's view of the forest with a dappled, intoxicating curtain of pale violet and green.

"The truth is, I've come to enjoy the wisteria," Ellen said. "I don't do much work out here, anymore. But it's a peaceful place to sit and enjoy a few minutes alone." Ellen took a spade and a pair of gardening gloves from the pocket of her apron, placed the spade on the ground beside her, and put on the gloves.

Daisy sat pensively on the soft ground, watching as Ellen knelt in the dirt and plucked weeds from around the plants. Beyond the garden in the clearing she saw the scattering of upright sticks and rocks that marked Ellen's buried children, not carried to term. Daisy counted, saw that there were no more than she remembered being there before she had left home.

Ellen followed Daisy's gaze, her eyes sweeping over the little assembly of voiceless companions. A spirited shiver crept up her spine, a ghostly whisper that was more welcoming than foreboding.

"Nobody ever told me I had a sister."

"Daisy, I've always had a terrible time with pregnancy. You know that."

Daisy tugged up a dandelion by its roots, wondering if one of those buried babies had blessed the ground with flowers.

"I know I told you that your father was engaged when we met. I knew it was wrong for me to fall in love with him, but I couldn't help it."

"Okay," Daisy said. "I'm listening."

"She was a lovely woman, Daisy. She had a little daughter—Eden. I was ready to call things off with your father when I learned she was pregnant again. But then, when she was giving birth, something went wrong. She didn't make it. Incredibly, the baby was healthy."

"And then what happened?"

"Eden went to stay with her aunt, but there was nobody to look after her newborn. Tracker and I got married, and I got to raise her as my own."

"What was the baby's name?"

"I named her Daisy," Ellen whispered. "It was you."

Daisy uttered a few words, shards of incomplete phrases: "Who? Me? My mother?" stammering until Ellen laid a cool hand on her cheek.

"Your father was heartbroken," Ellen said, "to lose your mother. He couldn't look at you for the first few weeks."

Daisy pressed her hands into the soil, leaning forward to try to keep her head from spinning. "And what about losing Eden? How did he take that?"

"You were there, Daisy. You know how hard it was. All those times you thought he was sneaking out?" Ellen took a steadying breath. "Going on hunting trips? He was really visiting your mother's grave."

"I knew there was something I didn't know." Daisy's eyes began to mist as she spoke, though she could not have put a name to what she felt. "But I had no idea it was something like this."

"I tried my best," Ellen continued. "I loved you right away. More than my own flesh and blood. You've always had such a bright, strong spirit. That was why I chose your name."

"And my—my mother?" Daisy stammered. "What was her name?"

"Her name was Dahlia. Earlier, I thought God wanted me to have more children. After all, he had blessed us with you. But maybe he meant for you to be enough. Or maybe for me to spend years focused on what I wanted instead of what I had." Ellen tugged a blade of grass up by the roots from next to a rosemary plant. "I thought I had some idea what God wanted. That's a problem in itself, whether it's a sin or not. Do you remember this?" She reached inside the collar of her dress and pulled out a ring hanging on a thin chain.

"What is it?" Daisy leaned closer, close enough to smell Ellen's pressed flower perfume, and felt her heart shift as she saw the inscription on the band: 'Ephesians 6'. The sight of the letters, more than the word itself, brought her back to the day of the fire. This was the ring that had slipped loose from the girl's hand into Daisy's clenched fist, then suddenly disappeared.

"Here," Ellen said, trying to offer it to her. Daisy saw that Ellen's fingers shook as she fiddled with the clasp, then, in a show of frustration Daisy had never seen before, gave the chain a solid tug and broke it, dropping the ring into Daisy's palm. "It was a gift from your father. When Eden moved back to town that summer, he wanted her to feel welcome, I guess, so he took it to give to her." Daisy scoffed and shook her head, then, seeing the openness in her mother's eyes receding, amended her expression.

"And that was how I happened to see it, that day," she said. The ring was tarnished, still, with age now more than smoke.

"Most of the passage is outdated, backwards nonsense." Ellen's eyes widened, then broke into laughter. "Can you believe I just said that about the Bible?"

"Go ahead, Mama," Daisy grinned. "It's true. But the first line is the one about honoring your parents, right?"

Ellen's smile trembled, as if it were too heavy a weight to hold. "And I couldn't even be honest with you about who your parents really were."

Daisy sat on the ground near Ellen, not knowing what to say. She started plucking weeds and twigs from the garden bed, tugging the green tendrils from around the plants, Ellen's little gravesites. Still damp from the previous night's rain, dirt clung to her fingers.

"Daisy, I let you down. I'm sorry. It doesn't matter that I tried, or that my intentions were loving."

Daisy picked up Ellen's spade and dug a small hollow into the earth, between the rosemary and columbine. She placed the ring, broken chain still laced through, into the ground and patted a handful of soil over it.

"The love was there," Daisy said. "It was always there, regardless. I always saw that."

"It didn't make much difference, in the end."

"That wasn't the end." Daisy tugged a dandelion from the ground where it had sprung up between the roots of a rhododendron bush.

"I appreciate the thought." Ellen lifted one of her thin shoulders in a shrug, waved away a gnat that had flown near her, a motion that seemed to dismiss Daisy's forgiveness.

"I mean it," Daisy insisted. "Maybe that was the middle of things. Maybe it still is."

A morning rain began to fall, sounding a hushed patter against the leaves above. The drops that fell through pulled the sweet, sharp fragrance of the wisterias down to the soil.

"Look at those clouds." Ellen spoke with a beaming lilt, a note of praise in her voice for the summer weather. "It'll pick up shortly here. I should get back inside and start on dinner for your father."

Daisy swept her hands across her knees, rain-softened soil crumbling from her palms. She rested her hand on Ellen's wrist, just at the hem of her glove. "Alright, Mom."

When Ellen's eyes landed on Daisy's, twinkling almost violet in the soft light, Daisy knew that she had understood. Nothing had changed. Ellen was still her mother.

"Oh." Ellen's face brightened. "You could stay for the afternoon and eat with us."

"No, but thanks anyway. I'm going to head back to the inn and get some rest." Daisy saw that Ellen had made the only choices she could have made. That, in some ways, her own choices were easier, kinder, because of Ellen's.

"I know," Ellen answered. "But I'll always offer. Are you leaving town again?"

"No," Daisy said. "I'll be here."

CHAPTER FIFTY-FOUR

Now

Finally, some time alone. In all of Anderson's years, he had never had such a simple thing as his own house. The home he'd owned with Daisy was theirs together, but that was different. After working for years in order to afford a comfortable life, it wasn't luxury he craved, so much as his own space.

The first few days felt downright lavish. Anderson stocked the fridge with nothing but his favorite foods, booked a vacation with Charlotte, purchased a new television. It was decisively pleasant to have a girlfriend, rather than a life partner: when Charlotte wasn't there, she just wasn't there. But he found that, oddly, the sense of guilt that had come to accompany his interactions with her hadn't lifted, even now that their relationship was in the daylight, out of the context of cheating. He had assured himself it would feel normal with the passing of enough time.

Suddenly, seated on the couch trying to figure out the new remote control, he realized: it always took a few attempts, these days, working out some new gadget. *Age comes for everyone*, he thought, forcing a smile as he pressed the buttons. But it didn't feel funny. After so many months of longing for solitude, it seemed an odd way to spend his time. Was the upcoming holiday only an attempt at leaving his newfound independence? And what was a new TV set, if not a tool to fill the silence? He brushed the thought away.

With Daisy gone, the house in Santa Fe was silent, as if it continued to hold its breath for her return. All of Daisy's neediness aside, he had enough of a conscience that it had felt distinctly bad to lie. But the affair had seemed to happen bit by bit, and at each small step, he had reassured himself that one more day of concealment, one additional lie, was only barely more wrong than the step that had preceded it. It took considerable work: not only hiding an entire relationship, but the secret score Anderson kept of Daisy's transgressions, her quirks and preoccupations, each one, in his mind, balancing some new wrongdoing on his part.

One of Daisy's more irritating habits, for instance, had been her insistence on drawing the curtains, in hopes of preventing those damned birds from flying into the glass. They had paid a premium to live in a house with this view, such a skyline: should it go unenjoyed, just to spare the neck of a few birds? Now, without Daisy, the curtains stayed open all day, letting in the beautiful city view.

Anderson consulted the product manual, continuing to push useless buttons on the remote, the quiet clicks echoing in the living room. Finally, the screen lit up. He had always appreciated watching his news. Reading the news, and writing it, had always seemed more like Daisy's territory. Anderson found CNN and leaned back on the sofa with pride. When he saw Daisy's picture flash across the screen, he sat straight up, blinking. He had fallen asleep, he told himself. Dozed off right away. Maybe he really was aging.

But as the news segment went on, Anderson leaned forward, glued to the television. 'Coming up at 11: Body discovered in 17-year coverup at Zion Chemical, site of a deadly fire.'

Anderson rose to his feet, as if the television could answer his exclamations. "She was right, all these years! No wonder she couldn't put it to rest." He sighed, smiling with pride for the woman she had become. *No*, he thought. *Not that she had become. That was the person she had always been.* "You did it, babe. That's my Daisy."

But she wasn't. Not anymore. Anderson turned the television off and went to pour a drink. As the quiet returned to the house again, he heard a faint noise from outside and turned his head in anticipation. *A bird. It had to be.* Anderson had braced himself in advance for what he imagined would be an inevitable moment: a bird would fly against the glass, fall to the ground with a scratch and a brief flutter, and there would be no Daisy to go outside after it, either shedding a secret tear at its death or beaming at its recovery. In a way, he had waited for it, a neatly planned-out moment of loss, of grief, for the woman he had spent nearly half his life with.

But Anderson hadn't expected this other thing, that came instead: more silence. These last few days, at any small sound, he had turned to the window, waiting for a bird to hit. But none did. *Maybe they were trying to fly inside to get to you, Daisy*, he thought, turning the television back on. *Maybe they saw something I was too careless to notice.*

CHAPTER FIFTY-FIVE

Now

Daisy had always taken pride in her self-discipline. There were things she knew about herself that she needed to be true: for instance, she never overslept. She knew how to ask the right questions. And when things were pulling her down, she knew that she had to keep moving: go running, get work done, clean the house.

But right then, as she felt her steps propelling her down the trail, despite all her weary numbness, she realized that it was a lie. To always keep moving was fine, unless you were running in circles to avoid getting to the point. Maybe it was truer that she didn't know how to sit still with her own mind.

The blank gray sky overhead seemed to scramble the time of day, the season: her arms trembled, clammy, and she felt cold down to her fingertips. The air, though, was summer-heavy and close, crowding her for breath so that she paused, finally, leaned against a pine trunk, and looked out at the hundreds of shades of whispering brown and green, bark and needles and foliage in all states of their life cycles. When she heard footsteps in the brush, she expected one of the police officers to have followed her. The forest was stark, yet serene, wholly itself. If only she could have blended in, avoided any more questions and answers.

"I thought you'd be here. I heard on the news that they were going to be at the plant."

At the sound of Jesse's voice, she nearly laughed with relief, turned to greet him. "I was afraid you were someone else."

"Daisy, what happened?" He reached out to her, hesitated, and she took a half step closer. His hand on her cheek was warm, the tip of his thumb tracing the tears under her eyes.

"They found her." Daisy placed her hand over his on her face, laced her fingers in between. She found she wanted to throw herself against him, block out the daylight. But she waited it out, drew in a deep breath instead. *I can sit still with my own mind*, she thought. "They found a body. And—"

"And?"

"I found out I was adopted," Daisy said. "The girl who died in the fire was my sister."

Jesse's embrace was tentative, his arms folding lightly around her back.

"Poor Mom," she wept, halfway smiling. "She was always saying that she did the best she could for me. She did, of course."

"Did what?"

"The best she could."

When Daisy heard Jesse's heartbeat through his shirt, the comfort of his presence, she drew back from their embrace. His hands slipped down her arms till they clasped hers.

We never figured out exactly what this was, she thought, studying his eyes. *We never had a chance to.*

They walked back to the Blue Ghost together in silence. Daisy stumbled once, then walked the rest of the path with her hand on his arm.

"I think I'm going to stay in town," she said.

"You are?"

"I'm going to look for apartments tomorrow."

"Glad to hear it."

"Thanks, Jesse."

"For what?"

"For being you. For believing me."

"Of course, Daisy."

Their pace slowed as they climbed the steps of the front porch. "I'll leave you here," he said. "Got to get back to work."

"See you around?"

"Definitely." As he turned to leave, he smiled back at her. "Maybe dinner and a movie? Next Friday?"

"Oh," she whispered. Jesse hesitated. "Yes," Daisy said. "Yeah, I'd like that."

Daisy walked up the stairs to her room, where the small assortment of her belongings and the passage of a week had created a sense of comfort, if not home. She let herself fall onto the bed, then stretched out with relief. It was not yet noon, but she was drained, exhausted in body and mind. The sky was linen blue under a thin haze of clouds, and the whisper of the nearby forest sounded nothing more than self-contented. As a rule, Daisy never took naps: they interrupted her days, gave too much opportunity to get lost in her thoughts. The mood of a dream or memory always stayed with her throughout the afternoon when she woke up.

Maybe, she thought, that wouldn't be such a bad thing to practice.

A LETTER FROM KELLY

Thank you for taking the time to read my book. If you'd like to stay informed of my future releases, please sign up for my email list below:

www.bookouture.com/kelly-heard

Writing this book has been a wonderful adventure, and I'm so excited to share it. I'm grateful to have the chance to connect with readers. If you'd like to talk about the story any further, please feel absolutely free to reach out to me online.

Sincerely,
Kelly

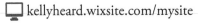 kellyheard.wixsite.com/mysite

 @heardkj1

ACKNOWLEDGEMENTS

This book could not exist without the great talent, input, and support from everybody at Bookouture: most especially my editor, the exquisite Leodora Darlington, and publicity gurus Kim Nash and Noelle Holten.

I am incredibly grateful to my family, who have supported me in every day through the writing of this book. My mother, Christy Campbell, my mother-in-law, Nancy Heard, and my aunt, Jamie Heard, have provided childcare and support when I was working to meet deadlines. My extended family and friends have shown interest in my work. Most of all I am grateful to my husband and children for tolerating the long nights and odd hours I've put in while writing this book.

Made in the USA
Middletown, DE
03 September 2020